The Glittering Art of Falling Apart

ILANA FOX

Also by Ilana Fox

The Making of Mia
Spotlight
All That Glitters

Dedicated to the memories
of Lesley and Nancy Fox

First published in Great Britain in 2015 by Orion Books,
an imprint of The Orion Publishing Group Ltd
Carmelite House, 50 Victoria Embankment
London EC4Y 0DZ

An Hachette Livre UK Company

1 3 5 7 9 10 8 6 4 2

A CIP catalogue record for this book is
available from the British Library.

ISBN (Mass Market Paperback) 978 1 4091 2090 2
ISBN (Ebook) 978 1 4091 2289 0

Typeset at The Spartan Press Ltd,
Lymington, Hants

Printed and bound in Great Britain by
Clays Ltd, St Ives plc

The Orion Publishing Group's policy is to use papers that are natural,
renewable and recyclable products and made from wood grown in sustainable
forests. The logging and manufacturing processes are expected to
conform to the environmental regulations of the country of origin.

www.orionbooks.co.uk

What's past is prologue.

WILLIAM SHAKESPEARE, *The Tempest*

Prologue

London, 1960

Everyone at the party had a Sidecar in their hand, and Lillie Tempest was determined not to feel left out. So what if she'd promised she wouldn't drink alcohol while she was in London? She was twenty years old, it was the start of a brand new decade, and life was just about to get exciting. She'd been one of the last debutantes to be presented, but Lillie was starting to think that the feudal class system her family lived by was old-fashioned. Hadn't the Prime Minister made a speech about a 'wind of change' at the start of the year? Lillie didn't pay much attention to politics, but she liked the sound of that, regardless of what Macmillan had actually been talking about. It was time for things to change and for her life to really start. She was determined to have some fun.

'Make me one of those drinks, won't you?' she asked a passing boy, while she smoothed down the satin of her milky-white cocktail dress. She'd bought it in Derry & Toms earlier that day, and at the time she'd thought it the height of elegance – but then she'd turned up to the party and found that all the other girls were in more casual dresses, or even trousers. She wished she'd worn something less formal, but she told herself that standing out was a *good* thing. After all, she was a Tempest

– which meant that people noticed her anyway – and this was the first time she'd been allowed to London without an escort. She wanted to make an impact. She told herself that her dress wasn't a fashion faux pas but a deliberate statement, and as she took a sip of her cocktail – which she didn't like, but never mind – she almost believed it herself.

Lillie looked around the party and allowed herself a tiny smile. She'd only recently met Petra and her rather fast set of friends, and she'd certainly never been inside a flat like this before. Unlike her own family home, or the sedate houses of the Tempests' friends, Petra's flat in Chelsea was modern and fun. Young people sprawled on low-slung sofas, a sparse buffet of cheese and crackers sat on top of a modern G Plan dining table, and people were dancing to the latest records. Everyone seemed incredibly happy and alive and bright. Petra's racy London life was so different to Lillie's staid, antiquated existence that she was quite overcome with envy. She wanted this for herself. Who wouldn't?

Just then the front door swung open and a group of young men walked in. Lillie watched them from under her eyelashes: all were attractive and sharp, with shiny duck's arse haircuts and slim-fitting suits. She knew that Petra was having a casual dalliance with one of them – was his name Marty? Ronnie? Something like that – but she hadn't met any of the others before, and she definitely hadn't ever seen the man emerging from the shadows. Lillie's eyes widened in surprise – he was the most handsome man she'd ever seen.

'We've made a new friend and we thought it would be rather fun to bring him along,' one of the men said with a smirk. Lillie turned to Petra to see her reaction, to see what she'd say about their gatecrasher. She hoped Petra wouldn't want him for herself.

Petra grinned. 'You always did know how to make a party memorable, Ronnie. Make sure your new friend gets a drink, and introduce him to Lillie here.'

Lillie took a deep breath and decided she wasn't going to wait for the stranger to be introduced to her. She was a modern girl, and that meant she could introduce herself. She knew that if her sisters were here they'd drag her away, would tell her to see sense, but Lillie didn't care for her sisters' approval. If anything, behaving badly spurred her on.

'I'm Lillie Tempest,' she said in a confident, practised tone. All around them people were dancing to 'Poor Me' by Adam Faith, but the moment Lillie locked eyes with the man it was as if everyone and everything disappeared. It was just him and her, and nobody else.

'Bertie Boyle,' the man replied in an accent straight out of the movies. Lillie realised she'd been gazing into his intense blue eyes for longer than was polite, but when she tried to pull away, tried not to look so keen, she found she couldn't. In that instant, she knew that meeting Bertie Boyle would change her life.

Was this love at first sight? If such a thing existed outside of romance novels, then yes, it was. Lillie smiled and stepped closer to Bertie, and as he put his hand on her waist she allowed herself to be blown away on her dazzling wind of change. Her life was changed forever.

Chapter One

London, recently

On a quiet road in Mayfair, half hidden by the shadow of a yet-to-blossom cherry tree, sat a tiny bookshop. The tea-green paintwork on the ornate window frames had started to peel, and the once-glittering gold lettering of the signage had faded to a brittle yellow. A considerable number of people walked past Heritage Books every day (tourists mainly, clutching at maps as they tried to find the former homes of Hendrix and Handel), but if you asked any of them if they'd noticed the bookshop, they'd have looked at you blankly. Most visitors to Heritage Books came by appointment; few stepped in because they genuinely wanted to buy a rare first edition for a loved one.

Inside the bookshop, and almost concealed by several wobbly towers of antique books in various shades and states, a young woman sat on a stool and allowed the sun to toast her face. Dust motes danced in the weak, muted sunshine that somehow managed to find its way through the dirty windows, and as Cassandra Alberta Cooke enjoyed the first warmth of spring on her skin, she closed her eyes. In the comforting cosiness and hush of the bookshop, Cassie felt cocooned; her chin dropped, her shoulders relaxed, and she was about to drift off to sleep when her phone vibrated across the wooden counter in a brittle hum.

She snapped open her eyes and checked the caller display: it was Safia, her best friend. She pushed her long hair behind her ears and tried to answer as jauntily as she could, but her words came out as a croak.

'You've been napping at work again, haven't you? You can't fool me, Cassie Cooke.' Safia's voice was little more than a whisper – she was at work too, at her desk, and clearly making a personal call when she absolutely shouldn't be – but Cassie could hear amusement in it.

'Only a little bit,' she admitted. 'It's just so snug and quiet in here. I've done all my work and Mr Heritage is away at an estate sale near Manchester. Not that he'd mind if I had a kip in between customers.'

Cassie thought of her boss and smiled to herself. Mr Heritage was in his seventies, with a shock of silken silver hair, and he carried himself with a posture that suggested that everything he did was done properly. Heritage Books had been on this street in London for as long as anybody could remember, but few could recall ever having a full conversation with the man who nipped into the shop every few weeks to deliver his latest vintage finds. He was an enigma. Cassie had worked at Heritage Books for over four years, but despite being entrusted with a set of heavy keys for the door and a smaller set for the safe, she still didn't know Mr Heritage's first name, and that suited her – she liked the formality of their relationship. She couldn't imagine ever having a job like Safia had; Saf regularly got drunk with her colleagues in Soho and often ended up mopping up her boss's drunken tears. It sounded like Cassie's version of hell.

'Anyway, what are you up to tonight?' Safia said. 'There's a party going on in Dalston, and apparently there will be loads of fit guys there. We'll be able to have our pick.'

Cassie trailed her finger across the cover of the book closest to her. It was from 1863 and was embossed with a gold-leaf emblem that shone in the sunlight.

'Would you mind if I didn't?' Cassie went out occasionally, but she never really enjoyed herself. London seemed full to the brim of drunk, leering men who acted as if she should be grateful that they'd spoken to her.

'Hiding yourself away in your bedroom is no way to meet a man.' Safia's voice was kind, but Cassie knew that her friend was mildly exasperated with her.

She gazed at the books surrounding her. Inside so many of the novels were the greatest romances ever to be read, but they offered little comfort. Characters in novels always found their one true love at the end of their journey, but Cassie didn't even know where she was going, or if she'd ever meet anyone who would be right for her: men like Mr Darcy, or Benedick from *Much Ado About Nothing* didn't seem to exist. She'd had a few relationships, but they'd all trailed away and the men had vanished in what felt like a puff of smoke, never to be seen again.

'I know,' she said quietly. 'But a party in some super-cool part of London just isn't my thing. I mean, come on – I wear normal clothes and I like normal things and I'm just not hipster enough. I'll be miserable.'

Cassie didn't believe she had the right sort of personality or looks to fit into the bars that Safia went to – and even if she did, she knew it wouldn't be enough. She wasn't pushy, and nor did she have the hard, glittering edge that so many girls in London seemed to be able to muster at the drop of a hat. On the rare occasion that she spoke to an attractive man, she found it hard to look him in the eye and ended up mumbling her words. She wanted to be able to turn on the charm, to be an extrovert, but she found she wasn't able to. She was too quiet and gentle for the City men who were looking for instant fun and gratification.

'So you're really just going to go home after work?' Safia asked.

Cassie confirmed she was. For despite loving her best friend dearly, all she wanted to do was to get the bus home, say hello to her family, and then hide herself away in her bedroom with a good book.

'Do you mind?' she asked, but she knew Safia didn't, not really. Saf accepted Cassie for who she was, and that was one of the reasons they were such good friends.

'Have fun with your books,' Safia replied. 'But remember, a book won't keep you warm at night.'

Cassie smiled as she ended the call, but she didn't spend any time wondering if Safia was right: when you found the right book, it could warm you in a way that love sometimes could not.

'Hello? I'm back!' Cassie closed the cherry-red front door behind her and stood in the hallway of the tall, spindly London town house that she'd lived in for most of her life with her parents and younger twin brother and sister. After university she'd shared a flat in south London for a few years, but she'd found the rent extortionate and had never felt quite comfortable with communal living with strangers. In the end she'd realised she'd do better if she moved back home to save her money, and that was what she'd done. She'd never regretted her decision, however loud her siblings could be.

Today, however, the house felt unusually quiet and still; the air was motionless and there was no noise, no chatter, no laughter. It felt as though it had not been lived in for a long time – which was ridiculous, as she'd seen the rest of her family at breakfast just that morning – and Cassie felt a shiver run through her body. This was how it would feel to be in Beaufont Hall, she thought, then pushed the image of the dilapidated mansion from her mind. She would not think of Beaufont. Not now.

'Is anyone home? Hello?'

'Cassie? Is that you? We're up here! Come and join us.' Alice's voice drifted down the stairs, sounding tiny, as though it were very far away. Cassie dropped her scuffed leather bag on the floor, pulled off her coat, and began to walk up the narrow Victorian staircase. From years of living in the house she knew which steps creaked when even the smallest of feet were placed on them, and it was these that she deliberately trod on as she climbed the height of the house. The squeaking floorboards accompanied the sound of her laboured breathing until she reached the very top, and it was then that she saw that the ladder to the attic had been pulled down.

'What are you doing up there?' Cassie called. For as long as she could remember, none of the Cookes ever went into the attic; it was used as a storage area for items that the family quickly forgot about.

'We're looking for clothes,' Alice replied. Her voice was muffled.

Cassie's eyebrows knotted into a frown; she tentatively mounted the ladder and stuck her head up into the attic. It had never been properly converted – the family wasn't well off enough to spend thousands on rooms they barely used – and it was under a single, bare light bulb that she saw Alice and her twin Henry rummaging through dusty trunks of clothing. Their cracked leather lids had been thrown open and the old Tempest family crest was hidden, but Cassie knew at once that the trunks had belonged to their grandmother Violet. Her heart sank as she saw puddles of delicate silk and vintage lace strewn across the dirty attic floor.

'Are Mum and Dad back yet?' Alice continued. She was

blithely unaware of the stricken expression on her sister's face. 'They said they were popping out to get a takeaway for dinner – Mum said she's too tired to make anything and that she fancies a treat.'

Henry turned to look at Cassie and misread the expression on her face. He grinned. 'Don't worry,' he remarked cheerfully. 'We won't get told off for being up here – it was Mum's idea.'

'It's not that,' Cassie said. 'I just don't understand what you're looking for. Are you searching for something specific?'

Henry shook his head. 'We need to make outfits for the school play and Mum said there might be something in here that we can customise.'

Cassie blinked at him. 'You're going to wear one of Granny's dresses for a school play?'

Henry rolled his eyes at her. 'We're going to use some of the material. I'm playing Oberon in *A Midsummer Night's Dream.*'

'And I'm going to be Hermia,' added Alice.

Cassie looked from the pleased expressions on the twins' faces back to the piles of dresses, skirts and blouses on the floor. She'd never met her grandmother Violet, who'd passed away before she was born, but she felt quite strongly that the twins shouldn't rummage through her clothes so nonchalantly and with such little respect – and that whatever they discovered shouldn't be cut up for something as trivial as a school play.

'"Lord, what fools these mortals be!"' Cassie muttered, but she didn't say it quite quietly enough and Henry put his hands on his hips.

'Puck says that, not Oberon or Hermia, and you might say well done! It was quite hard for us to get the parts.'

'Congratulations,' Cassie murmured.

'Thanks,' Alice said as she continued to dig in the trunk. She pulled out a champagne-coloured cocktail dress decorated with lace appliqué and threw it on to one of the piles without so much as a second glance. 'It turns out that having to listen to Shakespeare plays as bedtime stories had some use after all – I reckon we got the parts because we knew the characters better than everyone else.'

Cassie frowned and walked over to the dress that Alice had so swiftly discarded. It was beautiful. She lifted it to the light to examine it more carefully but was distracted by the sight of Henry tossing aside a crushed-velvet cape with a sparkling crystal clasp.

'Be careful with that!' she exclaimed sharply. 'You don't want to get it dirty.'

Henry glanced at his older sister and raised his eyebrows in amusement. He may have been ten years younger than Cassie, but both he and his twin had an outward confidence that she could never quite match.

'But everything is dusty anyway,' he said. 'Besides, all this stuff is really old. I don't know why Mum bothers to keep it.'

'Because it was Granny's, and because everything up here belonged to our family.'

'Oh not this *again*,' Henry muttered, and Cassie felt a familiar crossness tighten in her chest.

'Look, I know that being part of the Tempest family doesn't mean that much to you, but it does to me. We should show a bit of respect to Granny's things.'

'But she's dead,' Alice said in a neutral, matter-of-fact voice. 'She wouldn't mind nor care – and more importantly, Mum doesn't. And Violet was *her* mother, after all. Not yours.'

'That's not the point,' Cassie replied. 'When you're older, you'll understand. Our family heritage is *everything* and Granny's dresses are a part of that. We may be Cookes, but our mother was a Tempest and therefore so are we, regardless of our surname.'

Alice caught her sister's eye. 'The Tempest family no longer exists,' she said carefully and somewhat considerately for a teenager. 'Not how it used to, anyway.'

Cassie hugged Violet Tempest's cocktail dress closer to her.

'And that's why I think we should preserve the memory of it, even if nobody else is bothered,' she replied quietly, but either her siblings didn't hear her or they chose to ignore her, for at that moment her parents came home and called them all for supper and the twins raced to scramble down the ladder.

After a dinner of lukewarm Chinese noodles, the twins returned to the attic. Despite their invitation, Cassie opted not to join them. Instead she wandered into the living room with a book tucked under her arm and tried not to think about the activity at the top of the house. She hated that Alice and Henry had been given permission to shred up Violet Tempest's clothing, and she hoped the copy of *In Cold Blood* she'd borrowed from the shop would distract her from it.

Other than her bedroom, the living room was her favourite room in the house. It was the centrepiece of the home: a comfortable space that was furnished with happy family memories and crammed with photographs of all three of the children. The Cookes might not have had much money, but Rebecca had always made sure that the kids had the best of childhoods, and as Cassie looked at the pictures of her and the twins grinning broadly in the hot English summers that they no longer seemed to have, she couldn't help but smile back. Alice and Henry had been adorable babies, complete with curly blond hair and innocent wide eyes. In that respect, they took after her parents: all four were pale, with hair that shimmered with honey, caramel and vanilla tones. In comparison, Cassie was tall and dark like Violet Tempest had been, although she had the same wide blue eyes as her mother and siblings.

The more Cassie thought about her grandmother, the more she yearned to look through photographs of her extended family. She already kept a collection of photos in her bedroom, photos that her mother hadn't included in the albums, but she wanted to look at the 'official' family pictures. She put her book to one side, opened up a cupboard, and pulled out the albums full of sepia-toned photographs that she'd looked at so many times she'd practically committed the images to memory. In the photos, the older generations of Tempests were unspeakably elegant; they were always smiling, always fashionable, always well groomed. In particular, Violet and her sister Aster were beautiful: their long dark hair tumbled to their shoulders in waves and they were effortlessly glamorous. Cassie might not have the sophistication her grandmother had clearly possessed, but she hoped she had a fraction of her looks.

Almost all the photographs that Cassie cherished had been taken at the family home: Beaufont Hall. The mansion – for it was large enough to be a mansion, albeit a small one – was hidden away in the depths of the Buckinghamshire countryside, but nobody lived there any more. After Violet had died, the house had been passed down to her daughter, Rebecca, but the Cookes had never lived there, and instead Rebecca had let her cousin Lloyd stay – albeit in relative poverty. It had only been a few months previously that he'd had a drunken fall on some ice and had passed away. Since then the house had stood empty.

Cassie had only been to Beaufont a few times in her life, but those visits had captivated her. To her mind, it was not just a house; it was part of the family. Yet the remaining Tempests

– Rebecca and her three children – no longer went there. They'd just left it alone to slowly decay. Cassie couldn't understand why.

She continued to turn the crackling pages of the albums. There were photographs of her grandmother Violet and her grandfather Nicholas, of her great-aunt Aster and her children Rose and Lloyd, and of long-ago family friends whose names Cassie didn't know. There was even a faded photograph of her great-grandparents, Philip and Mary Tempest, standing proudly in front of Beaufont Hall with several Labradors at their feet. Cassie had stared at this photograph so many times that she felt as though she'd known both them and the house.

'You were mesmerised by that photo even as a toddler,' Rebecca remarked as she walked into the living room.

Cassie jumped – she'd not heard her mother enter the room – but then turned to her and smiled.

'I like the history in it,' she admitted. 'You can tell that Mary and Philip were happy, can't you? And Beaufont looks so majestic, like it could be the backdrop to a period drama or something.'

'It certainly would have been true then, but it's rather ramshackle now,' Rebecca replied.

Cassie tried to keep her expression neutral, for whenever her mother spoke about Beaufont – or of her life before she'd married Cassie's father – she sounded so uncomfortable and tense that Cassie had learned not to bring it up.

'Is that why we've never lived there? Or even visit it?' she asked quietly. 'It's such a shame that a wonderful house has been left alone.'

Rebecca picked up an out-of-date *Telegraph* from the coffee table and looked at the front page for a long moment. Cassie wondered if she was going to end the conversation without another word, but eventually she spoke.

'It is a shame in a way. But Beaufont is basically uninhabitable.'

'But Lloyd lived there.'

'Only because he didn't have any choice,' Rebecca said lightly. 'When he came back from jaunting around Africa, he had nothing and nowhere else to go. I offered him a room here, but he was too independent and proud to live with us, so I let him stay at Beaufont for peanuts instead. But he wouldn't have lived there if he could have gone anywhere else – really, I don't think it could have been particularly pleasant.'

'Is Beaufont really falling to bits?' Cassie asked.

'It is – but even if it wasn't, I doubt we could afford to ever live there. A house that size wouldn't be practical to look after; the upkeep would be eye-watering.'

Cassie put the photograph back in the album and let her eyes trail over the rest of the photos. However casual her mother sounded, Cassie could sense the edge in her voice. What was it about Beaufont and the Tempests that Rebecca so hated to think about? To talk about?

'I know that you idolise Beaufont and the family history,' Rebecca continued, 'but since Lloyd's passing, we really need to think about what we're going to do with the house. Your father and I have talked about it, and we've agreed we need to put it on the market.'

'You're going to sell it?' Cassie said slowly. She swallowed loudly.

'Times are hard – you of all people know that,' Rebecca replied. 'We may not be able to find a nice family who'd like to buy it, but we might be able to sell the place to a developer who could turn it into luxury flats.'

'But what if a developer wanted to knock it down?'

Rebecca paused. 'Darling, we can't afford to keep Beaufont

for much longer. When Lloyd was there, we felt like we couldn't sell it, but now he's gone . . .'

Cassie felt sadness grip her. Since she'd been small she'd had a fantasy that one day she'd return the family to Beaufont; that it would be at Beaufont that she'd raise her own children.

'Isn't there any way we could keep it? We could clean it up and rent it out, perhaps?' She hated the thought of another family living in their home, but it was better than having to say goodbye to Beaufont for good.

Rebecca shook her head. 'Your father and I have done the sums – we don't have any option but to sell it.'

'Then I'd like to go there to say goodbye properly,' Cassie replied firmly. The last time she'd asked her mother if she could visit Beaufont, Rebecca had refused. This time she wasn't going to take no for an answer.

To her surprise, Rebecca smiled at her. 'You always were a romantic,' she said fondly. 'But if you do go, it could also be for a more practical reason. The Winters have told me the house is a mess. I'm going to ask them to organise a local cleaning company to sort through Lloyd's old belongings and to get it in some sort of order. But I hate to ask them to do more than they already do, perhaps you could oversee the cleaning?'

The Winters were an old Beaufont village family who'd worked as staff in the house when Philip and Mary had lived there. When the Tempest family fortune began to dwindle away in the 1970s, so too did the staff, until the only person left was Mrs Winter, who'd remained as housekeeper until Violet Tempest had passed away. Several of the new generations of Winters had made names for themselves – one as an actor on a prime-time TV crime show, another in the City – but many had chosen to stay in the village. Rebecca kept in touch with Mrs Winter's son, who – despite his arthritis – remained a part-time handyman and groundskeeper. He'd done the best he could at patching the house up on the little the Cookes could spare.

'You mean I can actually visit Beaufont?' Cassie asked slowly.

Rebecca nodded. 'I didn't think it was appropriate for you to go when Lloyd lived there – he hated to be disturbed, as you know – but now he's passed away I don't see why you shouldn't, especially as we have to let the house go.'

'I can definitely oversee the cleaning company,' Cassie replied quickly. 'And actually, if it's not too big a job, maybe I could even do it myself at weekends. I'd like to help – especially if it means I can say goodbye to Beaufont properly.'

Rebecca looked at her daughter carefully. 'You don't have to, you know. We *can* afford to pay some cleaners, although lord knows how much it will come to.'

'But I want to do it,' Cassie said.

Rebecca laughed, but Cassie could sense her mother's hesitancy behind her smile. 'The keys are in the desk drawer in the study – why don't you see what sort of condition the house is in before you offer to clean it up?'

Cassie nodded, but she barely heard her mother or the warning in her voice; her eyes were trained on the photograph of her grandparents standing outside their family home. She was finally going to Beaufont.

Chapter Two

Buckinghamshire and London,
recently

Cassie drove her rusting Renault Clio along Beaufont's private driveway, but she struggled to keep her eyes on the road. Through the gaps in the thicket of trees she could see the mansion, and the closer she came to it, the faster her heart raced. When it properly came into view, she felt slightly emotional. Here it was! This was the home that had sheltered generations of her family for over a hundred years; the house that had played a part in the making of the Tempests' legacy.

Yet as much as she romanticised Beaufont Hall and its historic inhabitants, Cassie knew that it wasn't the prettiest of buildings. Ramblers who stood on the threshold of the grounds often remarked that they thought Beaufont was too forbidding, too dark and too gloomy to be attractive. Cassie could see that it was functional-looking rather than handsome, but she liked the contrast of the stern, intimidating house against the gentle rolling Buckinghamshire valleys. Beaufont Hall was a solid mansion, and regardless of how it looked she could never dislike it, or disregard it. It was important to her and her family history.

She decided to park some distance from the house so she could approach Beaufont on foot, and as she pulled up the handbrake and turned off the engine, she couldn't stop beaming. For years she'd longed to visit Beaufont Hall, but her mother had never been keen. Instead, Cassie had driven up here several times without her family knowing, but there had been little point in getting close to the house – to do so without being able to go in would have been like teasing herself. Today was the day that everything would change: she had the keys to the front door in her hand, as well as a valid reason to be here.

As she walked up the path, she felt as though this was some sort of homecoming. She quickened her pace and drank in the splendour of the dark grey double-fronted exterior. The sun peeped out from behind a cloud, and as Cassie looked up at the house she could see its reflection glinting against some of the windows, but she also noticed that many of them had been boarded up, and that years of water damage had curled the stained MDF. As she got even closer, her good mood began to falter, and by the time she neared the front door and the step on which her great-grandparents had stood to have their photograph taken, her smile had completely vanished.

The Beaufont Hall that Cassie had imagined for so many years no longer existed; in its place stood a soulless shell, a house with rotting window frames, crumbling bricks, overgrown gardens and a sense of long-ago abandonment.

'It's not as bad as it looks,' a male voice said, and Cassie whipped her head around.

Walking towards her was a man, but it wasn't the man she'd been expecting – Mr Winter. This man was tall rather than stooped, he had auburn hair rather than dull silver, and his eyes glinted a perfect moss green behind his glasses. He was in his thirties rather than his sixties, and he was attractive; he was more than attractive.

'You must be Cassandra Cooke,' he said when he reached her, and stuck out his hand. 'Edward Winter – Ed. My father normally looks after the house, but his aches and pains have been playing up so I've been doing it on his behalf.'

Cassie shifted the keys from her right hand to her left and shook his hand. She'd been expecting an elderly man to show her around a mansion that – in her mind at least – looked quite different. She felt thrown.

'My grandmother was the housekeeper here in your grandmother's day,' Ed continued. 'And my father practically grew up here, although he's a fair bit older than your mother.'

'Yes,' Cassie managed to say. 'My mother told me about the family connection.'

She gazed up at the windows again and tried to focus on what needed to be done so she'd not be awkward about her shyness, but the more she looked at the house, the more dismayed she felt. She'd known that Beaufont wouldn't be in the condition it once was – of course it wouldn't be; they'd not had the money to look after it for over a quarter of a century – but she hadn't expected this. It looked so forlorn.

'Shall we go inside?' Ed asked her, and Cassie looked at the front door. Now she was here – and now that she'd seen the reality of what Beaufont Hall looked like – she wasn't sure she wanted to spoil her fantasies any further. The house looked rundown, heartless, cold. Had she been naive in thinking it would feel welcoming or special to her because she was a Tempest? Possibly. But she hadn't considered that it would be like this. It was as though it had no soul.

'I suppose we should,' she said quietly. She noticed that Ed had a set of keys in his hands too, and she gestured for him to open the door.

'Are you sure?' he replied. 'It's quite stiff, but I'm happy for you to do the honours.'

Cassie shook her head and silently watched Ed turn the keys in the heavy, rusting locks. He pushed at the rotten front door with his shoulder, and when it gave, he stumbled slightly. Cassie looked past him and inside the house, but all she could see was darkness.

Ed turned to her and raised an eyebrow, but Cassie found that the last thing she wanted to do was to step over the threshold and into Beaufont Hall. She wanted it to remain a fantasy, the image of a majestic mansion where her family had grown up and laughed and loved. She wasn't sure she could bear to see it looking so lost.

'After you,' she said eventually, and as she watched Ed's figure retreat into the gloom of the house, she forced her feet to follow.

The air inside Beaufont Hall felt heavy with dust, and as Cassie allowed her eyes to adjust to the shadows, she found she was holding her breath. Whereas the outside of the house was ugly and brutal, the inside was fragile with lost beauty. Thick furry cobwebs hung from every corner of the ceiling and the smell of old dust stung Cassie's nose. The grubby rug underfoot was coated in grime and the walls were greasy with dirt, yet the floorboards were clearly a beautiful oak, the rug was antique and oriental, and the wallpaper was sea green and had an intricate pattern made up of unopened flower buds and overripe fruit.

'It's stunning,' Cassie whispered to herself, and Ed looked over at her and grinned.

'Most people would only see the dirt and the expense of restoration,' he said.

'But I'm not most people,' Cassie replied. She pulled her eyes away from the Victorian cornicing of voluptuous bunches of grapes on twisting vines, and glanced at Ed. 'And I've wanted to come here for ever.'

Ed glanced at his smart-looking watch. The gold face glinted in the dimness. 'I've got a bit of time before I have to get back for a call – shall I give you the tour?'

Cassie wanted to explore Beaufont Hall alone, but she knew she was thinking with her heart rather than her head. She couldn't predict the state of each room, and if they'd be safe to enter or not, whereas Ed clearly knew the house and how dilapidated it was. She'd wanted to see Beaufont for so long that anything was better than nothing.

'Please.'

As Ed showed her around her family's old home, she was struck by how beautiful Beaufont Hall must have been – and how tragic the state of it was now. In the depths of the gloom he led her through several anonymous rooms. They were all empty, and could barely be seen because of the boarded-up windows, so she couldn't work out what each had been used for. Rebecca had had the electricity turned off after Lloyd's passing to try to save money, but Cassie needed light to really understand what she was peering at.

'I don't understand how the house can be in such a bad condition,' she remarked. 'I'd already assumed Lloyd wasn't house-proud, but surely this level of dirt and decay is older than that. There was some flat in Paris that was abandoned during the Second World War and was recently discovered. That was dusty, but it wasn't . . . like this.'

Ed cleared his throat. 'I think Lloyd only used a few rooms. I'll show you them in a bit.'

'And where is the furniture? Do you know where it could be?' Cassie asked.

Ed looked down at her. 'As far as I'm aware, Rebecca sold most of the furniture Lloyd wasn't using – which was the majority of it – and gave him the money to live on,' he said. 'There are a few bits and pieces dotted about, but nothing of any value – a wooden chair, a cracked mirror, things like that. The rooms Lloyd lived in are fully furnished, in a way, but . . .'

'Can we see where he lived?' she asked.

Ed led her down several corridors until they were standing outside a closed door. He looked at her.

'What you need to understand,' he began gently, 'is that Lloyd wasn't very well – either physically or mentally. My family kept an eye on him at your mother's request, but, well, we never interfered, because it wasn't our place – and we certainly never invaded his privacy by entering the house or his rooms.'

Cassie looked at him. 'I'm not sure I know what you're trying to say.'

Ed looked stricken. 'I suppose what I'm trying to say is that we didn't realise that Lloyd lived like this until after he passed away.'

Cassie pushed the door open and gasped. Unlike the rest of the house, the windows in here hadn't been covered with MDF, and in the spring daylight the room appeared chaotic. The plasterwork of the ceiling was water-stained an ugly weak-tea yellow, and in the middle of it was a hole where there had obviously been a leak. Through it Cassie could see wooden beams and the darkness of the underside of whatever room was above. But her overwhelming first impression was the smell: a deep, dank, musty smell of rotting floorboards and raw, flourishing mould.

'I don't understand,' she whispered as she tried not to blanch at the stench.

'There was a flood,' Ed admitted. 'There was a hole in the roof but we don't know how long it had been there — water seeped through every floor into this room.'

'Did my mother know about it? Did Lloyd tell her?'

'He didn't. It was only after my father glanced in these rooms after Lloyd's death that he realised. He and I tried to fix it up the best we could, but . . .' Ed stopped talking when he realised that Cassie wasn't really listening to him.

'A hole in the roof doesn't explain the rest of this, though,' she said quietly. A small single mattress lay in the middle of the floor, and surrounding it were piles and piles of rubbish. Empty, faded crisp packets were stacked in colour order, towers made from discarded Coke cans leant perilously against the peeling wallpaper, and there were countless supermarket bags dotted around. She peered inside one and saw pages of newspapers from several years earlier. Another held metres and metres of dirty brown string. Around these were old cardboard boxes full of more rubbish: junk food containers, grease-stained pizza boxes, hollowed branches from fallen trees, and scraps of meaningless paper. There was very little floor space for Cassie and Ed to tread.

'I don't know what to say,' Ed said. 'We always knew that Lloyd wasn't quite . . . *right*, but nobody knew he lived like this. Did you ever meet him?'

Cassie shook her head. She could vaguely remember once meeting a jolly, red-nosed man when she'd been small, but she hadn't known her mother's cousin. Not really.

She suddenly felt guilty. If they'd known how Lloyd had been living, they'd have tried to help him.

'It's so sad,' she said. 'Are his other rooms like this too?'

Ed nodded. 'He used this as a bedroom, but the other room – his living room – is full of empty wine bottles and beer cans. It doesn't seem as though he ever threw anything away.'

Cassie pushed at a carrier bag with her foot. Underneath it was a beautiful leather-bound book. Realisation dawned on her.

'This room used to be a library, didn't it?' she said with a start. She'd been so busy breathing through her mouth to avoid the smell, so busy taking in the piles and piles of rubbish that Lloyd had hoarded, that she'd failed to see the beautiful mahogany shelves – or the old books that remained upon them. She pushed her way through the debris on the floor and ran her hands over the spines of the books closest to her. Many had been water-damaged, but others seemed to be in perfect condition. She suddenly wondered if any of them could be valuable.

'You know, when I was driving over, I had fantasies of being able to spend proper time here. I knew that cleaning the house and getting it in order to sell it would take some time and effort, but I'd hoped that it would be in some sort of habitable condition. I'd even hoped I might be able to stay the night one time. Silly, really – it would be like squatting in a derelict house.'

Ed smiled at her. 'We can get the electricity turned back on – you'll need light so you can see what you're doing if you're serious about cleaning the house by yourself. And if you like, I don't mind mucking in. Getting rid of all this rubbish will be hard work.'

Cassie walked to one of the windows and stared at the gardens beyond. All she could see was an overgrown, unmanageable knot of weeds and thorns that looked like a fortress but didn't protect the house from either the weather or the outside world.

'You're being very kind,' she said in a small voice, 'but

you really don't have to offer to help. I'm happy to do this by myself.'

Ed shrugged. 'I used to work in the City, but I'm taking a couple of years out to "find myself".' He gave a sharp laugh and shook his head at the thought. 'Helping you would give me something to do . . . And besides, I've nearly watched everything there is to watch on Netflix.'

Cassie smiled at him. 'Thank you, but Beaufont is my family home and my family's problem.'

'In a way it was my family home too,' Ed replied. 'Look, I really would like to help. I need something productive to do; something to stop myself from wallowing in self-pity.'

Cassie looked at him for a moment, but she didn't ask him to elaborate on why he'd left his job. Instead she thought about the magnetic pull Beaufont Hall had on her, and she knew that Ed could feel it too.

Cassie stretched her arms high above her head and glanced at the clock: it was getting late. She'd taken some of the books from Beaufont back to London with her, and while she didn't think any of them would be particularly valuable, there was no harm in checking – not when the family could do with the money. She put aside one book and picked up the next one – *The Good Fairy*, by F. J. Harvey Darton. It was a first edition, published in London in 1922, and considering its age, it was in fairly good condition. The original red wrappers were a little rubbed and nicked, and the pages were tanned with age, but it didn't detract from the overall appearance. Cassie wasn't an expert, but she guessed she could sell it for about £100 – possibly more.

She gently placed the book back in one of Lloyd's old cardboard boxes and moved it to a corner of her bedroom. She wanted to keep looking through the books, but she also wanted to talk to Rebecca. As far as she was aware, her mother hadn't been back to Beaufont since Lloyd had moved in, and she wasn't sure she fully understood the true condition of the house. She was just getting to her feet when there was a knock on her door: Rebecca.

'I was just coming to find you.' Cassie smiled, and gratefully accepted the cup of tea her mother offered. 'I brought some books home from Beaufont, and I think we could get something for them. We haven't got a first-edition A. A. Milne or Daphne Du Maurier, but I think one of them could be worth at least a hundred pounds.'

Rebecca perched on the edge of Cassie's bed and gazed at the cardboard box.

'A hundred pounds is a lot of money for a book,' she began, 'but I don't think there will be anything much left in the library. After my mother passed away, we removed everything we thought was valuable.'

As she spoke, Cassie looked at her carefully. She seemed tired and drawn.

'Tell me about the house,' Rebecca continued. 'What sort of state was it in?'

Cassie tried to describe Beaufont Hall as best she could, but when she came to telling her mother how Lloyd had lived, she found her voice wavering.

Rebecca looked horrified. 'That poor man,' she said, taking a sip of her tea to steady herself. 'I knew he wasn't well – he'd been an alcoholic for years and he'd spent all his money on his travels – but I had no idea it was that bad. How awful.'

Cassie didn't know what to say. She knew her mother would blame herself for not being aware of how Lloyd's life had unravelled in his later years, and she also knew that she shouldn't: Rebecca had been raising a family in London and couldn't be held responsible for her reckless, reclusive cousin in Buckinghamshire. She changed the subject back to Beaufont.

'The good news is that the rest of the house seems okay, but it was hard to see it properly in the dark, especially because lots of the windows are boarded up. Could we get the electricity turned back on?'

'Of course,' Rebecca said, but Cassie knew her mother was still thinking of Lloyd.

She reached out and placed a hand on her arm and took a deep breath. 'Mum, please – I'd really like to know more about what it was like to grow up at Beaufont Hall. It would help me see past the sadness of how Lloyd lived there.'

Rebecca fixed her gaze on her daughter and considered her words before she spoke. 'It was wonderful, in a way. Idyllic. As you know, my father passed away when I was a teenager – not long after my grandparents died – but when the grieving got easier it was actually quite fun. For so long it was just my mother and me, yet the house was rarely empty: my aunt Aster and Rose and Lloyd were there practically every day when I was younger, as well as my friends from school. My mother was a stickler for tradition, so we used to dress for dinner every night – only Rose and I wore outrageous ballgowns, which enraged Mummy. She knew we were mocking her but she could never prove it. And Lloyd obviously looked incredibly handsome in his suits. When we eat supper as a family now, I sometimes remember it – it seems so ridiculous in hindsight.'

Cassie could picture her mother sitting at a long table in the dining room, dressed up to the nines. She'd have looked beautiful, despite her outlandish outfits.

'And what was Beaufont like? Was it glorious?'

'It was,' Rebecca said simply. Cassie saw sadness in her eyes, and she knew it wasn't just because she was remembering Rose, who'd passed away from breast cancer when Cassie was small, or Lloyd, whose life had ended up so insular. 'My mother was the eldest daughter, so she'd always known the house would be passed down to her, but by the time she claimed it as her own, the money had started to run out. In a way that didn't matter – we were a small family and we didn't need much in the way of staff. Mrs Winter looked after the house and us, and her husband looked after the grounds. So long as we kept up appearances to the rest of the world, my mother was happy. Obviously I didn't care too much about that.'

'Did you use the whole house?'

Rebecca considered this. 'Not really,' she said. 'We didn't do so intentionally, but some doors remained closed for years – purely because we didn't go into those rooms. We used the drawing room and dining room for entertaining, but we mainly kept to the smaller rooms, which were warmer. There was a small den with forget-me-not wallpaper on the ground floor that we spent lots of time gossiping in . . .' Rebecca's voice trailed away, and Cassie noticed that her mother had paled; that her shoulders had tensed.

'What is it?' she asked, but Rebecca shook her head.

'It's nothing,' she said, and she stood and gathered the empty teacups. When she noticed that her daughter didn't look convinced, she offered her a smile. 'Really, it's nothing. It's just that sometimes it's painful to recall memories – even if they're good ones.'

Cassie looked puzzled. 'But why?'

Rebecca sighed and stood in the doorway. 'I suppose it's

because it hurts to think one will never experience those tiny moments of pure joy again,' she concluded.

As she walked out of the bedroom, Cassie wondered what it was about Beaufont Hall – or the people who'd once lived there – that so haunted her mother.

Chapter Three

Buckinghamshire, recently

Cassie picked her way through the maze of corridors at Beaufont Hall, trying to retrace the steps she'd taken with Ed to find the rooms in which Lloyd had lived. In one hand was a roll of black bin bags and a bucket and mop; in the other was a holdall filled with several wind-up lanterns, a thermos and a lunchbox of sandwiches. Under her arm was a wooden broom, and in her heart there was a steely resolve to clean the former library as thoroughly as she could. Her arms ached as she lugged everything with her, but she knew it would be worth it. She wanted to spend a decent amount of time working through everything Lloyd had hoarded in his time at the house, and she needed to be prepared if she was to do it properly.

When she eventually found the library, she was dismayed to see that it looked worse than she remembered, although Ed must have opened a window so it wouldn't smell quite so bad. She knew that house-elves didn't exist in real life – and if they did, she'd immediately present them with clothes so they could be free – but she wished she lived in a Harry Potter land where the whole of Beaufont Hall could be fixed with a flick of a wand. She looked longingly at the books hidden behind piles of Lloyd's rubbish, but she knew that cleaning the room came first. Only when it was clean would she allow herself to look at the volumes her family had collected and treasured.

'Need a hand?' Ed's footsteps should have alerted Cassie to his presence, but she was so lost in thought that the sound of his voice made her jump. She turned around and smiled.

'I do . . . but I have no idea where to begin,' she admitted. She looked at the mountains of rubbish on the floor and tried not to feel overwhelmed.

'If in doubt, start at the beginning,' Ed said with a grin, and he took the roll of bin bags from Cassie's hands, opened one, and began to fill it with crisp packets from a pile close to his foot. Cassie watched him uncomfortably.

'I know this may sound a bit odd,' she began slowly, 'but did this stuff *mean* something to Lloyd? Are we casually throwing things away that he put a lot of time and care and attention into?'

Ed put the bin bag down. 'I know this is hard,' he began, 'and maybe Lloyd *did* care about the things he collected, but at the end of the day, everything here is rubbish. We need to clear it away.'

Cassie knew she was being overly sentimental and ridiculous; she hadn't even known her mother's cousin. 'You're right, of course you are, but it just seems so cold and heartless. I've never had to clear things away after someone's death. It's not as easy as I thought it would be.'

Ed gave her a wry smile. 'But we're talking about crisp packets and pizza boxes, not photographs and mementos from his life. And if we find personal things like that, we won't throw them away.'

Despite herself, Cassie smiled. 'I'm being stupid, aren't I?'

Ed shook his head. 'You care about family,' he replied. 'You're showing you have a heart.'

Cassie could feel a blush rising on her neck and she ducked to hide it. As she unravelled a bin bag of her own, she told herself to get a grip. She so rarely spoke to good-looking men that she felt unsure of herself, and she wished she had that courage, that charm, that Safia had. Because Ed *was* good-looking; he was the sort of man she went out of her way to avoid in London because he seemed so self-assured and at ease with himself. He was the opposite of her.

'Everyone has a heart,' she muttered into the silence – and then she set to work and lost herself in the rhythm of scooping up tatty carrier bags, sifting through them, and discarding them as quickly as she could. Every so often she'd glance up to see how Ed was getting on; he was as quiet and methodical as she was, and they worked in companionable silence, speaking only to ask how the other was doing.

'There's something quite meditative about filling bin bags and clearing a space, isn't there?' Ed said after several hours of working through the rubbish.

Cassie had been daydreaming about meeting a Captain Corelli type from Louis de Bernières' novel, and when Ed's voice cut through her thoughts, she found herself feeling awkward around him again. She was thankful for the darkness of the room as the afternoon sun began to sink in the sky.

She straightened up and turned away to survey the room until her blush had faded. To her surprise they'd got rid of nearly all the rubbish, and as Ed wound the lanterns, she could see the library clearly, could picture it as it would once have been. Despite the smudges of dirt and dust, the artificial light of the lanterns picked out the rich tones of the wooden floor, and even though there were marks on the flocked wallpaper and the room was freezing cold, it felt cosy and comforting. Cassie could understand why Lloyd had chosen to set up camp here, and she wondered which of her other relatives had used the library. Had her grandmother Violet? Her grandfather Nicholas? Or perhaps it was her great-grandfather Philip who'd had a desk in here. The room was heavy with masculinity, but Cassie liked to picture her mother curled up in an armchair, a blanket on her lap and a Shakespeare play in her hands – even though Rebecca rarely read for her own pleasure and much preferred to visit the theatre to watch plays in action.

'Cleaning up is meditative *and* satisfying,' she replied once she'd gathered herself and her thoughts. 'And, you know, I can't quite believe how many books were hidden behind all Lloyd's stuff. I thought there'd only be a handful.'

Ed had been clearing the shelves of Lloyd's plastic bags of miscellany, and Cassie walked over to one of them to work out how the books were organised, but if they were in any sort of order she couldn't make sense of it, for they weren't arranged alphabetically. She supposed they might have been shelved to the Dewey Decimal System, but she didn't know how that worked; she wished she'd paid more attention in the school library when it had been explained to them.

'Can you spot a valuable book quite easily?' Ed asked, breaking into her thoughts.

Cassie shrugged. 'It depends,' she said. 'If I've heard of the author, that's a good start, but sometimes first editions can go for thousands if they're in a niche subject. I like reading fiction, but collectable first editions of novels are hard to come by.'

Ed nodded. 'What's the most valuable book you've had in the shop?'

Cassie lit up at the memory, and all feelings of self-consciousness vanished; enthusing about books was the most natural thing in the world for her. 'It was *The Sun Also Rises* by Hemingway,' she said. 'We didn't sell it in the shop – it was far too valuable to keep on the shop floor – but it went for a hundred and twenty-five thousand at auction.'

'Fuck.' Ed's eyes widened as he contemplated this figure. 'What was it that made it so valuable?'

'Several things. It was a first edition and a first printing, and it was in the original dust jacket – it hadn't been damaged at all. But Hemingway himself also inscribed it. When I looked at it I couldn't quite believe it – the idea that one of my favourite authors had held that very same book blew my mind.'

Ed grinned. 'That does sound kind of special. Do you think there might be something of that value on these shelves?'

Cassie shrugged. 'I doubt it, but there's no harm in looking. My mum doesn't think there is, but she isn't really into reading – she's into the theatre and plays rather than books. She adores Shakespeare but only when she's watching it or performing it. She's dyslexic, you see. My brother and sister and I are named after Shakespearean characters too – the twins are called Henry and Alice.'

'Where's Cassandra from?'

Cassie grinned. 'Have you heard of *Troilus and Cressida*? She's a character from that. Although it could have been a lot worse. Mum wanted to call me Ophelia until my father put his foot down.'

Ed chuckled. 'Is your mother an actress?'

'She was, although she was never a household name,' Cassie replied. 'She does behind-the-scenes stuff now – long hours for little pay, but she loves it.'

There was a long silence. Ed was watching her. She could see in his eyes that he recognised her shyness, and that he was assessing if he should leave her be or not.

He stretched out his arms and rubbed at his shoulders. 'I

think I'm done for the day. Are you going to stick around for a bit longer?'

Cassie's back ached but she wanted to go through the books on the shelves, wanted to see if there really was anything more valuable than the ones she'd already taken home.

'I think so,' she replied. The air in the house was now bitterly cold, and she rubbed her hands together to try to keep them warm.

Ed noticed her discomfort. 'I've got some blankets in my car,' he said. 'Shall I go and get them?'

Cassie nodded gratefully. When Ed returned, he was carrying some heavy, itchy-looking throws that smelled of damp but would keep her warm.

'I found these in the glove compartment too,' he said, offering her a pair of woollen mittens. They were a deep indigo and were far too small for Ed's own hands. 'They belonged to my ex-girlfriend but I doubt she wants them back.'

Unlike the blankets, the mittens were beautifully soft – they had to be cashmere.

'I'd hate to get them dirty.'

'I really don't mind if you do,' Ed replied. He looked as though he was on the verge of saying something about their previous owner, but then changed the subject. 'If you need anything else, just give me a ring. If you can't get a signal in here, you should be able to in the east of the house. I'm around all weekend.'

Cassie was immensely grateful for all Ed's help – there was no way she'd have been able to clear the library so quickly without him – but as he left, and his retreating footsteps disappeared into silence, she found herself breathing a long sigh of relief. However kind and friendly Ed was, Cassie found she couldn't quite relax around him, and therefore she couldn't enjoy the fact that she was finally at Beaufont Hall.

But now that she was alone – truly alone for the first time since she'd arrived at the family home – she felt her tense body uncoil. She draped one of Ed's blankets around her shoulders, pulled on his ex-girlfriend's cashmere gloves, and took a deep breath. Underneath the damp and decay was the true soul of Beaufont Hall, and it was so close she could almost touch it.

Nightfall descended across Buckinghamshire, but Cassie was so entranced by the books on the shelves that she barely noticed the darkness or the sharp, biting cold. She didn't think that any of the hardbacks she'd found were particularly valuable, but nevertheless she'd organised them into three piles. On the left were the books that she knew probably wouldn't find another home; they were niche interest manuals that would sell for very little should they ever grace the shelves of a bookshop. In the middle were the novels she thought Mr Heritage might like to stock in his shop – these were the books that people would buy for themselves or for friends. They weren't worth very much and nor were they rare, but they *were* interesting. The final pile contained the sort of hardbacks that Cassie thought could raise a little money. It included a copy of *The Naulahka* by Kipling from 1908, a first edition of *A Kist of Whistles* by Hugh MacDiarmid, and a bound set of John Milton's poetry from 1983.

If she could have done, Cassie would have kept all the books for herself, but she knew it was pointless – she didn't have the space for them in her bedroom at her parents' house, and as much as she loved to hold real books in her hands, she adored her Kindle. There were a couple that she knew she'd not be parted with: a battered edition of *A Bear Called Paddington* from 1962 that *must* have been read to her mother when she was a child, and a copy of *Charlie and the Chocolate Factory* from 1964.

When she looked closely at the latter, she felt her heart beat slightly faster. She'd correctly recognised the distinctive purple cover as that of a first edition, and the book was in perfect condition, with dark-green coated endpapers and gilt edges. It would probably sell for a decent amount of money, but she didn't want to sell it. Having to say goodbye to Beaufont Hall itself was bad enough.

Cassie glanced at her watch and realised that it was now late evening; she'd missed dinner and yet she wasn't hungry. She knew she had to drive back to London, but she decided to finish looking at the section of the library she'd been working on. She continued to slide books from the shelves, but, disappointingly, there was nothing else that could be of any value. She was about to call it a day – it was pitch black outside now, and the wind-up lamps were beginning to dim as they ran out of energy – when she spotted a shoebox in the shadows of the shelves. Her muscles ached and her fingers were numb with cold despite the mittens, but she couldn't resist opening the box.

Inside was a collection of notebooks tied together with a grubby pale-pink ribbon. Cassie slipped the top notebook out and stared at it for a moment. It was a diary of some sort, but in the fading light of the room she couldn't be sure who had written it, or when. Could it have belonged to a Tempest? She hoped so. She balanced the dusty box on top of the piles of books she wanted to show Mr Heritage, picked the brightest lamp up from the floor, and slowly made her way back to her car.

'What have we here?'

It was several days later, and Mr Heritage was looking through the collection of books in front of him. Despite being in his mid-seventies, Mr Heritage was keen on new technology

– he'd learnt how to use Skype so he could chat to his son, who'd emigrated to Australia, and he always responded to his emails from his iPhone. The bookshop looked as antique and traditional as many of the books they stocked, but Mr Heritage loved the Internet and often sold mid-level valuable books on eBay. Whenever Cassie wanted to get in touch with her boss, she knew that email was her best option, and when she'd asked if he could come to Heritage Books to see what she'd discovered in Beaufont Hall, Mr Heritage had been happy to oblige.

'I thought these books might be valuable, and wondered what you thought. I found them in the library of my family's old home and I'd like to sell them. We can't keep them; we just don't have the space.'

Cassie found she was holding her breath as Mr Heritage picked up the first edition of *The Naulahka*.

'This is a beautiful copy,' he murmured as he carefully examined the book. 'But I doubt it's worth much – some copies of this have only sold for twenty pounds on eBay.'

'I was hoping it would be worth more,' Cassie replied. She was unable to keep the disappointment from her voice.

Mr Heritage gave her a rare smile. 'Twenty pounds is still twenty pounds,' he remarked. He continued to look through the books until he uncovered a copy of *Études de Nu* by Germaine Krull. Cassie had included it as she'd noticed it was a first edition, but she knew nothing of the author and had never heard of the book.

'Now *this* is a find,' he pronounced as his blue eyes lit up with enthusiasm. 'There was only one printing of this, possibly because a collection of nude photographs – however tasteful – would have been considered rather racy in its day. Krull was believed to be quite the radical photographer. Now, there are over twenty full-page photographic plates, though the portfolio is a bit dusty, and there's a stain on the pastedown . . . I'd say it could fetch up to seven thousand pounds. From memory, this title is incredibly scarce.'

Cassie's heart leapt at the news. 'I had no idea,' she murmured. 'That would be fantastic. Do you think we could find a buyer for it?'

'I think so,' he replied. 'Now tell me, are there any more books like this?'

Cassie nodded. 'Some. I spent most of the weekend going through about half of them, and these were the ones I thought looked the most valuable. I'm planning on going back next weekend to carry on cleaning the house, but I also want to see what else I can find.'

Mr Heritage paused for a moment, then gave Cassie a long look and raised his bushy white eyebrows. 'I can source buyers for these books fairly quickly, but you need to be certain you *want* to sell them. *Are* you absolutely certain?'

Cassie hadn't explored much of Beaufont Hall yet, but she assumed there was very little of the Tempests left in the house. Her family – her *ancestors* – had bought these books, read these books, but she knew it was pointless to be sentimental about things she couldn't keep.

'I'm certain,' she replied as firmly as she could. 'And I'm sure my mother would be grateful for any money we raise.'

Mr Heritage nodded, apparently satisfied with her answer.

'Leave these with me, and I'll work my magic.'

Chapter Four

London, 1978

Eliza Boyle wasn't in a particularly good mood as she walked home languidly from school. She was failing her lessons (which was surprising considering she'd done quite well in her O levels), was sick of being treated like a child by her teachers and her parents, and the weather was still hot. Really, really hot.

As she tilted her face towards the blazing afternoon sun, she wondered if her parents would still be acting secretive and strange. Unlike so many of the girls at school, Eliza's parents were blissfully happy; Lillie and Bertie were madly in love despite their different backgrounds. But something was going on, something *adult* that Eliza hadn't been told about. She didn't know what it was, and she guessed it wasn't anything too serious, but she didn't like the fact that her parents were pretending everything was okay. They'd always said it was important to be honest and open with each other, but for several weeks her mother's once beautiful face had been pinched and drawn with obvious worry, and her father was distracted, stubborn clouds of pensiveness floating across his usually sunny expression. They put on an act when Eliza was around, but she wasn't a child any more; she was seventeen, and she knew something was amiss. She just didn't know what they were protecting her from – or why.

As Eliza's tatty flared jeans trailed against the sticky melting tarmac of the pavement, she wondered if other families were as unconventional as hers. Maybe they were behind closed doors, but she doubted it. Her parents had met at a party only eighteen years before, and according to her mother it had been love at first sight. They'd had a seductive whirlwind romance, and a mere two months after their first hot, sticky encounter, they'd discovered Lillie was pregnant. A swift wedding followed, and Eliza Pearl Boyle was born to parents who were still in the throes of their first flush of sexual attraction. They didn't have much money, but Lillie and Bertie adored each other, and they loved their daughter with a crushing ferocity.

Love – along with a council flat – was apparently enough.

Eliza slowed to a stop when she reached the promenade of shops under the flats in which her family lived. She was suddenly aware that sweat was creating a little pool in her bra, but she didn't rush inside to change into something else. Instead she gazed up at the windows of their tiny flat and wondered – for what felt like the hundredth time – how it compared to the mansion in which her mother had grown up.

At Beaufont Hall there had been staff, fresh flowers daily, and Lillie had had everything she'd ever wanted . . . until she'd run off with Bertie Boyle and her family had turned their backs on her. She had hoped her parents would forgive her in time, but they never had, and therefore Lillie's little family was poor and alone and had to make ends meet on the wages that she and Bertie managed to pull in.

Eliza tried not to care, but it was hard. Her mother always said it was better to have integrity than money, but as Eliza felt the sweat begin to ruin her only good blouse, she wondered if this was really true.

'You're later than normal,' Lillie Boyle remarked as Eliza walked into the kitchen. Eliza's legs were heavy, her shoulders ached from carrying her full school bag up the concrete stairs to the flat, and her face was shiny with perspiration. She desperately wanted a drink of water, then to take all her clothes off and wash the sweat from her body, but before she could do anything, Lillie reached for her and kissed her sticky forehead. Eliza squirmed. Lillie had been brought up in a cold, unaffectionate household and she was determined that her daughter would know what love was. Eliza didn't mind her mother being demonstrative in private, but she *did* mind being treated like she was ten years old. She pulled away and slouched against the kitchen counter as she gulped down a pint of tap water.

'It was too hot to rush home,' she replied after she'd downed most of the glass.

'And how was school today?' Lillie had asked Eliza this same question every day for years and years, and without fail, Eliza would reply that school was fine. The reality was a bit different – she hated most of her classmates, she didn't want to bother with sixth form and she wanted to get a job – but she knew her mother didn't want to hear that. She looked at Lillie as she finished her glass of water and thought she saw tension on her mother's face. Something was bothering her, she just knew it.

'Yeah, it was all right,' she replied. She wondered if it was worth asking Lillie what the matter was; her mother could give vague answers to questions too. She decided to ease her way in. 'Is Dad around?'

Lillie paused. 'He's out – he won't be home for dinner,' she said. Her blue eyes darted around the kitchen, and she gave Eliza a bright, over-wide smile.

Eliza didn't know what to say. What could she say? She knew her mother was waiting for a response – one which was complicit to the evasive behaviour her parents had recently adopted – but Eliza wasn't the kind of girl not to ask questions, not to take things at face value. That wasn't how she'd been raised.

'What's he doing?' she asked eventually as she ran the cold tap and refilled her glass. She felt as though she were wilting on the spot, but she ignored it; she was going to get to the bottom of this. She was determined to.

Lillie feigned indifference. 'He's going to the pub with some friends from work,' she said casually. 'They have business to discuss.'

'He's been doing that a lot recently,' Eliza said. She could tell from her mother's expression that Lillie was telling the truth, but she couldn't work out what business her father would have to talk about – his job as a waste collector was fairly simple.

'I don't know what you mean,' Lillie replied, but her eyes couldn't hide the worry.

Eliza couldn't stand that her parents were keeping something from her, and she especially hated that her father was being secretive. She knew it was a cliché that she was a daddy's girl, but she couldn't help it. She and Bertie were exactly the same: they matched.

'Look, Mum, I know something's up, and I'm not a child,' she said. Her voice came out sounding more cross than she'd meant it to, and she softened it into a plea. 'Please tell me what's going on, even if you think I won't understand. It can't be *that* bad – it's not like you're getting a divorce or something.'

For a moment Eliza thought her mother wasn't going to answer. 'It's union business,' Lillie said eventually, with an exasperated sigh. 'Lots of the men are angry about Callaghan's plan to cap wages at five per cent and they want to do something about it. They all deserve pay rises but it doesn't look like they're going to get them. Your father is trying to organise something to force the government's hand.'

Eliza digested this. 'Like a strike?'

'Like a strike,' Lillie confirmed. 'But it involves getting all the men on side and some don't want to get their hands dirty in case they lose their jobs. Your father's trying to persuade them, as the union doesn't think they have any other option.'

'But if it goes wrong, will Dad lose his job?' Eliza asked.

Lillie hesitated, and Eliza swallowed hard. Even though Lillie worked too – she was a part-time seamstress in a local tailor's – they barely managed as it was.

'He won't if all the unions can work together and at the same time. It's not just the bin men who are considering striking – it's everyone. The country could end up in chaos by the end of the year if they're successful, but it would be worth it – everyone deserves a fair wage for a fair day's work.'

Eliza grinned at her mother. Everyone around here thought Lillie was stuck-up and spoke posh, but if they took the time to get to know her, they'd realise she was the biggest socialist going.

'I agree with that,' she said.

Lillie smiled at her daughter and ruffled her hair, and Eliza forced herself not to pull away. 'Of course you do. There's no other way to think. But I don't want you to worry about this. Your father knows what he's doing and he won't lose his job. He'll be okay.'

'Is that why you didn't tell me what he was up to? Because if the worst comes to the worst I could get a job in a shop or something. I saw a sign outside the grocer's, they're looking for someone . . .'

'This is exactly why we didn't want to worry you. You know how important I think school is, not least because my father didn't believe in education for girls. I want something better for you; I want you to shine like a star. Now, what do you want for dinner – I was thinking shepherd's pie?'

Eliza swallowed. She might have her father wrapped around her little finger, but her mother was a different story, and when Lillie Boyle wanted to change the subject, the subject was changed.

'Shepherd's pie would be nice,' she said, even though she secretly thought it was too hot to eat something like that.

Lillie made a start on dinner, chattering about her day at work. As she began to tell a story about a woman who'd wanted a dress altered because she'd put on too much weight, Eliza found herself wondering what had happened to the woman her mother had once been, the Lillie Tempest who'd grown up in splendour and had only learned to sew because that was what girls were supposed to do. It didn't happen often, but sometimes – especially when Lillie smiled or laughed – Eliza could picture her mother as her former, younger incarnation: a beautiful girl resplendent in diamonds and furs.

'. . . And after all that, she decided not to get the dress altered and said she'd go to Dorothy Perkins to get a replacement.'

Eliza nodded vaguely. 'Can I give you a hand with dinner?' she asked.

Lillie smiled fondly at her daughter.

'Thanks, darling, but I'd rather you made a start on your homework.' She began to slice some miserable-looking carrots. 'It won't be ready for a while, but I'll call you when it is.'

*

In the haven of her stuffy bedroom, Eliza peeled off her clothes until she was naked but for her ratty bra and knickers. She threw open the tiny window in a futile attempt to let in some fresh air, then fell on to her bed, her body slick with sweat. Her bedroom had always been her sanctuary, but recently she'd started to feel like a tiger trapped in a cage built for a kitten. There had to be more to life than this: a collection of battered Sindy dolls, roller-skates gathering dust, and thin posters torn from *Look-in* magazine. She looked up at the pictures of the Bay City Rollers and David Essex that she'd once hung so carefully on her walls, and tried to remember what she'd ever seen in the teen idols. They were so fresh-faced and *wholesome*. She resolved to replace them with photos of cooler bands, like The Clash and The Ramones. The music scene in London was on fire, and whenever Eliza read *Melody Maker*, she wished she was part of it. The songs that these bands played spoke to her; like her, they were enraged with the world they lived in. She didn't know much about politics, but she knew the government had messed the country up and that she was stuck on this estate, regardless of how she did at school. Her mother might want her to shine like a star, but unless she did something drastic, Eliza was going nowhere, A levels or not.

When she tried to talk about this stuff at school, her teachers told her that having strong feelings was part of growing up, but that studying hard *would* help her. They said that all teenagers felt like she did, but she didn't believe it for a second. Yes, her classmates had the same lack of prospects – they were all in this together, after all – but they didn't have the hollow feeling that Eliza had; they couldn't do. Because when it came down to it, Eliza was *supposed* to have prospects: she was supposed to be a Tempest.

Okay, so being a member of a society family and the

establishment was desperately unfashionable, and not something Eliza could quite imagine her father being comfortable with, but it also meant that her life could be very different. If she were a Tempest, she'd not have to worry about her one good blouse being ruined by sweat, and they wouldn't have to worry about Bertie losing his job, because he probably wouldn't *have* a job. Or not a job like the one he currently had.

Eliza lay back on her bed, squeezed her eyes shut and tried to fall into her favourite fantasy – the one where she lived in the parallel world of her dreams. In it, she and her parents would dine as a family in Beaufont Hall. They'd drink champagne in the glorious rosy glow of the sunset, they'd eat meals prepared with ingredients from Fortnum's under a gleaming chandelier, and after dinner they'd sip cocktails and friends would come over and they'd all dance and have fun. Eliza had always imagined herself as a princess, and while she'd kind of outgrown that fantasy and would rather look punky, it was still her favourite one. She'd wear a silky emerald-green gown, with satin heels on her feet and pearls in her hair. In her fantasy she was beautiful, poised and refined, and the world was her oyster. She could do anything, she could be anything, and she was free.

But things weren't like that, were they?

Instead of living a comfortable life in the chocolate-box village near the family pile, the Boyles had a shabby council flat in a run-down part of Tottenham. Instead of wearing the latest fashions in luxurious fabrics, Eliza wore second-hand jeans that didn't fit properly. And instead of being in Buckinghamshire, where they were meant to be, the Boyles were outcasts.

Eliza knew she sounded like an entitled brat, but it was hard to be humble when her mother had been punished for absolutely no reason at all.

Of course, things weren't so terrible. They weren't homeless, or starving, and yeah, they all loved each other, but Eliza knew that her life could have been very different; it could have been a glittering whirlwind of fun.

Instead, Beaufont Hall and all that wealth belonged to the family who'd cut her mother out of their lives just because she fell in love with Bertie Boyle and not someone more suitable. She might never have met them, but Eliza hated the Tempests and what they'd done to Lillie with a burning passion.

She sat up, pulled out her diary, and tried to write her frustration away.

Chapter Five

Cassie gently placed the diary on her desk and stared at it. She'd started with the earliest notebook in the collection – the one with '1978' painted in Tipp-Ex on the red cloth-bound cover – and even though she'd only been reading it for half an hour, she was transfixed. She might not know who Eliza Boyle was, but she understood the raw emotions that bled from her writing. Cassie too had been frustrated and full of discontent when she'd been a teenager. Who hadn't been?

She opened her laptop and did a quick Google search of both 'Eliza Boyle' and 'Eliza Tempest'. For the former, several results came up, but Cassie quickly ascertained that the Eliza who had written the diaries wasn't a romantic novelist or an Irish immigrant from the 1800s. There was even less for 'Eliza Tempest'. Cassie frowned and tried searches for 'Lillie Tempest', 'Lillie Boyle' and 'Bertie Boyle'. Again, very little appeared on the results screen, and what there was didn't seem relevant. She closed her laptop and went back to the diary, wishing that her mother wasn't so reluctant to discuss the Tempests; that she didn't abruptly end every conversation Cassie tried to have with her about them.

Despite musing on it for years, Cassie didn't understand why her mother didn't share her enthusiasm for their family history. She knew that Rebecca had been close to her mother, and she'd assumed that it hurt to talk about her because she missed her. But it had been many years since Violet had passed away, and the doors to Beaufont Hall had been firmly closed to everyone but Lloyd. What haunted Rebecca so much that it made her hesitant to talk about the Tempests?

Of course, Cassie knew she could go downstairs and ask her mother if she knew who Lillie, Bertie and Eliza were, but she was also aware that Rebecca wouldn't wish to discuss it, regardless of whether she'd known them or not. They were clearly members of the family, but perhaps they were a distant branch – a branch who'd endured relative poverty while the others had enjoyed a life of luxury at Beaufont Hall. But that didn't explain how Eliza Boyle's diaries had ended up hidden away in Beaufont's library, or why Eliza was so angry at the unspoken misfortune that cast a shadow over the Boyles.

Cassie pulled out the box of old family photos that her mother had said she could have: pictures that Rebecca considered unflattering, or too over- or underexposed to be included in the formal family album. The photographs were mainly of Violet and Nicholas from the 1960s, and there were also plenty of snaps of Rebecca growing up at Beaufont – ones that Rebecca hated because she thought she looked podgy or had a terrible 1970s haircut. However, there were several photographs of other members of the family: one of Rose and Lloyd taken in Beaufont's formerly impressive gardens, and several of Aster, sitting serenely under an apple tree. As Cassie flicked through the pictures, she was struck by melancholy; Lloyd had been the only surviving Tempest other than her mother, and he was gone now, too.

She continued to leaf through the photographs until she

found her favourite one of her mother. It was a black and white portrait that had become bleached with age, and it had been discounted by Rebecca because she'd been caught mid-blink, but that didn't detract from her beauty. Her hair was loose around her face, her fringe was in need of a trim, and she looked happy. Free. Cassie stared at the photograph and wondered when her mother's face had become tired and pinched, when her hair had lost its lustre. What had happened to Rebecca to make her so weary of life . . . or was it just life itself that had done it to her?

As she tidied the photos away and climbed into bed, she remained lost in thought. She thought of Rebecca's idyllic childhood at Beaufont Hall, of Eliza's more difficult one on a council estate in Tottenham, and she wondered what Eliza Boyle was up to now. She planned on finding out.

'We should have the power back on in about an hour,' the electrician informed Cassie, who was sitting cross-legged on the recently washed floor of the library, surrounded by books. She glanced at Ed through the unboarded window – he and the roofer were in the garden, in deep discussion about how to replace the slate tiles – then turned and grinned at the electrician with the triumphant smile of someone who'd achieved something deemed impossible. She was proud that it was she who'd discovered the books that Mr Heritage had sold, and proud that she'd managed to persuade her mother to spend nearly £7,000 of the proceeds on Beaufont Hall. The house was a long way away from being in a marketable condition, but at least there would be no more water damage, and there was electricity so she could turn the lights on and start to clean the rest of the house properly.

'Thank you so much,' she said.

The electrician smiled at her. 'The electrics aren't in great shape – the whole house could do with an overhaul and some modernisation – but they should keep for a while. I'd get some mouse traps down, though; try to stop the buggers from chewing through the wires.'

Cassie nodded, and made a mental note to find a more humane way to deter the mice. In the absence of any Tempests, a family had moved in and made the house their own.

'Tommy reckons he'll be a few more days on the roof,' Ed said as he walked into the library. He nodded at the electrician, who took a sip of tea from his thermos and went back to work in the depths of Beaufont. 'The damage isn't as bad as we originally thought, so you may be able to get it under the quoted price.'

'That will keep my mother happy,' Cassie said.

'Speaking of which, have you found any more books that you think you could sell?'

Cassie chose not to tell Ed about the hardbacks she'd placed carefully in her bag, which included a 1924 copy of *Public School Verse* by Auden, *From Sea to Sea* by Kipling from 1901, and a book that excited her above all others – *Rumour at Nightfall* by Graham Greene. The copy she'd unearthed was a first edition and first printing from 1931, and it was impeccable – from the dust jacket to the original red cloth. Cassie knew that a similar version had sold at auction for £40,000, and she dared to hope that this one would be just as valuable. She didn't want to say anything until she'd spoken with both Mr Heritage and her mother.

Instead, she gazed over at the piles she'd made and shook her head. 'There's a couple of interesting novels, but I'm not sure yet,' she replied.

Ed looked genuinely crestfallen for her, and Cassie remembered that he had feelings for Beaufont too. 'That's a shame,' he said. 'Maybe now the lights are on it will be easier to see the books. Work out if they're worth more than you thought.'

'Maybe,' Cassie replied, and smiled at him as she brushed her dusty hands on her jeans.

'Anyway, I nipped back home and brought you a kettle,' Ed announced. His auburn hair blazed red under the newly switched-on lights, and his green eyes shone emerald behind his glasses. Cassie was momentarily struck by how attractive he was. It rendered her slightly dumb.

'That's brilliant,' she replied as warmly as she could, although she was squirming with shyness from his direct gaze. 'You're really looking after me, and I appreciate it.'

'It's what my family have been doing for yours for a long time,' Ed said lightly. 'Besides, I want to help – I hate seeing Beaufont in this state. Can I make you a cup of tea? I left a couple of mugs and some tea bags in the kitchen.'

Cassie shook her head. 'I'd love one, but now that the power's on, I'd like to see more of the house.'

'Then let me show you around properly,' Ed suggested firmly. 'The first time I did it, you weren't able to see very much at all.'

As Ed introduced Cassie to the Beaufont that was now lit by bright electric light, she was struck again by how beautiful and wonderful the house must have been – and how tragic it had become. Each room was dirty, the air thick with dust, but she could see that the house couldn't have changed much since her grandmother Violet's death in 1990. Furniture had been removed, and any paintings worth any money had been auctioned long ago, but the house had a timeless quality, and she thought that if she listened hard enough she might even hear the echoes of footsteps from years ago. Were there any lingering memories of laughter and joy? She hoped so, but she wasn't sure. Beaufont had an unmistakable air of despondency.

Yet despite this, she felt euphoric when she walked into a room and noticed a detail she'd not spotted before: the velvety flocking on the grubby wallpaper of the ruby-red sitting room; the vibrant jewel tones of the floor tiling under the dirt in the pantry; the intricate cornicing on rooms so large they could only have been used for entertaining.

When they came to the Great Drawing Room, Cassie found she was holding her breath in excitement. The formerly palatial room was a shadow of what it must once have been, but when she squeezed her eyes tight, she could imagine how it had been when her mother was small, spending childhood Christmases huddled in front of the fire as the family trimmed the tree. She could picture a long table on the stone floor, and oil paintings and tapestries hung high above the wooden panelling. She could see a rich, intricate rug running the length of the room, gleaming white antlers above burnished gold mirrors, a roaring fire within the marble fireplace, and candles dotted against a Christmas tree, casting shadows on the faces of those who entered the room in their formal attire.

However, in spite of her active imagination, she still couldn't conjure up the spirit of the Tempests who'd used this room as their own; she didn't feel close to the members of her family who'd once lived in this house. She'd hoped to sense their presence or share the feelings they must have had, but they were as distant as ever.

'Can we see the bedrooms now?' she asked suddenly, and Ed blinked at her. 'Can we go upstairs? I want to see some of the rooms that weren't used for receiving guests.'

As Ed led Cassie up the main staircase, she tried not to look at the rotting wood of the banister. Would whoever bought the house be able to restore it to the opulence and grandeur that the previous inhabitants had once been used to?

'We can't know, of course, who used which room . . . but this is one of the master bedrooms, so one of your relatives must have slept in here,' Ed said, his voice cutting into Cassie's thoughts. 'What do you think?'

Cassie thought it was unmistakably elegant, yet she was disappointed. For despite the hardwood oak floors, the soft grey marble fireplace, and the creamy-white dado rails and skirting boards, it was just another anonymous room. Perhaps her grandmother had slept here, or even her great-grandparents, but if they had, Cassie felt nothing. She realised she was being naive in thinking she'd be able to conjure some closeness to the family members who'd stood in this doorway before her.

'Are they all like this?' she asked. Her voice was quiet, yet it still sounded troubled.

'What do you mean?'

'Are all the rooms so . . . empty?' she elaborated.

Ed watched her carefully for a moment. 'There's very little furniture left, yes. There are a few bits and pieces – a rug here, a side table there – but the majority of the rooms are completely free of furnishings. Unless you mean something else?'

Cassie was surprised at how perceptive he was, but chose not to react to it. Beaufont Hall mystified her. It was bewitching but stern, a house where her family had created memories for over a hundred years yet that now felt abandoned and cold. It was nothing like she'd expected it to be . . . and yet it was also more. Under the smudges and stains she could sense it was ready to be awakened; that it was full of possibility and hope.

'I don't know what I mean,' she concluded, to draw an end to the conversation. It was one too personal to have with Ed.

Despite his kindness, he was a relative stranger. She drew a deep breath and made herself stand tall and determined. 'Shall we start making a move?'

Ed nodded in agreement and shut the bedroom door after them. It closed with the slightest and softest of clicks, and they made their way back down the stairs.

'So, this Ed guy sounds hot,' Safia remarked as she toyed with her straw, prodding at the slice of lemon floating amongst the ice cubes to squeeze the juice into her gin and tonic. 'He's either really into Beaufont or he's really into you – no man would help out a stranger like that without an ulterior motive.'

Cassie smiled at Safia's cynicism. 'He probably has a girl-friend – he definitely has an ex, anyway – and he's assisting me because his father was meant to but can't because of his arthritis. His family used to look after Beaufont Hall when my family lived there, so I suppose he feels duty-bound to. It's that or he's bored.'

The girls sat on the red leather bar stools of the Dean Street Townhouse in Soho. Their elbows rested on the dark wood of the bar; their toes grazed the reclaimed oak flooring. If they'd wanted to, they would have been able to see their reflections in the mirror behind the bar, but they were too engrossed in their conversation.

'I still think he sounds keen. What does he look like?'

Cassie described him as best she could. 'He's tall and fairly broad – maybe six foot two? Something like that. And he has auburn hair and green eyes.'

'It's a sign that you fancy him if you notice the colour of his eyes.'

'I notice the colour of his eyes because he wears glasses that magnify them. It means nothing!'

Safia raised her eyebrows but remained silent. Cassie felt her face grow flushed.

'Even if he doesn't have a girlfriend, I'm fairly sure I'm not his type,' she continued. 'Ed is . . . he's one of those men who's confident, you know? He's not like me – he's at ease with who he is in a way I don't think I could ever be. When I'm around people I don't know, I'm just so awkward—'

'Yet self-aware,' Safia interrupted.

'Oh, believe me, I can't *not* be aware of how awkward I am. I'm sure Ed likes me, but not in that way.'

Safia sipped at her drink. 'Whatever you say,' she replied airily.

Cassie shook her head. She wanted to tell Safia how comfortable she felt knowing that Ed was somewhere else in the house when she was in the library, how his eyes had lit up when she'd shown him a beautifully bound first edition, and how his small acts of kindness – from making her a cup of tea to carrying books to her car – made her feel warm inside. But instead she remained silent. She knew consideration did not equate to attraction, and that Safia could blow her thoughts out of proportion.

'Anyway, now I've got the roof fixed and the electricity turned on, I can start to clean the house properly. I can't restore it, obviously, but when it's in a more reasonable state, we can put it on the market.'

Safia gave Cassie a small smile. 'You don't want to do that, though, do you?'

'No,' she replied immediately. 'Of course not. I mean, I like the idea of Beaufont being lived in again, but *I'd* like to live in it.'

'You can't actually *live* there,' Safia objected. 'From what you've said, it wouldn't even be fit for squatters.'

'It isn't right now. But if I had the money and the time, it could be beautiful. And I know it's a romantic daydream, but it feels like I *should* live there. Beaufont Hall has been in my family for generations, and soon it won't be. Right now it feels like a ruin, a haunted house where village kids go to hunt down ghosts and to spook each other, and I can't stand the thought of it being like that.'

The girls sat in silence for a moment. A waiter in a starched white apron rushed past with a tray of drinks, and Cassie lost herself in the lavish, humming atmosphere of the bar. Unlike so many London hotspots, there was something about the Dean Street Townhouse that sang to Cassie. She loved the decor – the dining room was a homage to the original Georgian facade – and she adored the upholstered vintage armchairs, the rich ox-blood-red leather of the booths, the perfect crisp white tablecloths. She couldn't remember what had been in the building before it had been transformed into a hotel and restaurant – had it been a cheesy pub? Possibly – but whenever she walked into the Dean Street Townhouse, she felt an immediate sense of calm, a sense that she was being looked after. It was a feeling not dissimilar to what she experienced when she was at Beaufont.

'When I realised there were lots of books left in the library, I'd hoped I'd be able to find loads of first editions that would somehow sell for hundreds of thousands of pounds so that I could restore the house and live in it,' she admitted. 'Childish, I know.'

'That's not childish. But it sounds as though the best thing you can do for the house is to clean it up, make it look as good as you can, and then say goodbye to it,' Safia said.

'I know. But the thing is, I *did* find some books. Mr Heritage thinks they could be worth thousands and thousands.'

Safia stared at her. 'Enough to fix up the house?'

Cassie shook her head and gave Safia a wry smile. 'From what my mother says, Beaufont is like a bottomless pit when it comes to money – there would never be enough.'

'So what are you going to do with it?'

Cassie paused. 'I don't know. I've got a couple of ideas, but the books and therefore the money belong to my mother, so ultimately it's up to her. She'll probably want to put it towards the twins' university fees.'

'And you'd rather spend it on Beaufont, I bet.'

'It's a hard one.' Cassie shrugged. 'There's no point putting the money back into the house if we sell it . . . but what if we don't sell it? What if we could invest the money so that we made enough to keep Beaufont?'

Safia looked quizzically at her friend. 'I don't think I understand.'

Cassie grinned. 'I have a couple of ideas, but that's all they are right now – ideas. All I do know for definite is that I'm not ready to say goodbye to Beaufont just yet.'

'Do you have a deadline to get the house ready by?'

Cassie shook her head. 'My mother wants to get on with it as soon as we can, but I don't think there's any great rush. If there was, she'd insist on us using a cleaning company rather than letting me do all the hard work.'

'Then take your time,' Safia said with a shrug. 'It's your house too, in a way.'

'Not for much longer,' Cassie said sadly. She shook herself out of feeling maudlin. She was grateful to be able to spend a small amount of time at the house, and even though the chance of being able to keep Beaufont in the family was slim, it was still there; it had to be. She raised her glass. 'To Beaufont Hall, and to whatever the future holds for it.'

'To Beaufont Hall,' echoed Safia. 'And to spending a bit more time with this mysterious Ed guy, too.'

Cassie didn't comment, but she'd been raising her glass to that too.

Chapter Six

London, 1978

Eliza Boyle was angry a lot of the time. She hated being in the sixth form; she hated the relentless studying, the boring lessons, the organisation of homework and the back-wrenching weight of the books she had to carry around all the time. But she loved her new best friend. Alison's parents had recently divorced, and Alison had moved to Tottenham from Manchester with her mother, but such was her beauty, she may as well have been transported from Hollywood. She was exciting and charming and fearless, and there was an energy that radiated from her that made everything an adventure. Eliza thought Alison was glamorous and sophisticated, but the best thing about her was that she'd chosen to be friends with Eliza.

'I can't stand this any more,' Alison pleaded as they sat in a particularly dull maths lesson. The weather was still unbearably warm, and the stuffy, still air in the classroom felt suffocating. 'I need to get out of here and I need to have some fun. *Please* will you bunk off with me?'

Eliza looked at her. Alison's long blonde hair tickled the straps of her teal vest, her hips were slim in tiny sugar-pink shorts, and although they were half hidden by the desk, her bare legs were clad in bright red boots that Eliza coveted with all her heart. If Eliza was considered dark and sultry – Alison's words to describe her, not her own – Alison was a gorgeous golden drop of sunshine. She looked like a model in her make-up, and it didn't take much imagination for Eliza to picture her half naked on the cover of a Roxy Music album. She just oozed sex. If sixth-formers were made to wear uniforms, Alison would have made hers look disturbing with a tilt of her head and a coquettish smile.

'We've only got a few more weeks until the summer holidays, and then we'll be free for good . . .' Eliza began, but Alison gave her a withering look.

'I can't wait that long. I need to get out of here right *now*.'

Eliza had never played truant from school before; it had crossed her mind several times, but she'd never had the guts to do it. Today, however, in the blazing heat and boredom of the classroom, the mere idea of it set off a rush of adrenalin she couldn't ignore.

'Where should we go?' The shops were out – Eliza would have to hide in the shadows so as not to cross paths with her mother, who wasn't working today – and there was nowhere else to go in Tottenham. Nowhere.

'Soho,' Alison said immediately. Her bright blue eyes were wide, and her eyelashes so long and thick that Eliza was momentarily distracted by them. 'What do you think?'

Lillie had made it clear that Eliza was never to go to Soho; she was adamant that gangsters and prostitutes were waiting to suck her into an underworld from which she'd never escape. And while she knew that her mother was scaremongering, Eliza had obeyed her. But she was sick of being babied. Other people went to Soho and they were fine; why wouldn't she be? Besides, what her mother didn't know wouldn't hurt her.

'My God, yes. Of course. But I haven't got the Tube fare . . .'

'I'll lend you the money.' Alison smiled and Eliza nodded in response. Nobody ever said no to Alison – it was impossible.

'We're in London – the greatest city in the world – and there's more to life than boring old Tottenham. Soho is freaky now, and I want to see it; I want to be part of it and I know you do too.' Alison's voice was quiet, so that the teacher wouldn't hear her, but despite her low tone, Eliza couldn't fail to hear the petulance in her tone. Alison was used to getting what she wanted, just like Veruca Salt in *Willy Wonka and the Chocolate Factory*, a film that Lillie had taken her to see when she was a kid.

'Do you know where to go?'

Alison laughed out loud, and this time the teacher noticed that neither she nor Eliza was paying attention to the mathematics on the blackboard. He paused for a moment, gave them a pointed look, and then continued with his algebraic equations. A cloud of white chalk puffed from the blackboard as he angrily rubbed out some space for the next sum.

'Well, you've heard of The Roxy, right? There's also a club called PX, and something called Louise, although I have a feeling it might be for lesbians . . . I don't know. I think when we get there we'll sense where to go. We might even meet some people worth knowing, unlike this lot.' Alison gestured to the rest of their classmates.

She had a point. They were only a few miles from the centre of London – the centre of the universe and the music scene, as far as Eliza was concerned – but they weren't a part of it. Reading in *Melody Maker* about what was happening was one thing, and listening to Bowie and the Sex Pistols and The Clash was another, but walking right into that sort of glamour uninvited – like anyone could do it – was inconceivable. But they *could* do it; of course they could. The *Daily Mail* had recently declared that if you ventured into Soho you'd best pretend to have a pierced nose in case you were surrounded by skinheads, and the papers were full of stories of kids getting kicked in the head by rough men in cherry-red Doc Martens. But as Eliza imagined bumping into Poly Styrene or Siouxsie Sioux, or even Vivienne Westwood, she knew she didn't really have a choice. She pushed the newspaper stories and her mother's worries out of her mind. If Lillie found out that she had bunked off school to go to Soho there would be hell to pay ... but weren't teenagers supposed to be rebellious? Besides, if she got into trouble, she knew her father would calm her mother down; he was always on her side.

'Let's go today. Now,' she whispered, and when Alison grinned back at her, Eliza felt like she was on the verge of doing something that would change her life for ever.

Soho attacked and overloaded Eliza's senses until she couldn't help but feel dizzy with euphoria. The streets were as noisy and dirty as those in Tottenham, but they were also exciting and carnival-like, with loud music blaring from shops, men wearing make-up, and fishwives screaming profanities at each other as they wobbled drunkenly on fat ankles.

There were market traders yelling about apples and pears on Berwick Street. There were girls sunbathing in minuscule bikinis on the yellowing, sun-bleached patches of scrappy grass in Soho Square. And tired-looking waitresses poured tea for glamorous women behind the grubby windows of tiny European-style cafés. Eliza thought Soho smelt of rotting fruit, spilled beer, and something else, something she couldn't quite put her finger on. After deliberating for a while, she finally worked out what it was: Soho had the scent of late nights and sex and *fun*.

As the two girls walked past dark little pubs filled with smoke and red-nosed alcoholics, they couldn't help but peer in excitedly. Alison kept grinning at the coolness of it all, and Eliza wondered if these were the places she wanted them to hang out. She couldn't quite believe they were. These particular pubs didn't look any different to the pubs in Tottenham, and while she'd only caught glimpses of the people sitting at the bars, the clientele didn't look young or thrilling.

'Are we going the right way?' she asked eventually, as they came across Soho Square for a second time. Alison had a London A–Z in her school satchel, but she refused to pull it out. It didn't matter that they didn't know a soul in Soho – she didn't want anyone to think she was a tourist. But Eliza had removed her bright pink ankle socks on the Tube – an adult wouldn't wear them, so why should she? – and the cheap leather of her shoes was rubbing her skin raw as they walked around in circles.

Alison frowned. Even when she looked cross, she was still beautiful, and Eliza wished with all her heart that she too was blonde and blue-eyed instead of a boring brunette. Life would be so much easier if she resembled Farrah Fawcett.

'I think we need to go down here,' Alison said confidently, and after several twists and turns they found themselves on Dean Street, standing in front of a club called Gossips. 'This is the place I wanted to find!' she exclaimed excitedly.

Eliza gazed at the white Georgian building in front of her, trying to work out what she was looking at. There was a sign spelling out 'DISCOTHEQUE' above the closed front door, and on the wall to the side of it were the black-painted words 'GOSSIPS: FORMERLY BILLY'S'. However, there was no sign of life either inside or out. This building, this *club*, was an anticlimax. Eliza didn't understand Alison's elation.

'But it's closed. What do we do now?' she said. They were attracting curious looks from people walking by; some were builders or tourists, but the majority of those who slowed to stare at the girls were the men who came to Soho for the sex shops, the dominatrix studios and the walk-ups. Eliza wondered if their faithful wives thought they were at work. 'Shall we get a drink or something? If we're gonna bunk off in Soho, we should see if we can get served.'

Alison beamed at her. 'And this is why I consider you to be my best friend. We should *definitely* get a drink. I need a lager. Or a cider. Or a Campari with soda, with lemonade, with tonic . . .'

'But always with pleasure.' Eliza finished off the advertising campaign that had been everywhere that summer, then linked arms with Alison excitedly. Not only was she about to go inside a pub for the very first time, but she was going to do it in *Soho*. She'd been waiting for her adult life to start, and if it wasn't going to come any time soon, she was going to thrust herself right into it, and sod the consequences. The thought thrilled and terrified her all at once.

'Right, now that we have alcohol – and no need to thank me – we have to work out how we're going to get into Gossips tonight,' Alison announced after she'd returned to the table with their drinks. 'And we also need to think of how we can meet some boys before then; ones who look like Adam Ant or David Bowie, preferably. No Bill Grundys allowed – what a fucking rotter.'

Alison had flirted effortlessly with the man behind the bar at the Coach & Horses, and after just a few minutes of laughing and flicking her hair, she had two halves of cider and blackcurrant in her hands. The barman had refused to accept payment for them. Eliza didn't think Alison was going to have any problem finding herself a boyfriend when she decided she wanted one. First stop alcohol; next stop – the rest of the world.

But as Eliza took a sip of her drink, she couldn't ignore the tiny voice in her head that said it was ludicrous for her to think she'd get into Gossips. It whispered gleefully that she wasn't sophisticated or hedonistic enough, and then it revelled in the idea that she wasn't good enough and would *never* be good enough. She forcefully pushed the voice away with another large gulp of her cider. Gossips might be the Beaufont Hall of nightclubs, but it wasn't run by the Tempests, and the only thing the doorman would be bothered about was whether she looked right. The problem was that she didn't.

'Do you think we'll really be able to get in?' she asked Alison as casually as she could. She didn't want to seem in any way worried; she wanted to emulate Alison's breezy fearlessness.

Alison had pulled a tatty copy of *Melody Maker* from her bag and was peering at the cover photo of Elkie Brooks singing into a microphone.

'What?' she said in a distracted tone. 'Are you kidding? Of course they'll let us in. We're young, sexy and beautiful. Being underage is a virtue, not a crime. We'll be put right at the front of the queue . . . that is, if there is one. I'm sure there will be. According to the fanzines, Gossips is the hottest new place to hang out right now; it's where *everyone* is going.'

'But look at what I'm wearing,' Eliza said slowly. When Alison didn't appear to be listening, she was forced to raise her voice. 'Would they let me in looking like this? Really?'

Alison raised her eyes from the newspaper, and both girls looked at Eliza's outfit. It couldn't have been more different to Alison's if Eliza had tried. Where Alison was wearing a teal vest, Eliza was wearing a faded, ugly mauve T-shirt from the market in Wood Green. It was misshapen and fraying, and

Eliza had only put it on that morning because she couldn't face ruining another good top in the heat with yellowing deodorant stains. Alison was in her sugar-pink shorts, but Eliza was wearing her old navy skirt. It was made of a horrible synthetic fabric and fell several inches past her knees. And instead of sensational red boots like Alison's, Eliza wore her school shoes: boring brown lace-ups from Clarks. Her parents had married for love, and for that it seemed their daughter had to dress like a pauper. Eliza burned with indignation when she thought about it. It wasn't *fair*.

'We could buy you an outfit,' Alison began tentatively. 'There are loads of shops on Oxford Street, or Carnaby Street.'

Eliza gave her friend a rueful smile. 'Believe me, if I had the money I would.'

There was a pause. 'I could lend it to you,' Alison said. 'I have ten pounds, which should be enough for something—'

'Thanks,' Eliza interrupted. 'But I'm fine, honestly. I would never be able to pay you back, and I can't ask you to do that for me. You've already paid for my Tube fair and you've said you'll shout me drinks.'

The girls fell silent, and without another word Alison went to the bar and came back with two more drinks – pints this time – and a pair of scissors.

'Stand on your chair,' she commanded.

'What?'

'Stand on the chair and down this drink,' Alison repeated.

Eliza did what she was told, trying to ignore the stares of the other customers, as though she did stuff like this all the time. As she drank her pint, Alison took the scissors to her skirt, cutting round it five inches above the hem. Eliza stared at her aghast and wiped her mouth. The cider bubbled in her stomach and she felt a bit sick.

'My mother is going to kill me when she sees what you've done,' she muttered.

'Your mother needs to stop buying you clothes like this,' Alison said simply. When she was finished, she looked at Eliza's T-shirt and made a slit at the front so she could tie it in a knot on her midriff. 'That's a bit better. It's a shame we can't do anything about your shoes, but we can sort out your hair and your face – make you into a punky schoolgirl. My compact mirror's not big enough for the both of us – let's go to the ladies.'

Eliza followed Alison wordlessly into the stinking, urine-deluged bathroom. The toilet was blocked and the mirror was cracked, but there was just enough room for Alison to pull out her sizeable make-up bag. Inside was a Rimmel lipstick in an inky shade of violet, electric-blue mascara and pink eyeshadow from Boots 17, and a deep red blusher from Miss Selfridge. Eliza stared at the make-up and then back at the mirror.

'Who do you want to look like?' Alison asked.

Eliza considered the question. She longed to resemble Farrah Fawcett or Debbie Harry, but her long brown hair meant she'd never even get close to their golden looks. Siouxsie Sioux was dark and punky, but Eliza didn't think she looked much like her either.

'I want to look like me, but make me look like I should be David Bowie's girlfriend. Make me a Child of the Revolution.'

'That song's so old,' Alison remarked, but she did exactly as Eliza asked. By the time the girls re-entered the bar, Eliza felt like she belonged in Soho. It intoxicated her, and for the first time in her life, she felt truly alive.

When the boys first entered the pub, both Eliza and Alison briefly wondered if they might be girls. Their peroxide hair stuck out in all directions, their eyes were caked in Egyptian-style eyeliner, and their thin wrists jutted out from the red shirts they wore with tight black trousers and skinny ties. Some of the older men in the pub shook their heads in disgust, but the girls were intrigued – they looked like they'd stepped off the cover of a Kraftwerk album. One of them caught Alison's eye and winked at her.

'Here's our chance,' Alison hissed.

Eliza could smell the sweet sourness of cider on her friend's breath under the Juicy Fruit she'd popped into her mouth. Alison's cheeks were flushed and her eyes were bright. She stood somewhat unsteadily, pulled down her vest so the top of her cleavage was visible, and sauntered over to them. Her body language was coy and her expression open and friendly, but there was no mistaking Alison's bright laughter for anything but flirtation. As her golden hair glowed red under the pub's lights, Eliza thought she looked like a sinful angel, and she wished she could be as uninhibited.

After only a few moments, Alison had got the boys to buy them some drinks and persuaded them to join them.

'This is Curt and, um . . .'

'Raven. Rhymes with John Craven, but I ain't no news-reader,' the boy said. He was carrying a sticky tray of drinks, which he edged on to the table.

Eliza smiled shyly and reminded herself that she wasn't boring old Eliza Boyle from Tottenham any more. She was in Soho and she could be whoever she wanted to be. 'I'm Eliza: Eliza Decay.'

Alison didn't bother to hide her laughter. Eliza chose to ignore her. Instead she focused her eyes on the lipstick stains they'd left on their empty pint glasses and wondered how much they'd drunk. It was either too much or not enough.

'So . . . what are you ladies up to tonight?' Curt asked

casually as he and Raven pulled up some chairs and sat down. He rested his elbows in a puddle of cider that Alison had spilled earlier, and Eliza watched the alcohol seep into his red shirt. She wondered if she should tell him but decided not to; he must be able to feel it and he must not give a shit.

'We're thinking about Gossips,' Alison replied airily, as if she went there all the time.

The boys grinned at each other and lit cigarettes. They looked like twins, and Eliza immediately thought of them as Tweedledum and Tweedledee.

'Funny you should say that, that's where we're heading too,' Raven remarked. He took a drag of his Silk Cut and blew the smoke out through his nose.

'Are you really?' Alison breathed.

'We are now,' Curt said, and put his hand over hers. Alison stared down at it for a moment, then turned to Eliza and laughed.

Eliza eyed Raven from under her electric-blue lashes and tried to copy Alison's sultry smile, but flirting felt awkward and odd. She'd had a couple of boyfriends at school – boys she'd held hands with and kissed a couple of times – but she had never really been into them, nor they into her. It was innocent stuff, but it gave her the confidence she needed to try to dazzle Raven. Yet despite all her make-up, and her stiff Harmony-hairsprayed quiff, Raven took a drag of his cigarette and then looked away from her. Eliza felt her heart drop into her stomach.

'I need to phone my mum,' she muttered, delving into her school bag for her emergency ten pence piece. 'I'll be back in a minute.'

Outside, the sun shone brightly on a couple of weary-looking prostitutes standing on the street corner. Eliza tried to avoid eye contact with them. They were smoking Player's No. 6

and drinking an unidentifiable liquid from plastic bottles, and they looked sad and bored. Eliza hurried past them and down Romilly Street in search of a phone box, but as soon as she found one, she wondered what on earth she'd say. She should have returned home from school by now, but instead she'd been drinking in a pub. She was light-headed from the alcohol, dizzy with adrenalin from being in Soho, and her happiness had been punctured because that Raven boy didn't fancy her. It was almost too much, and as Lillie answered the phone, Eliza thought she might be sick in the corner of the phone box.

'I'm sorry I'm only just phoning now,' she said. Her head felt like cotton wool and her voice sounded slow, strange. She hoped she wasn't slurring and that her mother couldn't hear the sounds of traffic, the yells and whoops of glee in the background. 'I went back to Alison's house so we could do some homework together.'

There was silence at the other end of the phone, and then Eliza thought she could hear her father in the background. His voice sound calm, conciliatory, but also distant.

'Hello?' she tried again. 'Dad, can you hear me?'

'I can hear you,' Lillie said. 'And yes, your father is here too. We were starting to worry.' Eliza could hear the fretfulness in her voice.

'I'm sorry,' Eliza replied faintly. And she was. She didn't want to upset her parents, but at the same time, she wanted to be free from school and homework and from being treated like a child. She wanted to be an adult; she wanted her life to begin. 'I think I'm going to stay over,' she said. 'We've got so much revision to do, and Alison's mum says it's okay for me to spend the night.'

Lillie didn't speak for a moment, and Eliza could hear the beeps from the pay phone signalling that she was about to run out of money. She knew that Lillie would have heard them too, and that her cover was blown.

'I'll see you tomorrow, then,' Lillie replied. She paused again, and Eliza held her breath. 'Have a wonderful time.'

The phone went dead, and when Eliza tried to hang up, she missed the cradle. The receiver dropped to the floor and dangled by its wire, and as Eliza tried to catch it, she found she couldn't focus – and not just because she could barely see straight. It was because her eyes had inexplicably filled with tears at the wistfulness she'd heard in her mother's voice.

Chapter Seven

London, 1978

Alison, Eliza, Curt and Raven stood in the queue that snaked its way along Dean Street. Night had descended, yet the sky wasn't that of the picture books Eliza had grown up reading. Instead of an inky blue blanket speckled with glittering diamond stars, all she could see was a dirty orange smog; not even the brightest star in the sky could break through the artificial light of the city. Eliza had lived in London all her life and she'd never really seen stars. She longed to see them, to touch them. She'd always lived under a dirt-filled sky.

'Eliza Decay, wake up!' Alison's voice cut through Eliza's drunken reverie, and she realised that they'd reached the doorway to the club after shuffling towards it for what had felt like hours. A man on the door eyed the girls carelessly as he smoked a cigarette. Eliza held her breath and prayed he wouldn't notice her shoes.

'Pay downstairs,' he said in a gruff, bored voice.

Alison and Eliza walked through the Georgian doorway and followed the boys down a tight staircase to the till at the bottom. Alison wordlessly paid for Eliza's entry – and then they were in. To an untrained eye, all they'd done was to be allowed into a sleazy-looking club in Soho, but to Eliza it was more than that:

they'd tramped through an enchanted doorway into their own version of wonderland. This was the milestone that marked her coming of age; this was where her new life would truly begin.

The basement club was — superficially and at first glance — dingy and bleak. The carpet was sodden and stuck to the soles of Eliza's school shoes, and there were ill-matched tables and chairs hidden in the shadows. A few grotty-looking booths to the right of the dance floor were filled with people drinking and laughing, there was a throng of people at the makeshift bar to the right, and the low ceiling nearly touched the heads of the crowd that stood underneath it.

But what a crowd of people it was.

'I Feel Love' by Donna Summer blasted from the speakers, and boys dressed as toy soldiers danced with girls who shimmied in their tight pencil skirts. The gold braiding and crystals on the boys' jackets caught on the pillbox hats and veils that adorned the heads of the girls, but nobody minded, nobody cared. They shuffled and jived in angular shapes; they laughed and sang and danced as though their lives depended on it. Sweat ran down their foreheads, carefully applied bright make-up smudged on their faces, but there was joy, a sense of belonging. A sense that this was where they should be — right here and right now.

'This is the future,' Eliza whispered. Nobody heard her above the music, but it didn't matter. She felt herself move slowly towards the centre of the dance floor, and before she knew what was happening, she was moving in time with the others. Alison, Curt and Raven joined her, and soon they were lost to the music.

A man stood on the edge of the dance floor and watched them from behind his dark glasses. Despite the humidity of the club, he wore a long trench coat, but Eliza was transfixed by his hands, for his fingers sparkled with diamond rings: lots and lots of diamond rings that shone like the stars hidden in the pollution-filled sky.

'That's Wally – he's the owner of this bit of the building,' Raven yelled into Eliza's ear when he noticed her staring.

Eliza just nodded and carried on dancing. They moved to 'Autobahn' by Kraftwerk; to 'Do the Strand' by Roxy Music; to 'The Light Pours Out of Me' by Magazine. Eliza felt as though she was filled with light, that she too was made of diamonds and stars, and when she jumped around and waved her arms about in the air, she felt like she belonged. She truly belonged.

Hours passed, but Eliza didn't stop dancing. She was fuelled by alcohol, by the adrenalin of being part of something bigger and more powerful than she'd ever known. She shared a cigarette with Raven, whose lipstick blended with hers on the dirty orange tip; she drank vodka and gin handed to her by Curt, and she embraced strangers. She loved everyone.

At some point in the night she found herself shut in the tiny bathroom with a shaven-headed figure. The cistern was broken, there was no toilet paper and the door didn't shut, but Eliza couldn't have cared less. The figure leaned in to kiss her, and Eliza found herself responding. Their mouth tasted of honey, ruined by the acrid taste of cigarette smoke that lined the inside of their cheeks, and it was only when Eliza pulled away that she thought the figure in front of her could be a girl and not a boy. She didn't care, for gender wasn't what this was about, and as she made her way back to the dance floor as Eliza Decay, she felt energised in a way she never had before. She felt as though she'd touched the meaning of life with her fingertips. She felt as if she'd worked out *everything*.

'We're going to go soon,' Alison yelled when Eliza rejoined her friends. Eliza stared at her.

'But why?' she asked. She didn't want tonight to ever end.

Alison smiled. 'Because this is the last song of the night.'

'Where Have All the Flowers Gone?' by Marlene Dietrich played softly into the nearly empty club. Eliza grabbed her friend and swayed in time to the music.

'Where have all the young men gone?' she sang drunkenly.

'When will they ever learn?' Alison sang back. Then she stopped swaying and became bossy. 'Curt and Raven have got a squat not too far from here and they said we can crash there if we can't face the night bus back to Tottenham.'

'They live *in* Soho?' Eliza asked. She couldn't imagine anyone actually *living* amongst the bedraggled and battered people who prowled the streets of Soho after sundown.

'A five-minute walk away, apparently. So what do you think?'

Eliza shrugged. 'Won't your mum worry when you don't come back?'

Alison rolled her eyes. 'My mum is nothing like your parents – she doesn't treat me like a baby. Besides, she's too busy trying to find a replacement for my dad.'

Eliza tasted sadness on Alison's booze-soured breath. She put her arms around her friend's neck. 'Let's do it,' she said.

As they drunkenly made their way to the squat, Eliza found herself marvelling that only twenty-four hours earlier, she'd been asleep in her single bed in Tottenham with no idea of what the day would hold for her. Her parents, her school, and the nights when she wrote in her diary when she should have been having fun seemed a lifetime away.

Gossips would become her new habit. Soho was destined to become her life.

'This is it,' Raven announced as they stood by a filthy, ramshackle block of flats on Silver Place. The squat was above a cobbler's and opposite a sandwich shop, and even though the white walls were dirty with the dust of London, and the carpets were damp with mildew and grime, Eliza thought it was perfect. The boys rushed around to light candles with stray matches that littered every surface, and in the flickering light the flat seemed romantic and artistic.

'You're so lucky,' she whispered.

'It's all right,' Raven agreed. 'It will do for now. The water's on and we have bedding – we don't need much else. Why would we when the streets of Soho are our living room?'

'It's brilliant,' Eliza enthused. She watched Curt lead Alison by the hand to another room, and then she turned to Raven, who seemed awkward and uneasy without his friend. They stood in silence for a moment, and Eliza began to feel a headache – her first hangover – forming behind her eyes. She tried to think of something to say, but before she could, Raven cleared his throat.

'It's not you, you know. I mean, you're a nice girl and all, but you're a girl, and I'm into men.' She could tell that he was trying to keep his voice light rather than defensive, but he'd not quite managed it. 'Mainly men, that is. It's complicated – I go for an androgynous look, but on men. Not women.'

Eliza knew she was being tested, knew it was important for her to act cool about Raven's declaration of his sexuality, but the truth was she couldn't have cared less about who he wanted to fuck. All she wanted to do was to sit down and take her shoes off.

'Then it's a good thing I don't fancy you,' she said. Her feet were covered in blisters but she couldn't feel any pain; she suspected that would change once the alcohol wore off and her hangover properly kicked in. When Raven didn't say anything, she looked up at him. 'I'm really thirsty. Please could I have a drink of water?'

Raven ran the tap and presented her with a mug of lukewarm

water. She tried not to think about how dirty it was and drank it greedily.

'My parents chucked me out a couple of months ago when they caught me being buggered in my bedroom. I somehow ended up here with Curt,' Raven continued conversationally. He acted offhand – as if he was telling a story that didn't involve him; as if it wasn't painful for him to share. 'I don't know him that well – like, who he was before he was Curt – but I know enough. We both believe in the same things; we both believe in living for now.'

He sat down on a pile of blankets and cushions and gestured for Eliza to do the same. She slipped her shoes off and stuck her bare feet out in front of her.

'What do you mean, before he was Curt?'

'Curt's not his real name,' Raven said slowly, as if this should be obvious. 'Just like Eliza Decay isn't yours.'

She grinned. 'Eliza actually is.'

'I'm surprised. Most people completely change their name when they come to Soho – along with everything else. These streets are the land of reinvention, where anything is possible. It's not about the clothes, or the occasion, it's about a way of life. It's not something you can dip in and out of – not if you really mean it, anyway. It's a lifestyle. But that's enough about me. What's your story?'

Eliza blinked at him. 'What do you mean?'

'Nobody comes here unless they're unhappy. What's wrong with your life?'

Eliza remained silent.

'Abusive mother? Drug problem? Daddy won't buy you a pony? What?' Raven's tone was impatient, caustic, and his eyes had narrowed.

'It's nothing like that – my parents are great.'

'And yet you're here.'

Eliza shrugged. She could feel sleep pressing down upon her, but she didn't want to stop talking and she didn't want this night to end. 'I just want to start my life, I suppose. I'm sick of feeling trapped and mollycoddled. I want to escape and do something new and exciting. I want to feel alive.'

'We have a spare bedroom, you know,' Raven said conversationally. 'And I don't just mean for tonight. Do you work?'

'I'm doing my A levels,' she replied. 'But I'm nearly eighteen.'

Raven lit another cigarette and Eliza watched the glowing tip in the faded light of the room. He passed it to her and she inhaled deeply. She'd not smoked before tonight, but now she couldn't imagine not doing so.

'School is just a way for the government to keep you as a child of the state. They want to control you,' he said as he flexed his thin wrists.

Eliza took another drag on the cigarette and then handed it back to him. She'd grown up being told that she needed to be wary of the darkness of Soho, but in the flickering candlelight she felt comfortable in both her surroundings and her own skin. Raven might have postured and posed in his make-up and costume, but underneath the glitz and his over-intellectualising of everything, he was like her – struggling to become himself. He was so pale, so fragile, that Eliza wanted to take him in her arms, to warm him, to tell him he didn't need to prove anything to her.

'Nobody can control me,' she said simply, and Raven smiled.

Eliza forced the image of her parents out of her mind and crossed the line to the other side.

Eliza lay in her childhood bed and gazed out of the window. The moon had tumbled behind a low-rise tower block in the distance, but London had not yet come to life – the sun had not begun to soar. In the kitchen she could hear her father shuffling about before going to work, could hear the soft voice of her mother as she laughed and made his breakfast. Eliza concentrated on trying to hear her parents' words but she couldn't quite make out what they were saying. In many ways she didn't need to – she knew they were happy and that was the most important thing of all. It would make the blow that came next easier for them to deal with.

She took a deep breath, pulled on her dressing gown, and forced herself to be brave as she headed into the kitchen. She would be Eliza Decay; she would be fearless. But when she saw her parents at the table about to tuck in to toast and tea, her resolve stumbled. Her mother's dark hair was pushed behind her ears, and although it was early and she was clearly tired, she looked beautiful. Eliza stared at her for a moment. Even though she'd inherited Lillie's bright blue eyes, she knew she'd never be as breathtaking as her. She looked more like her father – she was handsome rather than delicate.

'You're up early,' Bertie commented with a smile.

Eliza tried to grin back but she felt too anxious. She watched her parents glance at each other. Eliza rarely got up before her father left for work.

Lillie immediately became concerned. 'What's wrong? Are you okay?' She rose to put her hand on Eliza's forehead to see if she had a fever, but Eliza took a step backwards so she was out of her mother's reach.

'I'm not sick,' she managed to say.

Lillie silently sat down again, but her gaze didn't move away from her daughter. Eliza caught her eye, and in that moment she could tell that her mother knew what was coming next. She knew that Lillie had spotted that something had changed inside of her.

Eliza didn't know how to say what she needed to. It had been days since she'd spent the night in Soho, and ever since then she and Alison had plotted and planned for this moment. Yet as much as you could prepare a conversation, as much as you could try to predict the script, you never really could. For to do so relied on knowing what the other person, or people, would say, and you could never foresee that – not even when you were about to speak with your parents.

'I'm moving out. Today. Please don't try to stop me.' Eliza's words fell out of her mouth in a rush, and even though she wished she could take them back, she knew there would never be a good time to have this conversation. There would never be the right way to say these words.

Bertie and Lillie Boyle froze. They stared at their daughter in horror.

'Alison and I have found somewhere to live and we're moving in today. I know you want me to finish my A levels, but I hate school – it's not for me. I want to be somewhere where I can be myself and grow up. I want to be an adult.'

Lillie opened her mouth to speak, but Bertie placed a hand on hers and she closed it again. Her parents glanced at each other again, and Eliza grew flustered in the face of their silent, non-verbal communication. Her body had tensed for the emotional blow – for the inevitable reaction of her parents telling her she was being stupid, that they would never let her ruin her life – and she didn't know how much longer she could wait for it.

'Well? Say something,' she pleaded. Her voice was high and thin. 'Tell me I'm throwing my life away; tell me I'm making a huge mistake and that you don't want me to go.'

'Of course we don't want you to go,' Bertie said eventually. The tone of his voice was steady.

Lillie stood abruptly, as if she wanted to run out of the room, but instead she placed two more pieces of Hovis under the grill on the oven. She had trouble lighting it, but after several attempts the gas ignited with a loud *whoosh*.

'Mum, I don't want breakfast,' Eliza protested. 'I hate breakfast.' The truth was that her stomach was in knots. She couldn't eat at a time like this.

'If you're going to move out, you need your energy,' Lillie remarked. 'Sit down and have a cup of tea before you go. Do that for me, at the very least.'

Eliza did as she was told. She'd been expecting anger and tears, a dramatic moment where her mother begged her not to leave, not to ruin her life. But instead Lillie was playing along, as if Eliza was six and she'd just announced that she was running away from home.

'Where are you planning to go?' Lillie asked conversationally. Her face was passive and her tone light, but Eliza wasn't fooled; she knew she was causing her mother heartache.

'A flat in Soho. It's just off Beak Street. We met some boys and they have a spare room. They gave it to us.'

Lillie blinked several times. 'They *gave* it to you? Who are these boys, anyway?'

Eliza chose to watch the flickering flames of the grill rather than look at her mother. She pretended to be fascinated by how the blue flames transformed to yellow as they flared above the bread. 'They're my friends – new friends – and the flat's not going to cost us anything because it's a squat. And I'm going to get a job in a pub or something.'

'You're only seventeen.' Lillie's voice sounded strangled, nearly hysterical, and Bertie coughed.

'I'll be eighteen in just a few weeks.'

83

The bread under the grill began to burn at the edges, and Lillie stood to flip it over. She kept her back to her daughter.

'I have to move out sometime,' Eliza said softly. 'And I know you'd rather I finished my A levels and that you think Soho is terrible, but it's not as bad as you think. I like it. I feel free there, like I can be anything and can do anything I want. You're both always going on about how the government is messing up the country, about how Callaghan is leading us all towards a crisis. I don't want to be part of that system. In Soho, I won't have to be.'

Lillie removed the toast from the grill and put it on a plate. She handed it to Eliza and sat back down again. She looked as though there were many things she wanted to say, but she chose not to say any of them. Instead she sat in silence as Eliza tried to eat her toast. Bertie had always been the peacemaker between his wife and his daughter, but there was hurt in his expression, too.

'I'm nearly the same age you were when you left home,' Eliza said eventually to her mother. 'You were twenty when you moved out to be with Dad, weren't you?'

'It wasn't quite like that,' Lillie said.

'Well, what *was* it like? You never talk about growing up at Beaufont Hall, or what your family was like – *is* like. You've never explained why I've never met them.'

Lillie stared into the distance. 'It's complicated,' she said eventually. 'There's not a day that goes by that I don't miss them – my sisters especially – but I don't regret leaving. The moment I walked out of Beaufont Hall, I became who I was meant to become, and it meant I could be with your father and that we could have you. You're worth more to me than being part of the Tempest family ever could be, than that house ever could be.'

Eliza looked her mother in the eye. 'Then you'll understand that I want to find that for myself. That I want to discover who I am and who I can be.'

Lillie nodded slowly and gave her daughter a wobbly smile.

'It's not far, it's only a couple of miles, and I know that if it doesn't work out, I can always come home again – can't I?'

'Of course you can,' Bertie replied.

All three of them knew they might as well make the best of the situation. Eliza took after both her parents: she was strong-willed and independent-minded, and nothing could stop her from doing what she wanted to do.

'We don't want you to go, of course we don't, but we understand. We just want you to be happy.' As Bertie spoke, he took Eliza's hand in his and squeezed it tightly.

For a moment, Eliza wished she was ten years old; that she could curl up in her father's arms and feel as though she was protected from the world. But she wasn't ten, she was nearly eighteen, and she wanted to go out into that world and make it her very own.

'Will you let us help you move into this flat? Let us see it for ourselves?'

Eliza nodded. Her eyes had filled with tears – tears of relief at how easy her parents had made this conversation, but also tears of sadness that she was hurting them. Yet at the same time she was filled with joy, with hope.

'Can you drive me and my stuff into Soho when you've finished work?' she asked.

Bertie nodded, and as the sun began to rise and shone its warm, summery light into the Boyles' small kitchen, Eliza felt as though her life was truly about to begin.

Chapter Eight

Buckinghamshire and London,
recently

Cassie swallowed hard in the silence of Beaufont Hall and turned the rusty handle on a door she'd yet to open. All was quiet but for a faint banging in the distance: Ed was working somewhere in the house. Earlier in the day he'd appeared in the gardens with a heavy pile of MDF and said he'd like to replace some of the rotten boards on the windows. Cassie had wanted to say that it wasn't necessary, but she also knew it was a job that needed to be done. She was grateful for Ed's help and his kindness — and for his presence. As much as she loved Beaufont Hall, she sometimes felt uneasy in it. When she wandered through the house, the sound of her footsteps echoed conspicuously on the grey flagstone floor. Beaufont Hall wasn't built for a solitary person to roam alone: it had been intended for families, for laughter.

The handle turned more easily than Cassie had expected it to. When she pushed the door open, she was surprised by what she found. Like the rest of Beaufont, the room was stale and cold, but there were no boards on the windows and she could see dust motes darting in the beams of sunlight. The floorboards were dirty and the faded forget-me-not wallpaper had begun to peel away from the damp, mildewed walls, but in this room there was furniture: a small, squishy sofa and a coffee table. Cassie blinked, remembering her mother mentioning a cosy den in which she'd spent a lot of time. Was this the room Rebecca had talked of? It could have been – it would explain why it had not been completely dismantled.

Cassie was exhausted from sweeping and mopping floors all day, and she gingerly lowered herself on to the sofa. A puff of dust rose from the cushions, but they were surprisingly comfortable, and Cassie wasn't afraid of dirt. She pulled Eliza's diary from her bag and gazed at it. The contents might not have given any indication as to how Eliza and Lillie were related to the rest of the family, but it had confirmed that Lillie Tempest had once lived at Beaufont, had possibly grown up here. If Eliza had been a late teenager in 1978, it meant she'd been born around 1960 or 1961, and that she was roughly the same age as Rebecca; and that Lillie was of the same generation as Violet. That Rebecca wouldn't have heard of Lillie or Eliza seemed unfathomable to Cassie, but something still prevented her from asking about them. She wasn't yet ready to admit she'd discovered the diaries; Beaufont belonged to Rebecca, and Cassie wanted the diaries for herself.

'I've done most of the ground-floor windows that needed doing,' Ed said, appearing in the doorway. His face was flushed from physical exertion and his glasses were in his hand. But when he took in the room, he put them back on so he could get a better look. 'You found some furniture?'

Cassie shrugged. 'This room must have been left alone,' she said.

Ed smiled. 'I had no idea,' he remarked. 'I didn't even know it existed. It's taken me about half an hour to find you – I assumed you were in the library, not in a secret living room.'

'It surprised me too. I actually thought this room was a cupboard,' she said. There was an awkward pause as Ed noticed the diary in her hands. He looked at it for a moment, and Cassie realised she wanted to tell him what it was, to confide in him about what she'd read. But something made her hold back. Ed thought of Beaufont Hall fondly, his family had worked here for generations, and the house was tied up with his identity almost as much her own was. Yet as comfortable as Cassie was beginning to feel around him, she barely knew him. She wasn't sure she wanted to tell any Tempest family secrets to a relative stranger.

'Are you hungry?' he asked. His words cut into her thoughts, and Cassie nodded. Without saying another word, he disappeared, returning several long moments later with a large wicker hamper and one of his scratchy blankets. 'My mother packed us a lunch – I think she may have gone a bit overboard.'

He carefully spread the blanket out across the floorboards and gestured for Cassie to join him. She sat down on the floor beside him and was touched when he began to hand her plates and food – roasted chicken legs and ham, pâté and cheese, peaches and grapes, and a still-warm loaf of bread.

'This is kind of her, but she really shouldn't have.'

Ed shrugged. 'What can I say? She's a feeder.'

Cassie tucked in, finding that she was hungrier than she'd thought. As she ate, she asked Ed about his parents. 'Did your mother work at Beaufont too?'

Ed shook his head. 'She was a teacher in the village school. It was my father's side of the family who worked here. When my grandmother retired, my father stayed on and did odd jobs around the house and garden until Violet passed away. He was very fond of your grandmother and mother, and I know he'd like to meet you, if you have the time. My mother would, too.'

Cassie smiled shyly. 'I'd love to meet them, and to thank your mother for this spread.' She thought of the diary and wondered if Mr Winter had known Eliza or Lillie. 'Could I visit them soon?'

'They'd like that. Let me speak to them about when would be the best time. I'm assuming it would be a weekend?'

Cassie nodded. 'I work at the bookshop full-time during the week, so it would have to be.'

Ed cut up a peach with his penknife and handed her a slice. His hands were calloused from the work he'd been doing around Beaufont, but they were warm, and Cassie tried not to react as her skin brushed his. It felt as though it was more than just a casual touch.

'I try to go back to London in the week too – to see friends and crash on their sofas,' he told her, 'but the more time I spend with my parents in the village, the less I want to go. I certainly don't miss my old life. Not any more, anyway.'

Cassie wiped peach juice from her lips. 'What did you do in London?' she asked.

'I worked in the City and invested in companies. I made good money and had everything I could ever want . . . apart from time. So I sold up and got out. I miss my mates, but I don't miss the rest of it, or the person I'd started to turn into. I used to wake in the night to find my heart pounding.'

Cassie leant back against the sofa. The den was the perfect place to share confidences – it was small and snug and cosy. No wonder Rebecca had spent a lot of time here.

'I've lived in London all my life and I don't think it's ever suited me. My family all love it – my mother especially adores the theatre and she used to plan all sorts of day trips when we were small – but I'm happier in the country. If I could live here, I would. I crave the silence.'

'I could fix up one of the bedrooms if you ever wanted to spend the night here,' Ed commented. 'It would be freezing, but there's no reason why you couldn't stay if that's what you'd like to do.'

Cassie had never even considered that she could sleep at Beaufont; that she could drive up on a Saturday morning and not leave till Sunday. She'd just been thankful that her mother had given her the keys, that she'd been handed the opportunity to explore her family home while she prepared to say goodbye to it.

'I'd love to stay over,' she replied simply. 'I can't think of anything I'd like more.'

Ed handed her another slice of peach. It was perfectly ripe, and the sweetness of the juice on her tongue reminded her of summer.

'Then let's go and choose a bedroom that you'd like to claim for yourself.'

Cassie followed Ed up the main staircase of the house and tried not to wonder if this was a bad idea. Her hand trailed over the Tempest family crest carved into the dark oak banister and she imagined generations of her family doing the same. Beaufont Hall might have technically belonged to Rebecca, but it was Cassie's heart that owned it, her spirit that wanted to claim it.

'Do you remember the main master bedroom I showed you last time?' Ed asked over his shoulder. 'Would you like to sleep in that one? I think your grandmother must have used it – and if she didn't, then your great-grandparents certainly would have.'

Cassie couldn't put her finger on why, but she knew she wouldn't feel comfortable in that room. She supposed she would like to discover which of the bedrooms had been her mother's, but there was no way of finding out without asking her, and she was hesitant to tell Rebecca that she planned to start sleeping at Beaufont at weekends. She was sure her mother wouldn't be keen, although she couldn't think why that would be.

'I think I'd like one of the smaller rooms,' she replied as they walked along the corridor.

They looked in several rooms, but each was as uninhabitable as the next. One had a broken window that needed to be boarded up ('I'll do this one next,' Ed said quickly as he noticed Cassie's dismay); another had floorboards that seemed perilously loose. Cassie felt a bit like Goldilocks as she stood in the middle of each room and tried it out for size. Some were too big and others were too small, and she was looking for one that felt just right.

Several rooms later, she found it.

'This is the one,' she whispered as Ed pushed open a door slightly away from the others at the far end of the corridor. The floor was covered by a grubby peony-patterned rug, two of the three windows had been boarded up long ago, and despite the staleness of the air – the feeling that nobody had been in it for a very long time – the bedroom felt happy. Cassie walked over to the one window that hadn't been covered and gazed out of it. Directly below was a rose garden that had grown into an intimidating tangle of black thorns, but further afield were the valleys of Buckinghamshire, awash with the golden yellow of corn and the pale greens of summertime grass.

'You'll need a blow-up mattress to sleep on,' Ed remarked. 'I think my parents still have the one I used when I had sleepovers as a kid – I can borrow it from them.'

Cassie smiled at him. 'That would be great. Thank you.'

'And I'll get this rug pulled up too – it's filthy.'

Cassie's smile began to falter. 'I'd quite like to keep it,' she said firmly. 'I'll bring a vacuum cleaner with me next time I come and give it a good clean.'

Ed gave an easy shrug. 'It's your house,' he grinned, and Cassie nodded back and gazed out of the window again.

Beaufont Hall had always felt like hers. Even when she was small, she'd been rather attached to it. She knew it *wasn't* hers, not really, and that it would soon be sold and would then belong to someone else, but she'd begun to realise that she couldn't stand the thought of saying goodbye to it; that she'd do anything she could to prevent it from being sold. It was now or never.

She took a deep breath and turned back towards Ed. 'Time for me to get back to the library,' she said lightly.

'I thought we were having lunch at yours today,' Safia said, kissing her friend hello at the bar of the Dean Street Townhouse. Although it was Sunday, Cassie had stayed in London instead of returning to Beaufont. She'd originally planned to make a family lunch – to which she'd invited Safia – but Alice and Henry's drama group had arrived to practise the key scenes of the play, and the house had become overrun with overly dramatic teenagers.

Cassie smiled. 'I know,' she said. 'But the twins and their friends took over the house and I couldn't bear the thought of asking them all to leave because we had a meal planned. We can nip across the road and get a burger if you'd prefer? Or we could cut through to Wardour Street for some Mexican?'

Safia wrinkled her nose. 'I much prefer the food here, and besides, I know this is one of your favourite restaurants.'

'It is. I fully admit to being drawn to this place, and to being a creature of habit.'

The girls were shown to their table. Once the water had been poured and the bread basket had been offered, Safia gestured to the notebook lying on the tablecloth.

'Is that one of the diaries you found?' she asked.

Cassie shook her head. 'It isn't, but it *is* related to Beaufont Hall. It's a log of the books I've found in the library – and my ideas about what to do with the money we've made.'

Safia took a sip of water and then picked up a butter knife. 'How much is there exactly?' she asked.

'A fair bit,' Cassie replied. 'Nearly fifty thousand pounds.'

Safia's eyes widened in shock. Her hand holding the butter knife stopped in mid-air. 'Fifty thousand pounds?' she echoed.

'Yes . . . minus the seven thousand we spent to get the hole in the roof repaired and the electricity checked over,' Cassie said matter-of-factly.

'That's a lot of money,' Safia said.

Cassie nodded. 'Though in sensible terms it's not nearly enough to restore Beaufont. It wouldn't stretch to replacing all the broken glass in the windows, or fixing the central heating, or installing a new kitchen, or getting new carpets . . .' Her voice trailed off and she felt despondent for a moment. 'But as I said, I have a plan,' she said brightly. 'It may not work, of course, and I'd need licences from the council, but I think it could help to bring in some money.'

'What is it?' Safia asked. They were momentarily distracted by the waiter asking for their order – smoked haddock soufflé and asparagus for Cassie, fish and chips for Safia – before Cassie continued.

'So many people open up their houses to the public like they're a museum – like the houses are already dead and all they're good for is being examined. But I want to breathe new life into Beaufont; I want it to be part of something alive and vibrant and current. So I'm thinking that if it would cost too much to restore the house, then a good place to start would be the grounds. The gardens and land of Beaufont Hall could play host to a craft fair, perhaps, or a small literary festival.'

Safia took a bite of bread while she considered Cassie's words. Cassie knew she had doubts and was trying to think what to say.

Safia smiled. 'It's a lovely idea,' she said. 'But I don't think fifty thousand will go too far in setting it up.'

Cassie nodded sadly. 'You're right,' she said. 'But it *can* go towards restoring the gardens, as well as a couple of rooms for me to stay in when I'm not in London.' She consulted her notebook again and drew a line through something she'd scribbled hours earlier. When she looked up again, her blue eyes shone. 'I know it will be difficult, but it's not impossible.'

After some time the waiter presented the girls' lunches with a flourish and then silently retreated. Cassie watched him as he walked back towards the bar.

'I admire your ambition,' Safia remarked as she nibbled on a chip. 'And please don't be cross with me for playing devil's advocate, but is this really the right thing to do? I know you can't bear the thought of it, but you could easily sell Beaufont to a property developer, who could turn it into flats. Your family would make a fortune.'

Cassie blinked. 'That's what my mother wants. I mean, she doesn't *want* to let Beaufont go to make money, but we just can't keep it on. I'm hoping that this money and my idea will persuade her to keep it in the family for a little bit longer.'

'You haven't told her about your idea for the festival?' Safia asked. 'Does she even know about the money you've made?'

Cassie shook her head guiltily. 'I don't want to talk to her about it until I have a solid plan in place, and a definite idea about the revenue I could bring in. My ultimate aim is to restore Beaufont to its former glory, but that could take years and years.

I know it's impractical and a long way off, but I like the idea of raising my own family there – of returning the family to the house.'

Safia didn't speak for a moment. 'I'm assuming you've not told her about the diaries yet, either?'

Cassie groaned. 'No, not yet. I know I should,' she admitted, 'but I can't. I want to read them all first. I don't know why, but I feel like it would be wrong to share them, to let Eliza's secrets be talked about without actually knowing what they are or who she was. I feel responsible for the diaries – like I'm their custodian.

'She had quite a difficult life, you know,' Cassie continued. 'But she was determined not to let that stop her. She quit school and moved into a tiny flat in Soho with her best friend – in Silver Place, sort of near where Wagamama's is now. I haven't read any further than that, but she's quite inspirational. She wanted to make her life her own, so she did it.'

'Silver Place isn't far from here,' Safia said, and Cassie grinned at her. Safia knew what was coming next.

Rather than the grotty street that Cassie had imagined and expected, Silver Place was a tiny alley tucked away from the bustle of the rest of Soho and lined with discreet beauty salons and art galleries. As she peered through their thick glass windows, she wondered what the street would have looked like thirty-five years ago. It must have been completely different.

A few minutes on her iPhone confirmed her suspicions. According to a property website, two-bedroom flats on Silver Place now rented for at least £650 a week, but a Google Image search of the street in the 1970s brought up black-and-white images of the alley slick with rain, with teenage boys loitering outside a sandwich shop and a locksmith. Had it looked like this

– more scruffy, and less moneyed – when Eliza had moved in? It must have done, but Cassie couldn't imagine it. She couldn't imagine Silver Place in any incarnation other than what it was right now, regardless of the photograph on her phone.

'I wonder which flat Eliza lived in,' Safia said as she stared up at the windows above them. Cassie leaned against an old-fashioned-style lamp post and did the same. Above almost every shop were three floors of residential space, and even though she knew it was futile, she tried to guess which one had been Eliza's home. Could it have been one of the flats above the white facade of number 1 Silver Place? Or had Eliza lived closer to street level? Could her face have appeared in the window behind the decorative iron window boxes that Cassie was currently standing in front of?

Cassie realised that she'd never know which flat Eliza and Alison had lived in. But if she had to select any of them for her own, she'd choose one opposite Ginger & White, the café from which a coffee-scented haze drifted on to the street. She imagined living a glamorous life in an airy, wooden-floored apartment with views over London, coming downstairs in the morning to grab a coffee and croissant to go. It was a different life to the one she wanted – now that she had the keys, she couldn't imagine not living at Beaufont Hall – but this was what Eliza had longed for: to be cosmopolitan and glitzy, to live a whirlwind life of fun and excitement.

'Tell me what you know about Eliza so far,' Safia said as the girls wandered up and down Silver Place.

Cassie began to relate everything she'd so far gleaned from the diaries, and they puzzled over how Eliza and Lillie could be related to the rest of the Tempests.

'The diary says that Lillie had once lived at Beaufont – but then she and her husband Bertie lived in relative poverty compared to the rest of the family,' Cassie said. 'There must have been some sort of rift, and it was one that made Eliza quite angry. She felt that the life she was meant to have, the life Lillie was meant to have, had been taken away from her and she didn't know why.'

Safia contemplated this. 'Maybe Lillie did something that angered her family. Do you know how she was related to the rest of the Tempests?'

Cassie shook her head. 'Not yet. I'm hoping that the diaries will tell me more, but in the meantime Ed has invited me to meet his parents. His father used to work at Beaufont in my grandmother's time; he's bound to have heard of Lillie at the very least.'

A smartly dressed woman left one of the buildings, and both Cassie and Safia watched her surreptitiously as she walked away on high stiletto heels. She was in her late thirties, so she was too young to be Eliza, but the sight of her made Cassie speculate whether Eliza might still live in Soho; whether she had even remained in that very building. She knew it was unlikely – impossible, even, for she'd lived there illegally – but that didn't stop her from wondering, from hoping.

She dragged her eyes away from the retreating woman and gazed back up at the multitude of windows glinting in the sun. She wished she knew which one had belonged to the squat, which one Eliza would have looked out of at the start of the day, or before she went to sleep. She wished she knew more about what Eliza had looked like . . . and how Eliza was related to her.

Chapter Nine

London, 1980

So much of Eliza's existence – and outlook – had changed in the two years since she and Alison had moved into the squat with the boys. When she thought about who she'd been when she'd lived in Tottenham, she felt nostalgic and protective of her younger self: she'd been so naive and childish. Back then she didn't know who she was; she only knew who she wasn't – she wasn't a Tempest, she wasn't herself, she wasn't who she wanted to be.

But life was so very different now. Every afternoon she'd wake up and feel energised in a way she'd never felt in Tottenham. Soho was alive – it was rich with history and characters – and she couldn't wait to get up and leave the squat. In the afternoons she was paid pennies for handing out photocopied flyers for club nights, and she'd stalk the streets: Lexington, Broadwick, Wardour, Dean and Frith. But it was after sundown that she truly came to life. When she wasn't working behind the bar at Gossips, she was in one of the other clubs in which she'd made her home. She didn't have a career – at least not in the traditional sense – but she was young and she knew there was plenty of time to think about that. She missed her parents, and phoned them from the office at Gossips several times a week, but she rarely went back to Tottenham. She just didn't have the time: life was so busy and perfect.

And it wasn't just Eliza's life that was different – it was her appearance too. When she looked at her reflection in the mirror, she barely recognised herself, and when she looked at her friends, it was as if she was gazing at a fashion shoot in *The Face* magazine. All the boys in their gang – known as the Meard Street Gang, after the tiny road they lingered on with the prostitutes at sunrise – made sure they looked the part of cool kids around town: they plucked their eyebrows, they wore their hair in quiffs under their outrageous hats, and they were always in eyeshadow and lipstick. But however amazing the boys looked, they had nothing on Eliza and Alison. It was the first time Eliza had had any money for herself, and although she didn't have much of it – and despite most of her clothes coming from charity shops – she always looked amazing. Both she and Alison crimped and backcombed their hair into messy nests, and they wore tiny lacy skirts, leggings, and ripped cropped sweatshirts. They were the princesses of the club scene, and the boys were their queens.

It was a happy, golden time. Maybe the cheap watered-down alcohol they drank had something to do with their joy, but Eliza didn't think so. It was the fact that for the first time in her life, she truly felt as though she belonged.

'If the DJ doesn't play "Enola Gay" by OMD, I may just die,' Alison remarked as she took a swig from the litre bottle of Woodpecker she'd shoplifted. They were sitting on a cold concrete step outside a closed café in Covent Garden, their faces glowing in the flickering orange light from the lamp post opposite. Alison passed the cider to Eliza, who took it gratefully. Winter was setting in, and the alcohol would warm her up. 'What do you want to hear?'

'God, anything but "Atomic",' Eliza replied. 'Gossips have played Blondie on repeat all week. Maybe "Broken English" by Marianne Faithfull? Or "Once in a Lifetime" by Talking Heads?'

Alison wrinkled her nose at Eliza's suggestions. It was Tuesday night, but it wasn't just any Tuesday – it was Blitz night. Curt had persuaded the girls to try out the new club, and while there was talk that Blitz was the natural successor to Gossips, Eliza thought it would just be a fad: nothing could replace Gossips.

'All right, ladies?' Curt's deep voice rang out, and Alison and Eliza lifted their heads to see him and Raven striding towards them. 'You both look lovely tonight, if I do say so myself.'

Alison laughed in delight, then stood and gave Curt a long, deep kiss. As Raven grimaced at their overt display of affection, Eliza grinned and gestured for him to sit next to her.

'Rumour has it that Spandau Ballet are playing at Blitz later,' he said conversationally as he took the cider from her hands. Eliza had seen the band several times at Gossips and was yet to grow bored of them.

'Brilliant,' she replied as she pushed her hair carefully away from her face. 'They're going to be massive, you know. I can feel it.'

Raven shook his head. 'You're only saying that because you fancy the singer. What's his name again – Tony, is it?'

Eliza blushed.

'Well I never,' Raven continued. 'Our little Eliza Decay has a crush. Maybe this Tony from Spandau Ballet will be the man to finally steal your heart.'

'He has a girlfriend,' Eliza muttered. 'Besides, I don't want a boyfriend. You know that.'

Alison pulled away from Curt long enough to give her friend

a long, hard stare. 'You say that, but when you meet the right boy you'll change your mind. You'll see.'

'I won't,' Eliza said defiantly. 'I mean, I want a boyfriend one day, of course I do, but not right now. I'm too busy having fun to start making compromises.'

Alison looked unconvinced, and Eliza tried to swallow away the lump that had formed in her throat. The painful truth was that she desperately longed for a lavish, romantic love to completely consume her, but it was elusive; she didn't know how or where to find it. Instead, she allowed men to buy her drinks and to talk her into drunken, shabby one-night stands. In the morning the men faded away as her hangover grew, and Eliza was left with nothing but an ache in her thighs and bruises on her ribcage.

'You know, Curt has a friend who—'

Whatever Alison was about to say was cut short as a terrified man ran past them, his oriental silk shirt ripped down one side and soaked with blood. He stumbled on the litter that surrounded them, but managed to round the corner. Eliza blinked, and in that moment a gang of skinheads sped past them like vicious hounds pursuing a fox. They had tasted blood and were going in for the kill.

'You fucking queer!' one of them called in a menacing voice. 'You shitting homo! Get back here so we can finish you off.'

They ran to the end of the road, and although they disappeared out of sight, Eliza could still hear their jeers over the pounding of her heart.

'Christ, did you see his face? It'll be black and blue tomorrow,' Raven yelped in alarm. 'We need to get out of here.'

'Shouldn't we do something?' Eliza said. 'We should try and stop them – or make sure he's all right at the very least.'

Raven stared at Eliza in bewilderment. 'And get our own heads kicked in instead? No *thank* you.'

'But we should help. We can't ignore what we just saw.'

Curt lit a cigarette and looked nervously towards the end of the street. The gang hadn't come back – not yet, anyway. 'He'll be long gone,' he said as soothingly as he could.

'Exactly,' added Raven in a shaky voice. 'It's probably not the first time he's been attacked, and it won't be the last.'

Eliza knew that Raven was thinking of an incident that had happened a month earlier. He'd been surrounded by skinheads, and the last thing he could remember was the shiny cherry-red boot of a boy who'd kicked at his face. Eliza had found him crumpled and bloody on the street, and had nursed him through his injuries until he was better.

'But what if he doesn't have anyone to help him? What if they catch him?'

'For God's sake, you can't save everybody, even though I know you want to.' Alison plucked the cigarette from Curt's mouth and offered it to Eliza. 'It's like that time you found an injured pigeon in the school playground and you wanted to take it to the RSPCA.'

Eliza knew Curt was right. They'd probably not find the wounded boy, and they'd only put themselves in danger. She brought the cigarette to her lips and inhaled.

As they walked quickly in the direction of Blitz, Raven put his arm around her shoulders.

'The problem we face is that society can't handle individuals,' he said. 'People are threatened by anybody who doesn't want to blend into the crowd, and it scares them. They can't handle it, and while we need to fight for our space, we can't fight for everyone.'

Eliza turned her head to look at him. Raven's expression was forlorn.

'You need to pick your battles wisely,' he continued. 'If you spend all your energy on someone else, what will you do when it comes to fighting for yourself?'

Eliza knew that he was trying to help, but she couldn't push the image of the bloodied man out of her mind. She'd been raised to fight for the underdog – to believe that everyone should have the same rights and freedoms – and not being able to help that poor man made her feel uncomfortable. But she also knew that Raven was right: sometimes you had to look after yourself first, just in case there was nobody else to do it for you.

The night the phone call came was just like any other. Eliza had been behind the bar for several hours; her hands were sticky with snakebite, her feet sore from heeled boots that looked good but pinched her feet. The crowd was especially excited tonight – they jostled and pushed each other on the dance floor – and the music was so loud you could feel it pulsating through your veins. The DJ played David Bowie, Cabaret Voltaire, Alice Cooper and Joy Division, and Eliza struggled to hear people's orders over the sound of the electric beats and the hum of excited kids. It was nights like these that she liked most; it was nights like these when she truly felt she was at the centre of something important, something significant.

'Missy, there's a phone call for you,' the manager yelled at her from the other side of the bar. Darren oversaw the club nights, but he spent most of his time at his desk trying to make the figures add up, although it was obvious that the club barely broke even. 'You need to take it in the office.'

Eliza glanced at the swarm of people trying to get her attention for drinks. She was the only person behind the bar and she knew she couldn't leave. She looked at Darren helplessly. 'Can you ask them to call back? I'm kind of busy here.'

He stared at her for a moment, but rather than walking back

to the office, he jumped over the bar and lowered his head to hers. 'I'll look after this lot,' he said into her ear. 'I think you should take the call.'

Eliza frowned at him, but she didn't need to be told twice. As she ran up the narrow linoleum-covered steps towards the office, she wondered who was calling her. Alison, Curt and Raven were all on the dance floor, so who could it be? The guy she'd slept with the week before? Not likely. Maybe Alison had slipped Tony from Spandau Ballet this number and told him to ring it.

She pushed open the office door and grabbed the receiver from where it had been placed face-down on the shabby desk. The cream coil was twisted and grubby, but she paid no attention to it.

'Hello?' she said breathlessly as she pictured Tony Hadley on the other end of the phone. There was a faint rustling and then a silence, so she tried again. 'Hello? Who's there?'

'It's Mum.'

Eliza's expectant smile froze, and she swallowed hard.

'Darling, can you hear me? It's Mummy,' Lillie repeated in a thin, tinny voice that sounded very far away.

Eliza sank into one of the threadbare chairs opposite the desk and pushed the phone closer to her face. The office was lit by a single bare bulb that hung in the centre of the room, and the shadows cast on the gloomy wallpaper swayed along to the muffled music coming from below.

She found her voice. 'Are you okay?' she asked urgently. Several drawn-out moments passed before Lillie gave a sob. 'Mum, are you okay? Is Dad okay?'

'You need to come home,' Lillie whispered. 'You need to come home now.'

Eliza had never heard her mother so distraught before. 'Is it Dad?' she said in a choked voice.

'Just come home,' Lillie managed to reply.

Eliza didn't need to be told twice. She gently placed the receiver back in its cradle and ran into the freezing night.

At about the same time that Eliza had started her shift at Gossips, Bertie Boyle was leaving his local pub. He'd had a few ales and pickled eggs with his colleagues, along with a good laugh and a game of darts. Most importantly, after two long years, the men finally felt as though they were on the cusp of getting what they wanted. The Winter of Discontent had come and gone, but the workers still weren't happy, and while Bertie didn't particularly want to add to the nation's woes, he wanted what was rightfully his. He wanted to make life easier for his Lillie; he wanted to give a little something extra to Eliza.

A blizzard swirled around him as he walked the mile home from the pub, and his boots crunched on the thick snow that settled underfoot. The orange glow of street lamps lit his way, and he paused under one of them so he could light a cigarette. It was then that it happened; it was then that he felt a growing pressure in his chest explode within him. Bertie was a big man – a strong man – and he thought it was nothing, but the pain got stronger, and then it began to crush him. He dropped his cigarette and struggled to take a breath. He knew there was a phone box in the distance, but he also knew he didn't have the strength to reach it. Beads of sweat appeared on his face and his eyes lost focus.

As Bertie fell, he was aware of his skull cracking on a concrete wall, but somehow he didn't feel it. All he could focus on was the crimson that seemed to surround him: the crimson of his blood that bloomed against the pure white of the snow on the ground. In days to come the snow would turn to grey ice, but for now it was clean and silken, and as he lay there, he was thankful for the softness of it, for the coldness that cushioned the pain in his chest and his head.

As Bertie drew his last breaths, he gazed up at the sky and knew he'd soon see the stars that were hidden behind the pollution. He thought of his daughter Eliza, so young, just starting her life; and of his wife, Lillie. He remembered dancing with her at the party where they'd met, and how beautiful she'd been as she glided in his arms, resplendent in her diamonds and pearls. He shut his eyes as he remembered that she had eventually sold those same diamonds and pearls to make ends meet, and he called out her name one final time ... but nobody heard him. Nobody came running to help.

Everything went black.

Eliza turned from her place at the front of the church and twisted her neck so she could take in the whispering, sorrowful congregation behind her. Her family had been coming to St Paul's on Park Lane in Tottenham for years, but this was the first time she'd seen so many people crammed into the space; the first time she'd seen grown men holding starched handkerchiefs to their faces to mop up their tears.

Lillie gripped her hand so tightly that her knuckles turned white, and Eliza reluctantly turned back to face the front. The vicar's eyes met hers as he said a prayer, but Eliza chose to look away and to stare at the statue of the Virgin Mary holding the baby Jesus instead. A drape of creamy, frothy lace had been placed so as to cover the statue's head, and Eliza wondered whether she and her mother should have covered their heads too, to show their respect to God. She was glad they had not, for if there was a God, he didn't deserve their respect. Not if he'd created the world in which they now lived.

Eliza knew tears were sliding down her face, but she couldn't feel them. Everything was numb, and she was glad of that: the pain would be unbearable if she had to suffer it, though she knew it would come eventually. The bronze handles of the coffin glinted in the weak wintry sunlight, as if to distract her from her thoughts, but there was no way that Eliza could look in its direction, not if she was to remain strong for her mother. For inside the wooden box lay her father. Her father, who'd had a heart attack on his way home from a union meeting at the pub, where they'd been on the cusp of forcing better working conditions and pay rises for all.

Eliza wearily surveyed her friends from behind the bar and wondered if she had the energy to serve them. She was back in her personal fairground of fun, surrounded by the scent of sex and sweat . . . only she couldn't feel any pleasure. It reached her, but it didn't penetrate her; she still felt numb.

She wondered what her mother was doing. Even though Lillie had insisted that Eliza return to her life in Soho, it had felt too soon. They'd only just buried Bertie, and it didn't seem right for them to try to resume their lives again yet. Eliza wanted to be with her mother, wanted to be there to comfort her – because God knows she had nobody else – but Lillie was adamant that she needed time alone to grieve. Eliza tried hard to respect her wishes, but it was all she could do not to jump on the night bus straight back to Tottenham.

'You look like shit,' Alison commented conversationally from the other side of the bar. Eliza chose not to respond; she didn't know what to say. 'You need to finish your shift and lose yourself on the dance floor. You need to forget about everything, just for a moment.'

'Day Breaks, Night Heals' was playing out of the speakers and everyone moved in time with the music. Eliza felt paralysed. When 'Number One Song in Heaven' by Sparks had come on, she'd barely been able to breathe. Everything reminded her of her father, and all she wanted to do was to curl up in a ball and try to forget what had happened, try to forget that she'd never speak to him again.

'Eliza's having her break!' Alison yelled to the other barmaid, who shrugged as she idly watched her drag Eliza out from behind the bar and into the bathroom. The acrid smell of urine made Eliza's eyes water, and Alison patted her arm awkwardly before perching herself on the broken sink.

'This isn't good, you know,' she remarked, taking a sip of her drink. Her wide eyes were bloodshot and dilated, and she scratched at her thighs nervously. 'I know you're having a shit time, but you need to force yourself out of it.'

Eliza nodded mutely. Alison watched her and sighed.

'Look, I know you're not into this, but Curt's got some new stuff in – it's guaranteed to give you a good time. It's giving me a great time.' She gave a sad, sharp little laugh.

Eliza fumbled with the packet of Silk Cut in her pocket and lit a cigarette. 'What is it?' she asked. She'd always been proud that she didn't take drugs, but right now she felt herself wavering. She'd give anything for a few hours' escape from the nightmare of grief.

'Speed. But it's not the dirty stuff. It's pure – it's practically medicinal.'

Alison pulled a wrap from her handbag. Eliza stared at her blankly. Alison was still beautiful, but she'd developed a hard edge in the last few months. Through the blue haze of smoke

Eliza saw her friend properly for the first time in months. Her skin was pallid and spotty underneath the make-up, and her lips had been drawn on as though she were drunk. Eliza wondered if, in her own way, Alison was as sad as she was.

Alison noticed the look on her face. 'It helps me get through the day,' she admitted.

Eliza and Alison never spoke openly about how Alison earned her money, but Eliza knew that Curt had introduced her to the same men he and Raven were linked with. Curt dealt drugs – everyone knew that – and Raven made his money on the back streets of Soho, where beautiful young boys got paid handsomely for their time. Alison had tried working behind the bar at the Coach & Horses, had wanted to get into fashion somehow, but she'd ultimately ended up posing for seedy photographs. Eliza was the only one who'd not slipped across the line, the only one who'd not let her soul darken in her pursuit of pleasure.

'I don't think this is a good idea—' she began, but Alison cut her off.

'Look, you've been there for me so many times, and now I want to be there for you. Let me help you.'

Eliza eyed her doubtfully. 'I need a hug, not drugs.'

Alison laughed. 'I'd hug you for the rest of your life if I could, but I need my arms for other things. This stuff isn't quite like a hug, but it can give you a boost in a way that nothing else can.'

Eliza rested her head against the cold, dirty tiles. 'How much is it?' she heard herself say.

Alison smiled miserably. 'It's on me. Share mine.'

Eliza watched her pour the powder into her drink and swill it around before taking a big gulp. She gestured for Eliza to do the same, but Eliza hesitated.

'Will this hurt me?' she asked in a small voice.

Alison laughed. 'It will only help you, I promise. Now down it before I change my mind.'

Eliza took a deep breath and did as she was told. If the speed tasted of anything, she couldn't detect it.

'You'll feel more like yourself soon; better, even,' Alison assured her. 'And if you want some more . . . well, you know where to come.'

Eliza stared at the bottom of the empty plastic beaker, then chucked it on the floor. As the girls walked back across the dance floor, she found herself examining the club more closely than she had for months. Bits of grubby black cotton dangled from the ceiling, pages from the *Daily Mail* and the *Daily World* had been stuck up on some of the walls, and a white sheet hung behind the stage area. For the first time she realised that Gossips wasn't as glamorous as it was in her mind, but it didn't stop her from thinking of it as home. Her refuge.

Nothing bad could happen to her here, and nothing could ever hurt her. Not when she was hurting so much already.

The speed kicked in and she suddenly felt a rush sweep through her body – it was as though she'd been dead and had come to life again. For the first time since her father had died she felt herself smile, and the music pumping through the speakers started to make sense.

Speed changed Eliza's life. She knew it wasn't good for her, and she wasn't proud to admit it, but when she took it – which she did daily, either in a glass of water or snorted hastily through her burned-out nostrils – she felt reborn, new, fresh. Her insides always felt dirty from the smoke and the alcohol and the drugs, but her blood flowed fast within her body and her heart pounded with renewed, artificial strength. Speed helped her feel alive; it helped her to stop feeling as though a part of her had died with her father.

When Bertie had passed away it had cast a shadow over her life. It was within that gloom that Eliza recognised the seediness of her existence for the first time. She lived with a drug dealer, a rent boy and a girl who took off her clothes for photographs, in a squat that was so cold in the winter that her bones physically ached; she lived on junk food and alcohol stolen from behind the bar at the club. She felt continual guilt that she wasn't in Tottenham helping her mother – although that was more Lillie's doing than her own – and she was fed up and bored. There was nothing glamorous or covetable about her life in Soho, and speed helped her escape from that reality. It softened the harsh edges of her life; it enabled her to laugh out loud when inside she felt absolutely nothing at all.

But the more speed Eliza took, the more in debt she became to Curt.

'You need to start paying for it,' he told her one night when they were at Hell. Eliza nodded and kept on dancing. She danced to 'The Girl From Ipanema' by Eartha Kitt, to 'Romeo Is Bleeding' by Tom Waits, to 'Shack Up' by Banbarra. Hell was more stylish than Gossips, with demonic murals, bright red walls and a graveyard at the back. The crowd was made up of gangster gays and predatory older men. David Bowie was rumoured to be hiding in the shadows along with Bianca Jagger and Helmut Newton, and people were having sex in the back alley, in the toilets, in the cloakroom. The scene was darker and spikier than Eliza had previously known, and that suited her. It was perverse, it was underground. Hell on Henrietta Street was where she could dance with the devil.

'I need you to start paying for it *now*,' Curt stressed.

Eliza caught his eye and saw that he meant business. But she didn't have any money – however many flyers she handed out, however many shifts she worked behind the bar at Gossips, she never had enough. Curt knew that.

'I'll pay,' she said blithely. She was on a high and she was determined not to lose it, not to let Curt ruin the evening.

'Talk to Ali and get some modelling work,' Curt said. Eliza nodded and tried to throw herself back into the music. Curt took hold of her arm. 'Talk to her *tonight*.'

Eliza shook him off. 'I will, all right? Just let me be. Jesus.' She wanted to stalk off to the toilets so she could snort another line, but a man she didn't recognise appeared at her shoulder. He wore simple trousers held up by braces and his shirt was adorned with a small black bow tie. A beret sat on top of his head, but his face was devoid of make-up. Eliza wondered how he'd been allowed in.

'Is this boy bothering you?' the man asked. His voice was deep.

Eliza looked up at him. 'What?' she asked distractedly. All she could think about was her next hit and getting away from Curt.

'Is this boy hassling you?' he repeated.

Curt shook his head in disgust and walked away. Eliza tried to make her way to the toilets, but the man blocked her path and smiled. Eliza often got approached by men – especially since she'd lost weight from taking so much speed – but trying to find love was the last thing on her mind these days. Even the faceless one-night stands she was used to seemed like a waste of her time.

'Look, thanks, but I'm not interested.'

The man's smile remained fixed. 'I'm not after that,' he began, but Eliza darted past him. 'Please – wait!'

Eliza paused and turned back.

'I'm a designer, a clothes designer. I'm mates with Malcolm – you know, McLaren – and he's helping me get my label off the ground. I'm looking for models.'

Eliza laughed. 'You'll want my friend Alison then,' she said, but the man was adamant.

'I want you. Look, I haven't got a lot of money, but I can chuck you a couple of quid and you'll have some decent photos. What do you say? You've got the right look.'

Eliza cocked her head. 'And I'll be wearing clothes?'

'That's the idea, yes.' The man looked puzzled, and Eliza suddenly felt a pang of sympathy for him.

He wasn't quite of this world, but he wanted to dress the inhabitants of it. Why not make a bit of money helping him out? It would keep Curt off her back, and her body away from the seedier studios that were hidden in the attics of the walk-ups.

'I'll do it,' she said breezily. She was already thinking about how many wraps she could buy with the money.

Chapter Ten

Buckinghamshire and London,
recently

The hamlet of Beaufont was a tiny, unassuming village nestled deep in the Buckinghamshire valleys. It comprised about forty cottages, a general store that doubled as a post office, a village hall, a little-used bus stop and a church on a site that had been a place of worship since Saxon times. The thick-walled flint tower of the church was home to a ring of six bells, and even though it had been rebuilt so often that the outer walls resembled a patchwork of stone, it was still majestic, still a talking point of the local area. If you were to climb it, you'd see for miles – and you'd undoubtedly spot Beaufont Hall in the distance.

The Winters lived in the shadow of the tower, just across from the crumbling Victorian headstones of the graveyard. Cassie stood with her back to the church so she could survey their cottage. It was low and squat, without any obvious modern extension, but it was also pretty, with walls a soft shade of vanilla, and a freshly thatched roof. Towering hollyhocks and delphiniums bordered the brick path that cut through the lush green lawn, and Cassie picked her way down it carefully before she pulled on the doorbell chain. Several moments later the front door opened and a woman with the same colouring as Ed smiled down at her.

'You must be Cassie Cooke!' she exclaimed.

Cassie nodded and stuck out her hand. Valerie Winter laughed and gave her a hug instead.

'We've so been looking forward to your visit! Ed hasn't stopped talking about you since you started to spend time at the big house. Now, are you thirsty? Hungry?' Valerie put her hands on her hips and cocked her head; one of her dangly earrings brushed against her shoulder. She was so warm and friendly that Cassie immediately liked her.

'Mum, maybe let Cassie in before you start plying her with tea and cake,' Ed's voice interrupted. He appeared in the low doorway and shot Cassie a grin. 'Come in, come and sit down.'

'He's always been bossy, that one,' Valerie confided as Cassie walked into the living room. It wasn't a particularly big room, but it was warm and cosy, with a cream patterned rug on the hardwood oak floor, soft powder-blue sofas, dove-grey curtains at the low windows, and ivory walls with exposed beams. On one of the sofas sat a man with tired green eyes behind thick-rimmed spectacles, perfectly combed white hair, and a big smile. He was probably in his late fifties or early sixties, but he seemed much older.

'Alan Winter,' he said as Cassie leant over to shake his hand. He patted the sofa cushion, and Cassie perched next to him. She felt slightly awkward despite the Winters' warmth. 'I used to work for your grandmother Violet. You're very like her. Tempests were either dark or blonde – their colouring was always extreme and there was little in between.'

Cassie smiled. 'My mother's blonde – as are my brother and sister. They're twins.'

Alan nodded at Cassie and simultaneously accepted a cup of tea from Valerie. His hands shook ever so slightly and a tiny amount of tea spilled on to the floral-patterned saucer. Ed settled on the sofa on the opposite side of the room. His jeans-clad legs stretched out so that they touched the coffee table; he looked too big for such a small cottage. Cassie tried – and failed – to imagine him growing up here.

'Edward tells us you've been cleaning up the house,' Alan said as he noticed Cassie watching his son.

Cassie nodded. 'My mother wants to sell it, as you know,' she replied. 'It's in a sorry way. It must have been magnificent when my family lived there.'

Alan sipped his tea contemplatively. 'It was. My earliest memories are of Beaufont Hall. The house is large, of course, but when you're a small child it can seem quite overwhelming.'

Valerie handed Cassie a slice of fruit cake, and Cassie smiled her thanks.

'My mother makes the best cake in the whole of Buckinghamshire,' Ed remarked as he helped himself to an extra-large slice and bit into it. 'She wins gold in all the village competitions, but she won't go on any TV baking shows. I think she'd win easily.'

'It would mean going to London, and you know how I feel about that,' Valerie said conversationally. 'I'm quite happy here, thank you very much. I don't need to go to the city to remind me how much I appreciate the countryside.'

Ed laughed. 'Subtle, Mum.'

'I don't know what you're talking about,' Valerie remarked, and then she laughed too.

'My mother always told me that I'd regret moving to London and that I'd hate working in the City, and ever since I moved back home, she parrots "I told you so" every single day.'

'I only mention it when you pop over,' Valerie said mildly. 'Which definitely isn't every single day, as you're suggesting.'

Cassie looked at Ed. 'So you don't live here?' she asked.

He shook his head. 'I wouldn't fit! No, I'm renting one of the cottages down the lane. I'd drive my parents mad if I lived here.'

'I can see why,' Cassie teased uncharacteristically. Ed grinned at her and she felt the creeping heat of a blush bloom on her cheeks. She turned back to Alan and tried to change the subject. 'Your mother worked at Beaufont Hall, didn't she?'

Alan nodded. 'She was the housekeeper for your grand-mother. She used to take me to work, and the family never minded me playing in the servants' quarters or in the grounds – there was plenty of space. My grandmother had looked after the house for your great-grandparents, you see, and my mother had been brought up in a similar way.'

'What was Beaufont Hall like when your mother was the housekeeper?' Cassie asked. She took a bite of cake while Alan considered his response.

'Glorious,' he said eventually. He placed his cup and saucer on a side table and settled back into the sofa. 'Well, it was glorious in lots of ways, but hard in others. Your grandmother was quite a lonely woman, despite having her daughter – your mother – living with her. She used to confide in my mother quite a lot, even though it wasn't really the done thing back then. Mum used to say that Violet thought of her as part of the furniture.'

'Did *you* meet my grandmother – or my mother?'

'I knew both of them. Violet Tempest was very Victorian – she came across as cold and haughty – but your mother was sweet. Because she was an only child, she spent a lot of time with her cousins, and I would often hear them laughing and running around the house. I was a bit older than them, but I used to wish I was younger so I could join in.'

Cassie thought of the photographs she'd seen of her mother as a child and smiled. She could easily imagine a young Rebecca speeding along the corridors of Beaufont Hall, her long blonde hair trailing out behind her.

'And were Violet and Aster close?' Cassie asked. She knew very little of her grandmother's sister – Rose and Lloyd's mother.

Alan paused for a moment. He nodded, but he looked troubled. 'They had to be, in a way,' he admitted.

Cassie put the remainder of her cake on her plate and balanced it on her knees. She glanced at Ed – who looked as confused as she felt – and back at Alan.

'What do you mean?' she asked cautiously.

Alan took off his spectacles, cleaned them on his shirt and put them back on. When he looked at Cassie, she could see his eyes glimmering brightly behind the thick glass.

'Because their younger sister disappeared.'

Cassie swallowed hard. 'Do you mean Lillie? Lillie Tempest?'

Alan nodded. 'You've heard of her then? I wasn't sure. When I was a kid, I was told never to mention her name – I certainly never heard any of the family talk about her.'

'But she didn't disappear,' Cassie said slowly. 'She lived in London with her husband and her daughter.'

There was a long silence then. Cassie was just starting to feel uncomfortable when Alan spoke.

'So your mother has told you about Lillie and what happened to her?'

Cassie shook her head. She hadn't planned to tell the Winters about Eliza's diaries – especially as she'd chosen not to mention them to Ed – but they were kind and welcoming and it didn't feel right not to confide in them, not least because Alan Winter might be able to help her discover what had happened.

'No – my mother doesn't really like to talk about Beaufont Hall or her family. I found some diaries in the library when I was clearing it out,' Cassie admitted. She looked over at Ed, who shot her a puzzled look in return. 'They belonged to Eliza Boyle – Lillie's daughter.'

Alan Winter sat extremely still. 'And you've not told your mother that you've found them?' he asked.

Cassie shook her head. 'I know I should have when I discovered them, but I wanted to read them first.' She didn't admit that she'd still not told her mother about the additional money she'd raised from the sale of the books, either.

'I've read several of the diaries, but there's no mention as to why Lillie and Eliza weren't a proper part of the family,' she continued. 'Do you have any idea what happened?'

Valerie stood to make another pot of tea, and as she walked past her husband she gently placed her hand on his shoulder. Cassie noticed that Alan looked uneasy, and she immediately felt apologetic.

'I'm sorry – I didn't mean to put you on the spot like that,' she said in a rush.

He smiled warmly at her. 'It's okay,' he said. 'It's natural that you're curious about your family.' He rubbed his forehead and gazed into the distance for a moment.

'All I know,' he said eventually, 'is that Lillie was there one day and the next she was gone. I never met her, of course – I was just a small child at the time – but her sisters were heartbroken. My mother said that nobody ever spoke of her disappearance, and the staff were told in no uncertain terms that they were never to mention her name again. Her parents closed her bedroom door and acted as if she didn't exist. Violet and Aster mourned her for a long time.'

'I wonder what on earth happened,' Cassie said. 'Do you know what year this would have been?'

Alan shook his head. 'It was the early sixties, but that's all I know. Your mother may be able to tell you more ... Family secrets often have ways of making themselves known.'

Cassie shifted her position and placed her plate with the half-eaten fruit cake on the coffee table. 'So I'm assuming you didn't meet Lillie's daughter Eliza?'

Alan looked down at the floor for the longest time. 'I knew of her,' he said eventually.

Cassie was about to ask him to elaborate when he raised his head and looked her straight in the eye. His gaze was unflinching and unsettling; she found herself looking away.

'I could tell you more about Eliza Boyle, but all I know is village gossip. If you want to know what happened to her, I suggest you ask your mother – she knows more about what happened, and if you ask me, I think it's time Lillie and Eliza stopped being the Tempests' dirty little secret.'

Cassie hovered nervously in the doorway to the kitchen and silently watched her mother loading the dishwasher. The drive back to London had been a long one – the Sunday traffic on the M25 had tested her patience along with her tense shoulder muscles – but she felt no relief at being back home. As much as she wanted to know what had happened to Lillie and Eliza, she also dreaded the conversation she needed to have with Rebecca. For in order to have it, she knew she'd have to admit to finding Eliza's diaries, and she wasn't quite ready to do so.

'Would you like a hand?' she asked. Her voice sounded loud in the relative silence of the house.

Rebecca turned to look at her. She gazed at her for a moment, then shook her head. 'No thank you. But I would like to talk to you,' she said.

Cassie felt the familiar apprehension that came before she had a row with her mother, but she pulled out a chair at the kitchen table and sat down. Rebecca finished loading the dishwasher, then poured two glasses of lemonade, which she carried to the table.

'I hear you visited Alan and Valerie Winter today,' she began. Cassie could see that her mother was trying to be light, conversational, but her lips were pinched and her eyes were hard. 'I didn't realise you know them.'

'I didn't,' Cassie said warily. 'But I've become quite friendly with their son, Ed, and he introduced me to them. How did you know I met them?'

'Because Alan phoned me as soon as you left. He says you're quite a credit to the family.'

Cassie traced her finger through the condensation on the glass in front of her. 'I wanted to ask him about his memories of Beaufont Hall. Since I've been spending time there, it's piqued my interest even more ... and I know you don't really like talking about Beaufont or your childhood.'

Rebecca ignored this. 'I've been meaning to ask you how the clean-up job is coming along. I've been making calls to estate agents, and several are looking forward to valuing the property as soon as you've finished.'

Cassie swallowed. 'Most of the downstairs rooms are finished, and Ed has boarded up all the windows that were cracked. I've started on a couple of the rooms upstairs too. In fact, I was hoping to stay there next weekend. Ed said he'd lend me a blow-up mattress ...'

Rebecca raised an eyebrow and Cassie stopped talking. There

was a silence then, an awkward, tense silence full of words not spoken, and Cassie knew that Alan had filled Rebecca in on their conversation about Lillie Tempest. She looked down at the table, and as she examined the grains of the distressed pine, she considered what she'd say next.

'Mum,' she began slowly. 'What can you tell me about Lillie Tempest and Eliza Boyle? I'd like to know who they are and how I'm related to them.'

Rebecca stared at her daughter for a moment and then her shoulders sank. When she spoke, her voice was no more than a whisper. 'Lillie was my aunt and Eliza was my cousin – but I gather from Alan that you now know this. They both passed away in the 1980s, before you were born.'

Cassie digested that. She'd had a feeling that Eliza was no longer alive, but it was still a difficult thing to hear. 'But why haven't I ever heard of them?' she asked. 'Why did you keep them a secret from me? From us?'

Rebecca sipped from her glass as she considered her answer. 'They've always been a secret. Lillie was no longer part of the family when I was born, and I grew up thinking that Aster was my only aunt.'

'You didn't tell me about them, though,' Cassie said quietly. 'I don't know why you kept them a secret from *me*.'

Rebecca looked drained, exhausted, and despite wanting to know more about her extended family, Cassie felt sorry for her mother.

'Alan says you found some of Eliza's diaries in the library,' Rebecca said. 'How many were there?'

Cassie wanted to be honest, but she knew instinctively that there was more to the story than Rebecca was telling her; that her mother was being evasive for the same reasons that she always had been when it came to discussing the family and Beaufont Hall.

'Just two,' she lied. 'One from when Eliza was seventeen, and another from a couple of years later. I've read them both.'

Rebecca nodded. 'And you didn't find any more?'

Cassie shook her head. 'Did you know Eliza, Mum?'

There was a long pause. 'I met her, yes. We were just getting to know each other when she passed away.'

Cassie could see it was discomforting for her mother to remember Eliza, but despite her stricken expression, Rebecca looked as though she wanted to continue to talk about her.

'She was a free spirit – wild in many ways. But she was also sweet and kind and full of love. She was beautiful, too, and she tried to make a go of it as a model, although she didn't really have the self-discipline.'

'Do you have any photos of her, or of Lillie?'

Cassie expected her mother to say she didn't, but to her surprise, Rebecca walked over to her handbag and took out her purse. From the depths of the many hidden compartments she pulled out a tiny black-and-white passport photograph of two women in their twenties. One of them was blonde – Rebecca – but the other was dark: Eliza Boyle.

Cassie pored over the dog-eared photograph. Rebecca and Eliza looked so young and so beautiful. There was no denying that they were related, despite Rebecca being a sunny blonde and Eliza being dark and more exotic-looking. They had the same shaped eyes, the same broad smile.

'You both look so lovely,' Cassie said with a smile. She handed the photograph back to her mother, who glanced at it and then squirrelled it away again.

'We *were* lovely, in that way you are when you're young,'

Rebecca mused. She looked up at her daughter. 'Could I please see the diaries?'

Cassie nodded. 'Of course you can,' she replied. 'And thank you for telling me a bit about Eliza and Lillie.'

Rebecca smiled, a sad, melancholy smile. She looked as though she were on the verge of saying something else, but instead she chose to turn away.

Chapter Eleven

London, 1982

It had been two years since Bertie Boyle's death, and two years since Eliza had started to take drugs to numb the pain of losing her father. Her life in Soho had always been glazed in glitter and fun, but as time went on, the sparkle had worn away; now only seediness and desperation remained, and it hung over everything like a thick, murky smog. Eliza was bored of working at Gossips and she'd begun to tire of the social scene. What had once been fun now felt stupid and childish. She longed to do something with a bit more meaning; she wanted to do something that would have made Bertie proud of her.

Because she knew her father would have wanted her to – and because she felt guilty if she didn't – Eliza had got into the habit of phoning her mother almost every other day from the cold, dark office at Gossips. She had always been more of a daddy's girl, but she felt a responsibility to her mother, felt that Bertie would have wanted her to try to grow closer to Lillie in his absence. But every time they spoke on the phone, the weary sound of Lillie's voice made Eliza feel helpless. She wished with all her heart that she could make the loss of Bertie easier for her mother, but it was impossible: Bertie had been Lillie's everything.

Eliza had never wanted her parents to worry about her and her life in Soho, so when she spoke to Lillie she hid the truth of her humdrum days. Rather than telling her that she was constantly broke, miserable and bored, she started to make up tiny lies in the hope that she'd hear a smile in her mother's voice. She elaborated the importance of her job – Lillie believed that Eliza was now a manager of one of the club nights, rather than just a beer-stained girl who worked behind the bar – and she told her that she'd moved from the squat into a rather more comfortable studio flat with working gas central heating. She didn't like lying to her mother, but when Lillie sounded pleased that Eliza was getting on well, it encouraged her to keep telling stories.

The reality was that Eliza felt trapped in the life she'd so gleefully run to, and every time she stepped behind the bar at Gossips, she wished she was somewhere else. She longed to be able to escape the life that she'd once loved so much, but it seemed impossible. Or at least it had done until the stranger had walked into the basement club and brought with him a glimmer of light and hope.

The evening had started like many others: Eliza had been slouched behind the bar as the crowds began to filter into the club with nothing but debauched pleasure on their minds. She had served them their usual drinks – snakebite, pints of beer, shots of vodka – but she was going through the motions. She'd taken a couple of lines of speed at the start of her shift to give her some much-needed energy, but the chemicals couldn't cut through the fog that had enveloped her brain. She didn't feel alert, didn't feel on form, and when the man on the other side of the bar tried to get her attention, she didn't notice him. He had to wave a five-pound note in her face for several seconds before she realised he was there.

'Can I have a drink?' he said in a loud voice for the second time, and Eliza snapped to attention as he came into focus. He had slicked-back brown hair, almond-shaped eyes, thin, smiling lips and a dimple in his chin.

'What can I get you?' Eliza wondered how she'd not noticed him before. Dressed in a light grey suit, he stood out amongst the regulars in their many shades of black.

'What do you suggest?' the man replied with a grin, and Eliza struggled not to roll her eyes.

'I dunno, how about a shandy? You look like a shandy kind of man.'

'A shandy kind of man,' the man echoed, his smile fading. 'Right. Well, to be honest, I'm not really a shandy *or* a Gossips kind of man. I'm actually here to talk to you. You *are* Eliza, aren't you?'

Eliza looked at the man warily. She was known on the scene – of course she was – but this man clearly wasn't part of it: not with his clean-cut looks and sensible haircut.

'How do you know my name?'

'I've been working with Devan, and I was looking through his archives when I saw the photos from the shoots you've done for him,' the man said. 'He told me all about you, and he suggested I come and have a chat.'

Eliza let her guard drop. 'You know Devan?' she asked.

The man nodded, and Eliza looked at him properly. When she'd been approached by Devan in Hell and asked to model for him, she'd been sceptical – but Devan had been legit. He was obsessed by Little Lord Fauntleroy and he created clothes he imagined the character would wear if he'd turned bad: the trousers were peg-legged and made of leather, the suits were covered in polka dots, and the hats were soldier's caps made from red PVC. Everything was covered in silver lurex piping, crucifixes, Stars of David and swastikas.

When Eliza had first modelled for him, she'd felt awkward and out of her depth, but whatever she'd done had worked – or at the very least it hadn't hindered Devan's progress, for he now sold his clothes at a new boutique opposite Kensington Market, and he was riding high with Dexter Wong and Pam Hogg. He could now afford to use real models, but every so often he asked Eliza to step in – he said that she looked more authentic because she was actually part of the scene. Eliza enjoyed her time in front of the camera, but despite Devan trying to encourage her to model professionally, she didn't take it too seriously. She had the right look for Devan's clothes, but that was all she had: a look.

'I've known Devan for a while,' the man continued. 'He uses my agency when he wants to book new girls to model his collections. But I'll be honest, I'm not here to talk about him; I'm here to try to persuade you to take modelling seriously.'

Eliza eyed the rolled-up sleeves of his loose-fitting suit and wondered if he was one of those yuppies that she'd read about in the papers.

'I don't understand,' she said honestly.

'Look, I don't do this often, but when I saw your photographs, I thought you had something special. I might be wrong, but there's something about your face that's very on trend for right now.'

Eliza started laughing – it was a nervous reaction to what he was saying and she couldn't seem to stop it. He frowned at her and waited for her giggles to die away.

'This is my card,' he said, and he slid a heavy cream business card across the sticky bar. 'Like I said, this isn't something I'd normally do, but the photos piqued my interest, and Devan said it would be worth talking to you to see if you wanted to do more work for other clients.'

Eliza picked the card up and stared at it. A crowd of boys with pink eyeshadow and heavy eyeliner were trying to get her attention, but she couldn't peel her gaze away from the business card in her hands. It read: *Jonathan Klein, Model Agent.*

'You're serious, aren't you?' she said. Her heart was racing – and not just because of the chemicals that throbbed through her bloodstream. 'But why would you want to help me? You don't even know me.'

Jonathan pushed his jacket sleeves further up his arms. 'Trust me, this isn't an altruistic visit. I'm in the business of making money, and with you on my books I think I could make a hell of a lot more. So why don't you go home, have a think about it and then give me a ring. That is, of course, unless you want to serve this lot for the rest of your life.'

Eliza gazed at the boys clamouring for her attention and then turned back to Jonathan. 'I don't need to think about it,' she said. 'If you think I could really do this, I'd like to give it a go.'

The morning that Eliza decided to visit Jonathan in his office was one she would remember forever. She woke early to the sound of the rubbish trucks driving up and down Lexington Street, and rather than going back to sleep, she pulled on her pixie boots and walked straight out of Silver Place. She strode through Soho with determination, past a haphazardly parked Austin Metro, past posters plastered on the walls for the general election and for an upcoming Iron Maiden tour, and past homeless people sleeping in doorways. When she got to Tottenham Court Road Tube station, she checked the map and plotted her route to High Street Kensington; it seemed a million miles away, and she hoped her visit wouldn't come to nothing. She wanted this.

Eliza was sick of being poor and sick of feeling as though her life wasn't going anywhere. In comparison, Alison appeared to live a charmed, golden existence. She always had enough money, always seemed to be able to afford anything and do whatever she wanted, even though all she actually did was hang out in Gossips with the rest of them.

Eliza wasn't shallow – she had been brought up with very little, and she knew that so long as she had enough of everything she needed, she was okay – but she was envious at how effortless Alison's life seemed next to hers. The girls didn't really talk about Alison's nude modelling, but Alison had once admitted how easy she'd found it once she got over her initial embarrassment. She took her clothes off, she spread her legs, and she smiled her glassy smile. The drugs she took helped her to get through the shoots – and then they helped her to forget what she'd just done.

Eliza found Jonathan's office easily with the help of her tatty *A–Z*, and gratefully accepted a cup of coffee from the receptionist. Jonathan greeted her with a friendly smile, but it was one she struggled to return because of her nerves. Her daydreams about modelling were either about to come true or be crushed.

'As I said at the club, I like what you've done for Devan, but I'd like to do some test shots to see you in a more natural style – without all that make-up you wore,' Jonathan said as he placed his elbows on his chrome desk and leaned towards Eliza.

Eliza stared at him and wondered if she'd heard him correctly. Despite his kind words, she still wasn't sure that he was right – she was tall, gawky, and her hair was brown and frizzy. She didn't really look like the glamorous models that graced the pages of magazines.

'Do you think I could really get work?' she asked. She'd already looked around Jonathan's office and could tell that he meant business. Black-and-white photographs of some of his more successful models hung on the walls, there was a plush grey and pink carpet underfoot, and an electronic typewriter shone on top of his desk. Eliza had never been anywhere as smart as this.

'If you worked hard, you could potentially earn thousands. One of my more popular models earned forty-five thousand last year – a record in the agency.'

Eliza's eyes widened. 'And you think I could earn that much?'

Jonathan nodded. 'I do. But you'd need to tidy yourself up a bit and lay off the chemicals. I'd be hesitant about sending you to go-sees if you were dressed like that.'

Eliza looked down at her ripped leggings and dirty lacy top. She'd not washed her hair in four days and her hot-pink nail varnish was chipped. She was loath to admit it, but Jonathan probably had a point.

'Even if I did dress smartly, I still don't think anyone would believe I was really a model. I mean, look at those girls in the photos behind you. They're all skinny blondes, and I look nothing like them.'

Jonathan glanced at the photos, then turned back to Eliza with a smile.

'The fact that you look different to the other girls on my books is a big plus point, not a minus,' he said easily. 'You have a sultry, continental look about you – but rather than having brown eyes, yours are bright blue. It's an intoxicating mix. Are your parents both English?'

Eliza shook her head. 'My mother is, but my father was American. He thought his grandmother may have been an Indian; you know, a Native American.' She felt the familiar pain when she thought of her father and swallowed hard. There was so much she hadn't asked him about himself and his family, and now she'd never be able to.

'Look, I can tell you're apprehensive, and that it's a lot to take in,' Jonathan said smoothly. He'd clearly noticed her discomfort but chose not to ask her about it. 'Why don't we go to the studio around the corner and do a few test shots? That way you can see if you're comfortable, and I can see if your features translate well to Polaroid.'

Eliza hadn't expected this. 'You want to take some photos of me right now?' she asked, and Jonathan nodded and stood up.

'No time like the present,' he said briskly, and looked at her shrewdly. 'After all, you don't want to be working behind that bar for the rest of your life, do you?'

Eliza could hardly believe it, but as soon as she stood in front of the camera and under the hot lights, something changed in her. She'd been photographed before, of course, but it hadn't felt like this – it was as if she'd come alive in a way she'd never experienced previously. It was like an awakening.

'Do you want some photos of me wearing make-up?' she asked Jonathan as he looked intently at the Polaroids he'd taken of her.

Before she'd got to the studio she'd thought she could take or leave modelling. Yes, she wanted the money and to be able to leave Gossips, but she didn't quite believe Jonathan when he said she had the perfect look for it, couldn't accept that this might be her way out of the world she'd managed to get stuck in. But now she found she wanted this more than she'd realised, and it wasn't just because it could potentially pay her well. It was because it was validation; a way to make her way in the world that her father would have been proud of, and a way to prove to everyone – including the Tempests – that she was good enough.

'That's not necessary,' Jonathan said as he waved a Polaroid in the air to help it develop faster.

Eliza bit her lip and wished she hadn't drunk so much the night before. She'd run out of speed so had compensated by knocking back glasses of vodka whenever her boss wasn't looking. It seemed like a good idea at the time – and it certainly made her shift go a lot faster – but she was paying for it now. She only hoped the photographs wouldn't highlight the bags under her eyes and the spot she could feel growing on her chin.

'I think I've seen enough,' Jonathan continued, and looked at her gravely. He stood out against the grubby white walls and dirty carpet of the studio; he reeked of ambition, of money, and even though he was square, Eliza couldn't help but think he was one of the most attractive men she'd ever met. He was magnetic. 'Would you like to see what you look like?' he asked.

Eliza felt her heart sink at his tone, but she was determined not to show it. Hadn't she told him she wasn't cut out to be a model? Today had been a complete waste of time. 'Okay,' she said as neutrally as she could, and walked over to the table where the Polaroids were laid out.

She picked one up and stared at it in shock. The girl in the Polaroid was completely different to the girl Eliza saw reflected in the mirror, but she could easily believe that this girl was a model – for as well as being exquisitely beautiful, she also had an edgy, don't-fuck-with-me attitude. The girl in the photo looked as if she'd been born into modelling and found it effortless. Eliza could barely believe it was her.

'What do you think?' Jonathan said, and Eliza heard amusement in his voice.

She looked up at him and shook her head; she couldn't speak.

'You look beautiful,' he continued, and Eliza felt pleasure blossom inside her. No man had ever told her she was beautiful – pretty and sexy, yes, but beautiful, no. 'You look delicate but strong, and there's something so interesting about your genetic make-up. I don't think anyone could resist looking at you. I know I could stare at your face for hours.'

Eliza blushed, but Jonathan suddenly became businesslike again.

'If you're happy with me doing so, I'd like to put you on my books as soon as possible. I'd like to schedule a time to do some proper head shots, and I'll need to get you measured – height, weight, shoe size, that sort of thing. Then I'll send your photo out to some of my contacts to test the waters. But I don't think you're going to have a problem getting booked. Your look is very now, very current.'

Eliza stared at him, and then back at the photos on the table.

'That sounds amazing,' she said softly. If she could get proper modelling work, it would keep her away from the doorway into Soho's underworld; keep her from tumbling into the abyss in which her friends already found themselves. Jonathan had rescued her.

'I'm assuming it won't be a problem to use your real name on the head shots?'

Eliza thought about it and frowned. Apart from Alison, the only models she knew of – such as Gia Carangi, Christie Brinkley and Paulina Porizkova – all had exotic, sexy names. Despite missing her father badly and wanting to do something to make him proud of her, she didn't want to use her surname. Boyle wasn't the most glamorous surname in the world, and as much as she'd like to, there was no way she could call herself Eliza Tempest. It would be like rubbing salt into the deep flesh wound that stood between her and the rest of the Tempests, and her mother would never forgive her for stirring things up.

'I don't want to be called Eliza Boyle, and I don't want to use my mother's maiden name either,' she said, thinking hard. 'I need a surname that sounds kind of alluring and interesting.'

Jonathan was silent as he considered it. 'How about Eliza Archer?' he suggested eventually, and Eliza's eyes lit up.

It was perfect.

Chapter Twelve

London and Buckinghamshire,
recently

Cassie did a Google Image search for 'Eliza Archer', and swallowed hard as the photos cascaded across her laptop screen. There she was, the girl whose diaries she'd been reading. But she wasn't just any girl – she was a model, one who'd soared for a brief moment in time before her skyrocketing career had quickly imploded on itself. Eliza Archer had been the girl everyone had wanted to be, before she'd mysteriously disappeared without a trace.

Cassie clicked on a photo to enlarge it, and a black-and-white image taken for *The Face* filled her screen. She drank in Eliza's perfect, beautiful features and wondered why her mother hadn't told her that Eliza Boyle had renamed herself Eliza Archer. All Rebecca had said was that Eliza had tried to be a model and had failed.

Cassie reluctantly dragged her eyes away from the photograph and pulled up Eliza's Wikipedia entry. Her eyes ran quickly across the words on the page, and she forced herself to slow down so she could fully digest everything that was publicly known about Eliza. Her heart raced, and concentrating felt impossible, but she read the entry again and again until she felt she'd memorised every line.

Eliza Archer, fashion model

Eliza Archer (April 1961–November 1989) was a British fashion model during the mid-1980s. Archer embodied the clubland look of the era and was relatively successful for a short period of time.

Archer appeared in several fashion magazines, including *The Face*, *L'Officiel*, *Gloss* and *Elle*. She also appeared in several issues of Japanese magazines between 1983 and 1985.

Early life

Archer was born in Tottenham, London, in 1961. Little is known about her early life or her parents.

Career

Archer was mainly known in fashion circles by her first name. She was spotted in a nightclub by respected agent Jonathan Klein. [1]

By 1984, she was an established model and had worked extensively in Asia, America and Europe.

Archer was a regular at Gossips nightclub in Soho, and later visited Embargo in Leicester Square.

Little is known or documented concerning the decline of Archer's career. Her last fashion shoot was in 1985.

Death

In November 1989, Archer died of unreported health complications at the age of 28.

Legacy

As Archer's career only lasted for a few years, little of her legacy remains. Photographs of her have appeared in various books about the 1980s music and fashion scenes in London.

'I'm looking for a book,' a male voice said.

Cassie hurriedly closed her laptop and smiled up at him.

'Do you have any early editions of *Little Lord Fauntleroy* by Frances Hodgson Burnett? The man who replied to my email enquiry said you did – a Mr Heritage? It's a birthday present for my partner.'

Cassie stared at him for a moment. Her thoughts were still with Eliza, whose friend Devan had designed his clothes with the fictional character in mind. She forced herself back to the present.

'Sorry, did you say *Little Lord Fauntleroy*?' she asked.

The man nodded. His face was ruddy above his tweed suit; he looked as though he lived in the country and had made the journey to Heritage Books especially. Cassie was pleased to be able to help him.

'We do have a copy. It's a first edition but not a first printing – it's a later issue.' She took a set of keys from the desk drawer and walked over to the glass-fronted cabinet where they kept some of the higher-priced books. She brought out a crimson-bound hardback and passed it to the man. 'It has marbled endpapers and gilt edges, and this version has several illustrations. There are a couple of marks, but it's in a good condition considering it's from 1886.'

The man looked elated. 'My partner will be delighted. His parents were disappointed when they found out he was homosexual – he rather identifies with the story about how Captain Errol was thought badly of for marrying who he loved.'

Cassie's thoughts immediately turned back to her own family. In the excitement of discovering that Eliza had been a model – a proper one rather than a soft porn one like her friend Alison – she'd completely forgotten that Eliza had told Jonathan that her father had been American. The parallels between *Little Lord Fauntleroy* – where the Earl was disappointed with his favourite son for marrying an American – and Lillie's life were too great to ignore. She wanted to get stuck into Eliza's next diary, but she knew she had to focus on the sale at hand.

'Last year I managed to get him Ricky Schroder's autograph,' the man continued. 'I didn't think I'd be able to top that, but I think I have now.'

Cassie nodded absent-mindedly. 'Sorry, whose autograph did you get?'

'Ricky Schroder,' the man repeated. 'He played Ceddie Errol in the film – the little blonde boy who lives in poverty after his father is disowned?'

'I'm sorry, I've not seen it,' Cassie murmured.

The man chuckled as Cassie wrapped the book in brown paper and tied it with string. 'I suppose it came out before your time,' he said.

He paid for the book with cash – £380, which Cassie carefully placed in the till – and left the shop with a smile on his face.

Cassie sat back down on her stool and reopened her laptop to the photographs of Eliza. She was lost in thought. Had Lillie Tempest been disowned for marrying an American? She couldn't help but think this was what had happened. And she was surprised to find that it was Ed, rather than anyone else, that she wanted to share the revelation with.

'So I think Lillie was probably rejected by her parents because she fell in love with an American,' Cassie remarked conversationally.

It was the following Saturday, a rainy autumn day, and the air smelled of damp lingering bonfires. She and Ed were getting a bite to eat in a café in the village closest to Beaufont which was home to many London commuters, and the café wouldn't have been out of place in Hampstead or Notting Hill. Homemade cakes took precedence on the serving counter alongside a Gaggia espresso machine, and several Boden-clad children clamoured for the attention of their weary-looking parents. Cassie wondered if Lillie had ever cycled over here when she'd been a girl; if she and Violet and Aster had sought refuge from the weather with cups of cocoa like she and Ed had.

Ed considered what Cassie had said. 'You could be right. From what I know of society families like yours – and bear in mind I know very little, and what I do know is gleaned from programmes like *Downton Abbey* – reputation was everything. Lillie may have been expected to make a good marriage for money.'

'That's what I thought. The Tempest name wasn't as well known as that of the Guinnesses or the Mitfords, but Violet and Aster did their best to shun the limelight as adults. I've been wondering if they did so because they didn't want to draw attention to the issue of Lillie being disowned.'

Ed shrugged. 'Perhaps,' he remarked. He took a bite of his sandwich and watched the rain fall heavily outside. 'Or perhaps it was because their father – your great-grandfather – was strict and decided it was more respectable for them to keep a low profile. Do you know much about him or your great-grandmother?'

Cassie shook her head. 'I know they were called Philip and Mary, and I've seen a few photographs of them, but that's all. I like to imagine them as stern but loving... Kind of how I imagine Beaufont Hall would be if it had a personality.'

'Beaufont Hall definitely has a personality,' Ed said with a smile.

Cassie watched him as he ate, and wondered when she'd started to find being around him so comfortable. The hours they'd spent at Beaufont in companionable silence had definitely helped, as had meeting his parents. Her shyness around him had all but disappeared – even if her attraction to him had not.

'But then I keep wondering if Bertie being American is a red herring,' she continued, pushing the romantic feelings she had for Ed back down into the shadows. It would be pointless for her to fall for him: men like Ed never went for girls like her. 'I worked out something else.'

Ed stopped chewing and looked at her. Cassie tried not to blush under his direct gaze.

'I think Eliza may have been conceived – and possibly even born – before Lillie and Bertie got married.' Ed raised an eyebrow and said nothing. 'I know that's not a big deal now, but it would have been back then. And from everything I've discovered, the family did seem quite Victorian in terms of their values. I wonder if Lillie got pregnant and her parents disapproved so strongly that they banished her from Beaufont.'

'Have you looked up Lillie and Bertie's marriage certificate, or Eliza's birth certificate?' Ed asked.

Cassie felt stupid. 'I hadn't even thought of doing that,' she admitted. She almost wanted to go back to London so she could jump on her laptop and order them immediately. 'Wikipedia gives an approximate date of birth for Eliza, but it would be good to get official confirmation.'

She rubbed a peephole in the condensation on the window and watched the rain fall even harder. She was thankful that they'd fixed the hole in the roof of the house, but she hated to think of the MDF covering the windows becoming sodden.

'I should get back to Beaufont in case this weather gets worse,' she said.

'Want company?' Ed asked as he gestured to the waitress for the bill.

Cassie finished her cocoa and smiled at him. 'That would be great.'

Cassie and Ed ran from the car to the side entrance of Beaufont Hall and pushed open the door so they could shelter in the dark servants' corridor. They pulled off their waterlogged shoes, but Cassie wished she hadn't: the stone floor was unforgivingly cold through her socks and she yearned for warmth.

'I can build a fire,' Ed suggested. 'I know you're keen to keep cleaning up, but you should warm up first.'

Cassie wondered how he seemed to read her mind as often as he did.

They walked wordlessly into what had fast become her favourite room after the library – the tiny den with the faded forget-me-not wallpaper. Ed began to make a fire with the stray pieces of wood and kindling he'd brought inside the week before, and Cassie curled up on the squashy threadbare sofa and watched him. Outside, the sky had turned dark grey and the rain came down in great sheets of silver over the bedraggled trees in the former orchard. Despite the cold, Cassie could think of nowhere else she'd rather be.

'Ed,' she began slowly, 'I was wondering if I could pick your brains. I've been thinking about what I'd do with Beaufont if we didn't sell it, and I keep coming back to the idea of holding a festival in the grounds. What do you think? Could it work? Would it be a good idea?'

'A festival? At Beaufont Hall?' Ed asked as he sat down next to her.

'Yes. There are acres and acres of fields we're doing nothing with, and we're not too far from London – it could be the perfect venue.'

Ed took off his glasses and wiped them on his thick grey lambswool jumper. 'What sort of thing are you thinking of?'

'I'd love to do a literary festival with a bit of folk music thrown in – something that's boutique and upmarket. In the last couple of years festivals have really upped their game; there are yurts for people to stay in, gourmet food vans from farmers' markets, Internet access, proper showers ... I want to do all that, but I'd like to give it a literary slant.'

Ed nodded. 'It sounds like an interesting idea and it would definitely give Beaufont Hall a purpose again, but it also sounds like a hell of a lot of work, *and* you'd need a lot of capital to get it off the ground.'

'That's one of the reasons I wanted to talk to you about it. You used to work in investment and funds and things – do you think I could get financing for this? I ... well, I found some books in the library that I'm selling through the bookshop, and it will make enough to tidy up the grounds and sort out some of the ground-floor rooms, but I won't have enough to do anything else. I've been making a list of things I'd need, and there's no way I could do it without some sort of investment.'

Ed gazed at her. 'How much do you think you'd need?'

Cassie leant over the arm of the sofa and pulled her notebook from her bag. The cover was covered in tiny patches of rain. She brushed the water off with her hand and flicked through the pages until she got to her sums.

'To be honest, it's all guesswork, but I think I'd need about a hundred and fifty thousand. I'd need to construct several stages and hire marquees and a generator, I'd need to pay for staff to help prepare and to run it on the day, and then I'd probably have to pay acts, and sort out tickets and marketing. But I think that amount should do all that comfortably. I know it doesn't sound like a lot, but I'm not looking to recreate Glastonbury. I want to do something small and friendly. Two hundred and fifty thousand people go to the literary festival at Hay; I want to put on something for about five thousand people. Beaufont has acres and acres of land – there could be several fields for things to do, and another one or two for people who wanted to camp.'

Ed took the notebook from Cassie's hands.

'And what about revenue?'

Cassie knew her answer from memory. 'I've done my research. The majority of revenue would come from sponsorship, ticket sales, and food, drink and merchandise sold on the day. I could charge food vans and merchandisers to set up in return for a flat rate and a cut of their profits.'

Ed examined Cassie's sums. 'I think you'd need more than a hundred and fifty thousand to get this off the ground,' he said eventually. 'But I can help you put together a business plan that you could show to potential investors.'

Cassie had secretly hoped that he would offer to help; without him she would be stuck. 'Would you mind?'

Ed shook his head. 'But if you're going to do this properly, you need to be fully committed. I know plenty of investors who would be interested if we can firm up your business plan and make it worth their while. But if you raised investment, you'd have to quit your job at the bookshop and your family would have to be one hundred per cent behind you.'

Cassie felt sheepish. 'I've not actually told my mother about the valuable books I found in the library . . . and nor does she know that I want to try to keep Beaufont in the family. I mean, she knows that I don't want to sell, but she doesn't know I've been working on something to try to save it . . .' Her voice trailed off and she swallowed hard. 'The other thing is that if we hold an event here – a yearly event that has the potential to get bigger and bigger – it would raise the profile of the family too: a festival at Beaufont Hall would bring the Tempests back into the spotlight. I kind of get the feeling that my mother wouldn't be keen on that either.'

Ed was about to reply when a huge gust of wind ran through the house and several doors slammed one after the other. The lights, which had been gently flickering, turned themselves off, and Cassie and Ed found themselves plunged into darkness with only the burning embers in the fireplace providing them with light and warmth. Glittering forks of lightning shot through the sky.

'I hope this isn't a sign that my ancestors don't want me to hold a festival here,' Cassie joked weakly, but as she spoke the words out loud, she wondered if it was true. No doubt her grandmother would have disapproved of the idea of opening up Beaufont's grounds to the public, and if ghosts really did exist, she'd definitely have something to say about the matter. Cassie guessed that Eliza Boyle would have been all for the idea, though.

'More likely it's proof that the weather girls on TV have got the forecast completely wrong again,' Ed said lightly. 'I found some candles in the kitchen a few weeks ago – sit tight and let me go and get them.'

Ed disappeared for what felt like an eternity, eventually reappearing with an old candelabra stuffed with dusty white candles. Their soft glow threw unusual shadows across the floral wallpaper, and Cassie found she was shivering again. She loved Beaufont Hall, but it was so large and creaky that she couldn't help but be a bit nervous. Ed, however, didn't seem remotely fazed.

'It's awful outside,' he remarked casually, as if he got caught in a forbidding mansion in a scary storm several times a week. 'I can try to fix the fuse box to get the lights back on, but I wouldn't recommend you driving back to London in this weather. The blow-up mattress is in the bedroom upstairs . . . unless you'd like to sleep at my place?'

Cassie was aware of Ed's body heat close to hers, and as the silence between them grew, so did her attraction to him. She tried to tell herself to stop thinking of him this way, tried to catch her breath and act normally, but she found she couldn't.

'That's kind of you, but I really should stay here,' she managed to reply. She knew Ed's eyes were on her and she momentarily wished he would lean forward and kiss her. She held his gaze, but just as she began to feel warm with attraction, he turned away to look at the flickering flames of the fire.

'I'll go and see if I can get the electricity back on,' he said abruptly. 'You can take the candles to have a look at the bedroom. Let me know if you think you'll need anything else, and if you do, I can drive over to mine to get it.'

Cassie tried to smile at him, but he'd already leapt up and left the room.

As she slowly made her way through the house, she tried to push aside her thoughts of Ed and how she'd longed for him to kiss her, to touch her. Instead she tried to get excited at the prospect of spending the night at Beaufont Hall. It was something she'd wanted to do forever, but she'd not imagined a terrific storm brewing outside the first night that she did.

It was 3 a.m. and Cassie couldn't sleep. The gale had quietened down, but the storm still rumbled above the fields beyond the house. There were fewer clouds in the sky now, but the ones that remained danced across the stars and moon so fast that the streaming light made patterns on the tired wallpaper. She knew she should shut her eyes and try to rest, but her mind was racing with thoughts of the festival, of Eliza and Lillie, and of Ed. The flame on the candle next to the bed winked every time the rotting window frames rattled in the wind, and in the distance an owl hooted. She wished yet again that she'd agreed to spend the night at Ed's cottage, though she knew that if she'd tried to kip on his sofa, she'd have been kept awake with very different thoughts and feelings. She longed for her attraction to him to disappear.

She forced herself off the blow-up mattress and walked to the window. The overgrown rose garden below was thorny and wild, and the fields in the distance had a ghostly air. She tried to imagine them in the sunshine, full of tents and stages, and she found the picture came easily to her. Past the fields and to the west of the house was Beaufont village, and she pressed her nose to the dirt-spotted glass to look in that direction. Only a few of the cottages had lights on at this time of night and she wondered if Ed was in one of them, and if he was awake and thinking of her like she was thinking of him. She told herself off immediately – Ed wasn't interested in her like that. As she reminded herself of this, she suddenly felt very alone and very cold.

Yet instead of hopping back into bed, she turned back to the room and tried to picture what it might have looked like when Violet, Aster and Lillie had been children here. Although she'd not mentioned it to Ed for fear of being thought strange, she'd chosen this room because she'd had a sense, a feeling, that it had once belonged to Lillie. She knew that in a house the size of Beaufont this was unlikely, but it didn't stop her from hoping that she was right. She felt as though she was getting to know Eliza from her diaries and the photographs on the Internet, but she still knew very little about Lillie Tempest, and it was frustrating.

She knew she should try to sleep, and she was about to get back into bed when a tiny glint of gold caught her eye. It came from the rug in the middle of the room. She frowned. She'd been planning on vacuuming the rug that weekend, but the storm and the lack of electricity had meant she'd not been able to. As she approached it, the glimmer disappeared, and she assumed she'd been seeing things. But just then the moonlight streamed into the bedroom, and she saw it again. She sank to her knees and felt something hard caught in the intricate woven strands of wool. She gently pushed her fingers into the faded magenta and ivory pattern, pulling the threads aside until she touched metal. She held her breath as she removed the object from deep within the rug, and held it up to the candle so she could see it better.

It was an earring – a gold earring with multicoloured stones. An earring that definitely wasn't hers.

Cassie climbed back on to the mattress and clutched at the earring as she tried to fall asleep. After what seemed like hours, her eyes began to feel heavy, and when she woke, Cassie found that the storm had finally passed and that the earring glinted golden in the day's bright sunshine.

Chapter Thirteen

London, 1984

Eliza Archer might not have been a cover star – not yet, anyway – but after two years of being on Jonathan's books, she was finally starting to make a name for herself. The first year had been a struggle: fashion editors seemed to still want tanned, blonde, corn-fed girls, like the 1970s hadn't gone away, and Eliza wasn't any of those things. She was dark and edgy; she was the opposite of mainstream.

Despite this, she persevered. She went on go-sees in the daytime, worked at Gossips in the evenings, and fell into bed exhausted. She still took speed – she needed something to get through the days, and caffeine just wasn't enough. She was just about to admit defeat when she got a booking . . . and then another . . . and after that, the phones at Jonathan's office didn't stop ringing. Since then, she had found work abroad as well as in England. She'd had lots of campaign bookings in Japan, where she'd got to grips with sushi, sake and skyscrapers. She had adored Tokyo, where she'd revelled in the frenzied pace of living. One day she'd even been recognised: a teenage girl had thrust a pen and piece of paper at her on the street in Shinjuku, and as Eliza had written her autograph for the first time, she'd felt the sharp glitter of stardom scratch at her.

Yet the more work she got, and the more successful she became, the more disjointed and uncomfortable her life outside of modelling became. She felt as though she was happy – truly, brilliantly, gorgeously happy – for the first time in her life, yet nobody else around her, with the exception of Jonathan, was pleased for her. Even Lillie, who'd secretly wished that her daughter would leave Gossips to pursue a proper career, had been dismissive of modelling when Eliza had booked her first job back in 1982.

'You're more than a pretty face,' she had said as she'd poured a cup of tea for her daughter. The Tottenham flat had been in the process of being packed up as Lillie prepared to move to Basingstoke for a fresh start, and Eliza had had to make do with sitting on a heavily taped cardboard box containing the living room cushions. 'Your father so wanted you to make a difference in the world; he wanted you to try to right the injustices that so many people face.'

'I know that,' Eliza had said softly. 'But I'm not as strong as Dad was, and I can't help with the battles my friends have to deal with – I can't do anything about homophobia, or that AIDS disease that so many gay men are catching.'

'Yes, but you're clever and kind and you have so much to offer. You have a voice, and it won't be heard in fashion photographs.'

Eliza had blown on her cup of tea and tried not to feel cross at her mother's reaction. She'd wanted Lillie to be proud of her rather than judgemental, but after Bertie had died, the tension between them had become more apparent, and nothing Eliza did seemed to please her mother. She still phoned home as often as she could, and Lillie was still affectionate towards her when they saw each other – which admittedly wasn't often. But despite everything, there was always an edge there, and Eliza often felt displeasure radiate from her mother. She wondered if it was because of who she'd become – or rather, who she was not.

'Look,' she had said. 'If I could help other people, I would, but I need to earn a living and take care of myself first.'

Lillie had looked as though she'd been on the verge of arguing, but instead she sighed and changed the subject. As she had chattered on about the job she'd accepted in a tailor's in Basingstoke, Eliza had watched her carefully. In the last few years Lillie had aged badly: her skin was dull, there were deep lines around her eyes, and wiry grey hairs framed her forehead. She still held herself proudly, but the struggle of life had beaten her down. Eliza had hoped that her mother would be pleased with her news – had hoped that it would delight her and give her something more exciting than a move to a dull town could provide, but it wasn't to be.

Her friends, in contrast, had initially been thrilled for her, toasting her triumph at Gossips with pints of snakebite and the wraps of MDMA that Curt was now dealing, and dancing the night away to 'Ceremony' by New Order, 'Memorabilia' by Soft Cell, and the Human League's 'Sound of the Crowd'. They'd believed that Eliza's success was the start of something good for all of them: Raven would become an artist rather than a rent boy, Alison would become a famous singer rather than a nude model, and Curt would have his own club. The future was bright, and it was tantalisingly within reach; prosperity was on its way.

Yet as the months went on, nothing much changed. Alison, Curt and Raven believed that if they sat back and waited, fortune would knock on their door, but in the meantime, they spiralled further and further out of control. Alison had climbed the greasy porn ladder to videos recorded on Betamax and VHS; Raven continued to service his clients in grotty walk-ups hidden in seedy Soho alleys; and Curt kept feeding their friends the chemicals that none of them were prepared to give up.

Eliza had tried to include them all in her success, and had even gone so far as to introduce Alison to Jonathan, but he had coolly assessed her and then remarked that she was pretty but not photogenic. Eliza had tried to make amends for this disappointment by lavishing money on her friend, buying her clothes, cosmetics, decent food and alcohol, but the more she spent, the more remote Alison became. Eliza was wise enough to know that she couldn't buy Alison's friendship, but she wasn't astute enough to realise that the gifts were pushing her further away.

It only took a few months until her friends began to avoid her altogether. Eliza knew that if her gang wasn't at Gossips, they'd be at the Camden Palace, or the Mud Club, or the Bat Cave, so she went to these places in the hope of finding them. She reasoned that if they spent time with her again, they'd realise she'd not changed; she was still Eliza Decay, regardless of how she earned a living. But despite her attempts at hunting them down, she never seemed to find them. She could sense them in the Soho twilight, and once she even heard Alison's peals of laughter surrounding her, but the three of them skulked in the shadows and refused to make themselves known. Without her friends by her side, the club scene lost its spark, and when they ignored her in the squat, she self-medicated with drugs to mask her loneliness and loss.

After one long and rather exhausting modelling shoot in Italy, Eliza came home to find that she had been replaced in the flat at Silver Place by a girl named Fiona, who'd styled herself on Sade. As she packed her meagre belongings into a bin bag, she attempted to catch Raven's eye, but he looked straight through her. She knew why he hated her: he thought she had become the establishment, the type of person the scene so hated, and she knew that nothing she could say or do would change his mind about her.

Before she said goodbye to Silver Place for the last time, she paused at the door and took out her purse. She counted out the crisp notes she'd taken out of the bank the day before, laid £250 on the coffee table they'd made from bricks and a rotten plank of wood, then scrawled a few words on a scrap of paper.

Alison,
I know you hate me right now, but if you ever need anything,
please find me via the modelling agency. This is for food, not
drugs. I love you and will always be there for you.
Ex

She placed her short letter on top of the pile of money, and as she turned away, she felt her eyes fill with tears. To the outside world Eliza Archer had it all: she was beautiful, successful, and had a healthy career that earned her plenty of money. But behind the sparkling facade her life felt empty. It *was* empty.

Not since her father had died had she felt so hurt and lost.

'I need somewhere to live that isn't a hotel or in Soho,' Eliza explained to Jonathan as they walked through the streets of Chelsea on their way to an apartment viewing.

She had spent a month living at the Carlton Tower Hotel, and in that time she'd tried to stop thinking about Alison; had tried to stop the familiar feelings of rejection from surfacing. But despite her best efforts, the brutal brush-off she'd suffered at the hands of her friends had brought back old emotions, and in the plush depths of her hotel room, with nothing to distract her, the anger at how the Boyles had been rejected by the Tempests had re-emerged. For years she'd been so busy with her social life and her career that she had barely thought about the Tempests and the impact they'd had on her own little family, but now she was struggling with the idea that she wasn't the right sort of person for either her friends or her mother's family. She needed a fresh start.

'I have to say, I was surprised when you asked me to join you on this viewing,' Jonathan admitted. 'Does this mean you're finally over your obsession with Soho?'

'I might be,' Eliza said with a weak smile. 'But I can't bear to live in the hotel any more. I can't get the bombing out of my mind.'

Jonathan nodded. The previous week, the Grand Hotel in Brighton had been bombed by the IRA, and the newspapers were still full of stories about the people who'd died and been injured. Eliza hated the idea that anybody could walk into her hotel and do something similar.

It was a beautiful, bright autumn day, and Eliza was grateful for the sun – it made the gorgeous tree-lined avenue seem dazzling, spectacular. It seemed so adult, so grown-up, that she felt slightly out of place, even if she didn't appear to be. When she caught her reflection in shop windows, she was slightly surprised that she no longer had the ratty hair or wore the dirty clothes that she'd settled upon as her Soho uniform. Since she'd moved out of the squat, she'd adopted a completely different kind of look; she supposed she dressed a bit like the yuppies she used to be so disdainful of. She no longer looked like an angry kid – she was on her way to becoming a successful professional model, and she dressed the part in outfits that could pass for Armani, for Jasper Conran, for Bruce Oldfield. Only Princess Diana could beat Eliza in the fashion stakes, and even that was a close call sometimes, as the lascivious stare of the estate agent waiting outside the mansion block they'd come to view confirmed.

'This apartment building has a fair bit of history, as does this particular flat,' the estate agent began as he pushed his hands through his slicked-back hair and led them into the building. The red-brick mansion block was on a quiet road, but it was only five minutes from the King's Road. It really was the perfect location. 'In the 1960s, there were lots of parties here – and one of Princess Margaret's extremely close friends owns the flat we're going to see. Apparently she hosted an awful lot of dinner parties.'

Eliza smiled. She couldn't quite believe that in the space of six years she'd gone from living in a scummy flat in Tottenham with her parents to viewing a flat in which royalty might have dined.

'Did Princess Margaret actually spend time here?' she asked as she cast her gaze around.

The estate agent winked. 'It wouldn't be discreet of me to say.'

But Eliza really didn't care if Princess Margaret had partied here or not. As she walked the length of the flat in her heels, she knew without a doubt that she should live here. She'd felt it the moment the estate agent had opened the front door, but now she knew for definite that this was the right place for her. It was kind of like when she'd first gone to Gossips all those years ago. Some buildings in London just had a feeling of home about them, and this was one of them.

As Jonathan asked all the pertinent questions – about the deposit, the rent – Eliza tuned the men out and tried to imagine what the living room had looked like in the 1960s when Princess Margaret might have visited. If she half closed her eyes she could almost see people in old-fashioned clothes doing the Twist to the strains of the record player, and imagine couples laughing and smoking and having fun. Her mother, she realised, would love this flat. Lillie had never visited her daughter in Soho, and Eliza hadn't wanted her to because the Silver Place squat hadn't been particularly pleasant, but this apartment was something to be proud of, and she knew her mother would approve.

'I've decided I want it,' she announced, and gave the estate agent the smile that never failed to melt the heart of whoever she directed it at. 'Tell the owner that I'd love to live here. I'll pay the deposit now along with the first two months' rent.'

'And will both of you be moving in?' the estate agent asked.

Eliza blushed. Her gratitude towards Jonathan for rescuing her from a probable future in the seedy sex industry of Soho had developed into something that definitely wouldn't be considered professional. She was aware of how good-looking he was, and how he was always fresh and clean in comparison to how grubby she felt. Eliza was instinctive and liked to live for the moment, and she had to struggle to keep her emotions in check when she was around him. Admitting how she felt about him – and having him admit that those feelings were unrequited – would have ruined their working relationship forever.

'It's just me,' she replied firmly. The estate agent smiled knowingly, but fortunately Jonathan didn't seem notice.

'I'll have to get back to you, but I don't see that an unmarried girl-about-town such as yourself living here would be a problem. Petra – the owner – was quite racy in her day, and I know she's keen to have the flat occupied as soon as possible.'

Eliza forgot about Alison, forgot about the Tempests, and pushed all her feelings for Jonathan out of her mind. Screw Soho, she thought. She'd finally found her home.

'You've improved since I last saw you,' the photographer remarked as Eliza stared down the lens of his camera.

The lights overhead scorched her skin and her pose was uncomfortable, but nothing would stop her from keeping the fire ablaze in her eyes. She glittered for a few more frames and then allowed herself to smile as Sebastian changed his film.

'I've been working hard,' she admitted.

She'd met Sebastian – a fairly well-known fashion photographer in London – on one of her first shoots. Back then she'd been nervous but happy, excited at the career that stretched out in front of her. Now she took her work in her stride. She had good days and bad days, but whatever her mood, everything became easier with cocaine – which was sometimes offered to her by a photographer, sometimes not.

'I've been doing lots of shoots abroad,' she continued. 'For some reason I get booked for international jobs, but I want to make it here. I want to become the best and the most well-known model in England.'

Sebastian gazed at her thoughtfully. 'The shapes you're creating and the looks you're giving me are fantastic. But if you want to make it over here, you really need to do something amazing, something special. Like I said, you've improved, but I think there's something missing. In fact, I know there is.'

They were doing some black-and-white editorial shots for *The Face*, and the theme was 'Destroy, Disorder, Disorientate'. For this particular shot Eliza was dressed in a strapless Galliano dress, with a blue-black feathered hat perched perilously on top of her head. A lit cigarette dangled between her fingers, and smoke swirled seductively around her, creating a translucent haze through which she was supposed to stare.

'Let's push this as far as we can,' Sebastian continued. 'We need to do something a bit different, a bit wilder.'

Eliza nodded. She desperately wanted some cocaine, but she'd run out and her dealer hadn't answered his phone for a few days. She was finding it harder and harder to work without it, but she was determined not to let it show. If Sebastian was going to offer her some, he would have done so by now.

Let's do what we need to do,' she said. 'What do you have in mind?'

Sebastian put his camera back on the tripod and walked over to where Eliza was standing. His footprints left dirty marks on the white paper that covered the floor, but he didn't seem to care.

'"Destroy, Disorder, Disorientate" – what do those words really mean?' he said. He took the cigarette from Eliza's hand and placed it in his own mouth. 'To me they suggest chaos . . . and while you're a decent model, the notion of chaos is lacking from this shoot. There's too much self-control, too much awareness of what you're doing. You're too uptight, too perfect. It's like you've buttoned up the real you and you're not letting go – you're not being yourself, your *true* self.'

Eliza considered this and tried not to feel defensive. She was so rarely criticised when on a shoot that she found it hard to take when she was – especially when the photographer had nailed exactly what was on her mind. She knew she wasn't the same girl she'd been when she'd started modelling; she wasn't the girl who threw caution to the wind and gave her soul to each shoot. But how could she be? She was older, she was wiser, and she'd been hurt by her friends' easy dismissal of her. She'd vowed never to let herself be unguarded again. She thought she was pretty good at faking vulnerability, but Sebastian had seen through her. If only she had some drugs. If she'd had some cocaine, she'd have been fine.

'You're right,' she agreed smoothly. She was determined not to show Sebastian that he'd unnerved her. 'There's not much disorder or disorientation in what I'm doing.'

Sebastian took another drag on the cigarette and then dropped it on the floor. When he stubbed it out with a drag of his foot, the ash left a dirty grey smear on the paper covering.

'I can create disorder, but you need to go with it. You need to feel it. Do you think you can do that?'

Eliza knew that if you were to make a shoot work, you had to completely trust the photographer. It wasn't easy – especially when the photographer treated you as a piece of meat rather than a person – but she prided herself on knowing how to perform trust without actually believing in it.

'Of course I can,' she said convincingly.

Sebastian put down his camera and rummaged in his pocket. He produced a wrap of something and threw it to her. Eliza caught it and opened it up, and tried not to let her heart sink when she saw it wasn't cocaine or speed.

'What is it?' she asked. She'd never seen brown powder before.

'Just something to relax you.' Sebastian walked over to a table and laid out some foil and a plastic tube. 'Come here.'

Eliza obediently moved from her position and handed Sebastian the wrap. He tipped some of the powder on to the foil and gave her the tube. 'When you see the smoke, you need to breathe it in, okay?'

Eliza nodded. Sebastian pulled out a lighter and lit the

underside of the foil. The powder began to burn, and she sniffed at the vapours but couldn't smell anything at all. She inhaled . . . and then she inhaled again. She lifted her eyes to Sebastian, who smiled down at her, and with his smile came a burst of chemical sunshine. Eliza suddenly found herself at peace – she was warm and happy, and she felt more relaxed than she had in years. Whatever she'd smoked was the opposite of cocaine: she had no nervous energy but felt as though she'd been lit up with euphoria. Her eyes dilated and she wanted to lean in for some more, but Sebastian led her back to her place in front of the camera.

'That was amazing,' Eliza murmured. 'What is it?'

Her eyes tried to find Sebastian, but before she could focus on him, she caught a flash of his wolfish smile, and then felt the bandeau top of her dress being yanked down to expose her breasts. She stumbled backwards, but she didn't try to cover herself or rub the stars from her eyes. She was aware of the camera flashing angrily at her, and she stood dumb, mute. Sebastian was forcing her to perform 'Destroy, Disorder, Disorientate' half naked, and he'd made sure she was too warm and full of love to care.

'I don't understand,' she said simply. Despite the artificial happiness, she knew her eyes were stinging from the tears that had gathered in them, but Sebastian didn't react, just wordlessly kept taking photographs.

Eliza wiped the tears from her face, and as she did so, she smeared her heavy dark eyeliner across the top of her cheek. Her eyes were empty, her collarbones jutted through the glitter pasted on her skin, and her dark pink nipples caught the light. She looked broken and beautiful, and when she looked back on her career, it would be this particular image that would stand out above all others.

For as well as being the most stunning and successful shoot of her life, it was also the one in which she'd been introduced to her downfall.

She'd fallen instantly and hopelessly in love with heroin.

Chapter Fourteen

Buckinghamshire and London,
recently

Cassie had barely slept after she'd discovered the multicoloured earring in the rug. The storm had quietened down to a gentle whisper, yet she'd been unable to relax. In the pearly-white morning light her eyes felt gritty and her head was heavy with fatigue. But despite her exhaustion, she found she couldn't bear to put down Eliza's diary for 1984, and she quickly turned each faded, ink-stained page to see if there was any mention of the jewellery she'd found the night before. She was disappointed, but not surprised, to find that there was not. Eliza's diary for 1984 had started so positively, yet by the end of the year her thoughts and her life were becoming darker; her handwriting became more scrawled, and there were weeks where she sometimes wrote nothing at all.

Cassie pulled her hoody on over the T-shirt and jeans she'd slept in, and wandered through the gloomy corridors of Beaufont. She might have cleared the house of dirt and dust and cobwebs, but with most of the doors shut and many of the windows boarded up, it was still dim and forlorn. She found herself fantasising about a time in the future when all the rooms would be open and bright, when new glass would replace the old, cracked windows and sunlight could shine into gleaming, clean rooms. She hoped she'd be able to turn Beaufont's fortunes around; she knew that if she didn't do it soon, it would be too late.

'Morning!' Ed's voice called out. Cassie screamed in shock.

'Shit, I'm sorry,' he said apologetically, and Cassie shook her head and laughed at herself. 'I wanted to surprise you but I didn't mean to give you a fright. I used my key in case you were still asleep. I hope that's okay?'

'It's fine,' Cassie assured him. Her heart was racing, but she was pleased to see him, even if she wasn't enamoured at being caught by surprise. She ran her fingers self-consciously through her hair and under her eyes – she was sure the mascara she'd applied so carefully the day before would have smudged during the night.

'It's a beautiful day, but it's still fucking cold,' Ed explained. 'I've lit a fire for you.'

Cassie followed behind him towards the den. When she walked into the room, she smiled. It was warm and bright, and she could smell coffee and bacon.

'I thought you might be hungry,' Ed said uncertainly as Cassie spotted brown paper bags and cardboard cups. 'I got them from the café, but they might be a bit cold now . . .' His voice trailed off and Cassie smiled at him. It was the first time she'd seen him anything but confident.

'This is lovely,' she said. She sat down on the floor with her back to the fire and took a sip of lukewarm coffee. 'Thank you so much.'

'My family has taken care of yours for generations,' Ed said with a shrug. 'I know you don't employ me, but I like looking after the house . . . and the people in it.'

Cassie bit into a sandwich in the hope that it would hide the blush she could feel creeping up her face. The saltiness of the bacon next to the sharpness of the tomato ketchup was exactly what she needed, yet it didn't distract her from Ed's kind words. She didn't know what to say, so she averted her gaze from his mussed-up auburn hair and bright green eyes and allowed the room to fall into an embarrassed silence.

'Did you sleep well?' Ed asked eventually.

Cassie shook her head in response, hoping it would also shake away some of her awkwardness. If Ed noticed her discomfort, it didn't show on his face.

'I found something in the bedroom last night, something that doesn't belong to me,' she said.

'I didn't think there was anything in that room apart from my old mattress.'

Cassie pulled the earring out of her jeans pocket. She placed it gently on the floor between them, and they both stared at it in silence. The top of it was a triangle of gold, delicately linked to a brilliant green piece of glass. Under this was a golden orb studded with tiny gem stones, ranging in colour from red to burgundy to jade to sapphire. Cassie didn't think the stones were real, but she thought the gold was. Could the earring be expensive, or designer? Possibly, but she wasn't sure.

'It was hidden in the threads of the rug,' she said. 'But I don't think it could have belonged to any of the sisters – Violet, Aster and Lillie, I mean. I don't know much about jewellery, but I don't think it looks old enough to have been theirs.'

Ed picked the earring up and placed it gently in the palm of his hand as he examined it. 'The last people to live at Beaufont were your grandmother and your mother,' he said after a pause. 'Perhaps this belonged to Rebecca.'

'Perhaps,' Cassie said, but Ed's suggestion disappointed her. She knew this was the most likely answer, but she'd so wanted the earring to have belonged to Lillie or Eliza, however impossible that might be. She sighed. 'I'll show it to Mum when I get home. Maybe she'll remember it.'

Ed drank some of his coffee. 'Will you be heading off soon?' he asked casually as he wrapped his hands around his cup.

Cassie listened for disappointment in his voice and tried not to feel disheartened when she heard none. The more time she spent with him, the more her feelings for him grew; her initial attraction had deepened into something more special. Sometimes she caught him looking at her in a way that suggested he felt the same, but other times – like now – she knew it was just wishful thinking on her part. Ed liked her, she knew that, but she also knew he didn't like her like *that*.

'I think so, yes,' she said. 'The weather has settled down and I desperately want a shower.'

Ed smiled. 'I know Beaufont isn't able to provide that for you, but I do have a lovely hot, functioning shower at the cottage that you're more than welcome to use. Why don't you come over and freshen up before you drive back to London?'

The desire for a shower and to see inside Ed's cottage was stronger than any lingering shyness or awkwardness Cassie felt around him.

'Could I really?' she asked. 'If you wouldn't mind, that would be great . . .'

'It wouldn't be a problem at all,' he replied warmly. He gulped down the rest of his coffee and Cassie finished the last of her breakfast, and ten minutes later she was following his old Toyota down the hedgerow-framed road towards Beaufont village.

Ed's cottage was smaller than his parents', but what it lacked in size it made up for in cosiness. It had been built in the 1850s for the farm hands who'd once worked the land around

Beaufont Hall and the surrounding villages. Over the years the various owners appeared to have done little to change the cottage's facade, and when Cassie stepped inside, she found she could easily imagine what it would have been like in her great-grandparents' day: there were lots of exposed beams, and the doorways were so low that Ed had to continually stoop so as not to bang his head. He looked like a grown man trying to move around in a doll's house.

'I know my furniture doesn't exactly go with the decor,' he said hurriedly as Cassie took in the black leather sofa and the chrome and glass coffee table. 'But the cottage came unfurnished and it made sense to bring my stuff from London. I didn't quite realise that what worked well in a converted warehouse in the city wouldn't look as good in a cottage in Buckinghamshire.'

Cassie smiled. 'It looks fine,' she said. If the cottage had been hers, she'd have decorated it differently, but there was no harm in it looking like a bachelor pad. It might be sweet and cosy, but it was full of testosterone: framed black-and-white photographs depicted deserted city streets, and there were few soft, curved edges or personal mementos.

Cassie spotted a photograph on the mantelpiece and walked over to it. The photo wasn't framed, but it took pride of place above the deep fireplace. It showed Ed with his arms around a slender blonde dressed all in white. She wore pearls in her ears and had a wide smile, but despite being beautiful, her brown eyes were hard and determined. She was typical of the women Cassie sometimes saw in the City; the type she avoided because they were sharp, overbearing and intimidating.

'Girlfriend?' she asked.

'An ex,' Ed replied lightly. He gazed at the photograph for a moment, then turned away. 'Grace: someone I hurt badly but still care for. But anyway, let me get you a towel – or do you need two? Girls always seem to need two.'

'One will be fine,' Cassie answered. As Ed left the room, she continued to stare at the photograph. There was no denying that he and Grace had made a good-looking couple, and appeared to have been blissfully happy. She wondered what had happened – just how he had hurt her.

Ed returned with a large, fluffy grey towel and led Cassie through the kitchen to a small wooden door that she'd assumed was a cupboard. Inside was a large wet-room with clotted-cream limestone tiles on the walls, soft grey slate underfoot, and a gleaming waterfall shower with a wooden bench underneath.

'I didn't quite expect this,' she murmured in surprise.

'I think this must have originally been the pantry,' Ed explained. 'The owners converted it into a wet-room before they started to rent out the property. There's a smaller bathroom upstairs, too.'

'It's beautiful,' Cassie said, but she eyed the futuristic shower cautiously. There were a multitude of buttons and she knew she'd not be able to work out how to turn it on, let alone set the temperature. Ed, standing next to her, noticed her expression.

'It looks like the cockpit of an aeroplane, doesn't it?' He smiled. 'But it's not as complicated as you'd think. Why don't you slip off your clothes and I'll show you how it works?'

Cassie stared at him in a stunned silence that was punctuated by both of them turning bright red.

'Shit, I didn't mean it like that,' he stumbled. 'I meant you could cover yourself up with the towel – it's a big one. I'll just tell you how to operate it now if you like, and you can try it out by yourself in private. Fuck, I'm sorry.'

Ed's voice was rich with embarrassment and Cassie could feel his breath on her neck. They were standing so close to each other that she knew she'd only have to shift slightly to feel his body brush against hers. She longed to touch him on the arm, to feel his bare skin on hers, but she quickly shook those feelings away. Ed wasn't attracted to her, and she didn't want to test their blossoming friendship. She couldn't bear the thought of not being friends with him purely because she had a small – hopefully fleeting – crush on him.

'I knew what you meant,' she said quickly. 'It's absolutely fine, really.' She tried to catch his eye, but he was fiddling with the knobs and buttons of the shower.

'I've set it to a medium temperature, and you just need to use this button here to turn it on . . .' There were several more seconds of silence before he coughed. 'I'll leave you to it,' he said finally, and he quickly left the room, closing the door behind him.

Several moments later, Cassie found herself standing underneath the most powerful shower she'd ever been in, but she found she couldn't stop staring at the wooden door – which she'd deliberately left unlocked.

Several hours later Cassie pushed open a different door – the front door to the family home – and breathed in the familiar scent of freshly brewed coffee, the lingering remains of Alice's overbearing perfume, and the chlorine-scented swimming bag that Henry had dumped in the hall the day before. She compared this to the stale mustiness that remained at Beaufont Hall. Despite the scent of home being a comforting one, she found she still missed Beaufont. She missed Ed.

She dropped her handbag next to Henry's swimming kit and walked through the hallway towards the conservatory. The crisp sun had risen high over London, and there, with a cup of tea in one hand and a half-read copy of the *Daily World* in her lap, sat her mother. A tall vase of stargazer lilies bloomed on a side table next to her, and Cassie was momentarily taken aback by their violent scent. She sat down on the wicker sofa opposite. She longed for a nap, but she knew she needed to have a serious conversation with her mother first; she needed to have the conversation she'd been putting off for a while.

Rebecca eyed her thoughtfully, as if she could tell that Cassie was gathering her courage to say something that might not be pleasant for either of them.

'Welcome home,' she said wryly. She looked as though she wanted to say more, but instead she took a sip of her tea and waited patiently for her daughter to speak.

'I was at the house yesterday, as you know,' Cassie began awkwardly. 'While I was there, a storm came, so I stayed at Beaufont rather than risk driving home. I didn't plan to, but Ed's blow-up mattress was there and it just made sense.'

'You must have been freezing,' Rebecca remarked.

Cassie nodded. 'It wasn't great – I'm shattered today, actually – but I'm glad I spent the night. I know I've been planning to stay there on Saturday nights until the house is ready to go on the market, but I never really thought I would.'

Rebecca's blue eyes gazed into hers, but she said nothing. Cassie knew her mother well enough to be aware that silence was Rebecca's tactic to weed out information from her children: she liked to remain mute so that Cassie or the twins ended up speaking to fill the tension-filled quiet.

'The thing is,' Cassie began, 'staying the night made me fall in love with the house even more . . . and the more time I spend there, and the more I clean it up, the more I realise I couldn't bear for us to sell it. I really, really don't want us to have to let Beaufont go.'

'Darling,' Rebecca began with a sigh, 'we've been through this. We simply don't have the money to keep the house going—'

'But I raised some money,' Cassie interrupted. Rebecca stared at her, and Cassie rushed to continue. 'I mean, it's nowhere near enough to keep the house, but we could do something with it . . .' She paused for breath and started from the beginning. She told her mother about the books she'd found in the library, about how much Mr Heritage had managed to sell them for, and then she tentatively outlined her festival plan.

'I know fifty thousand wouldn't go very far on the house,' she said quietly. 'But it would go a long way to fixing up the grounds and maybe several of the downstairs rooms so we'd have an office and somewhere to live.'

Rebecca took a sip of tea before she spoke. 'I'm not sure I understand. You'd like to host a festival at Beaufont Hall?'

'In the fields, yes,' Cassie said. 'A small literary one – not a loud heavy metal concert that would have the villagers up in arms.' She explained how Ed was going to help her put together a business plan and proposal before he introduced her to potential investors.

'But before Ed helps me, I need your blessing to pursue this,' she continued. 'After all, Beaufont Hall does belong to you, and if we do anything at all it may bring awareness of the family back into the spotlight. If you think holding a festival would be disrespectful to the family name then of course I won't do it – but I really do want to save Beaufont. I know the money from the sale of the books is yours, and if you'd rather we spent it on something else then I understand, but I can't let the house fall into ruin more than it already has. I won't. It's our family home, and even though you seem to hate it, I don't. As long as Beaufont stands, I will do everything I can to save it.'

Rebecca stared at her daughter for the longest time before

she sighed and tucked her hair behind her ears. 'That's quite a speech,' she said.

Cassie found she couldn't meet her mother's gaze.

'I can tell you now that my mother would have despised the idea, and her parents – your great-grandparents – would turn in their graves if they knew we were discussing such a thing. But I suppose it won't hurt to delay putting the house on the market while you explore the options.'

Cassie looked up and stared at her mother in astonishment. 'Do you really mean that?' she asked.

Rebecca looked uncomfortable, but she nodded. 'Your father and I knew you were up to something – you're not as subtle as you think you are, darling – but I don't think I quite realised the force of your feelings. I suppose that if we had more money, Beaufont House would eventually be yours anyway as you're the eldest, so I think it's only fair to give you the opportunity to try to keep it.'

'That's great news,' Cassie said faintly. 'I'm very pleased.' She'd spent hours having imaginary conversations about this with her mother, but she'd never thought Rebecca would agree to her idea, or at least not quite so easily. She didn't know what to say.

'Of course,' Rebecca continued, 'I'm unhappy that you've kept the amount of money you raised from me, and I'm not delighted that you've set up a bedroom in the house, but I do understand that you think Beaufont Hall is important – even if I don't quite share your sentiments about it.'

'But why do you hate it so much?' Cassie asked quietly.

Rebecca shook her head. She didn't speak for such a long time that Cassie thought she wouldn't answer the question.

'I loved Beaufont when I was growing up,' she said eventually. 'It was a lovely house, but we weren't well off, and as the years went by it fell more and more into disrepair. We tried to live in a way that my mother thought was fitting for the inhabitants of Beaufont, but I always felt we fell short of the house's expectations, of my mother's expectations. I suppose I always thought that *I* fell short.'

'What was Granny like?' Cassie asked.

Rebecca considered this. 'I loved her, but she was complicated – she was haunted by things that had happened when she was younger, and she never seemed particularly happy.'

'Things to do with Lillie?'

'Perhaps,' Rebecca said. 'She always felt that the Tempest family was cursed in a way, that the house was bad luck. When she was alive, I disagreed with her – your father and I even got married there – but before too long I was inclined to see her point of view. That's why we left Beaufont. It felt full of negative energy and it was the most horrendous drain on our finances. We both felt that moving to London would be a fresh start for the family, and we were right.'

Cassie had always longed for her mother to talk about Beaufont Hall, and to explain why they'd decided not to live there. Now that she'd been given an explanation, she felt sad. Cassie didn't necessarily believe in bad luck, and she disliked the fact that her mother associated it with their family home.

'Luck can change,' she remarked quietly. She decided to move the conversation on to something else. She rummaged in her jeans and brought out the earring, which she handed to her mother. 'I found this last night in one of the bedrooms. Can you think who it would have belonged to? Was it yours?'

Rebecca turned the earring over in her hands and looked at it for a long time. Her expression was downcast. 'It's definitely not mine. When I was growing up there I kept my jewellery fairly simple; subtle, even. Mummy preferred it that way. Where did you find it?'

Cassie described the bedroom she'd slept in. Rebecca's expression remained the same, but Cassie could sense a tightening in her jaw, a slight frown at her brow.

'That was Lillie's old bedroom,' she said eventually, and Cassie's face lit up in pleasure. 'My mother never went in there, but I used to. I used to wonder what Lillie had been like and why she'd disappeared. In my mind she was glamorous and carefree: the complete opposite of my mother.'

'So this earring could have belonged to Lillie?' Cassie asked excitedly.

Rebecca shook her head. 'It's almost certainly from the 1980s rather than the 1950s. Earrings like this were all the rage then. I never had a pair – they were much too gaudy for my mother's liking, and I never would have dreamed of wearing something that made her unhappy.'

'So whose could it be? Could it have belonged to Eliza?'

Rebecca didn't speak as she considered this, and as Cassie surveyed her mother's face she found it unreadable.

'I'm not sure,' she answered eventually, handing the earring back to Cassie. 'If it did, I have no idea how it would have ended up in Lillie's old bedroom.'

Cassie looked at the earring and wondered what secrets it held – for she was sure that it did.

'You look exhausted,' Rebecca said. Her voice cut into Cassie's thoughts, and she put the earring back in her pocket carefully and nodded at her mother.

'I am,' she confirmed.

'Why don't you go and have a bit of a lie-down,' Rebecca suggested. She'd picked up her newspaper, and with that one movement Cassie knew their conversation was over, that

Rebecca's thoughts on Beaufont Hall and her family were yet again closed off to her.

She got up and made her way upstairs to her bedroom. It was only as she was being carried off to sleep that she realised she'd forgotten to ask her mother if she had copies of Lillie and Bertie's marriage certificate, or Eliza's birth certificate. But before she could make a mental note to ask about them when she woke, she fell into a deep, dreamless sleep.

Chapter Fifteen

London, 1985

The *i-D* fashion shoot was not going well. Before he'd offered Eliza the job, Jonathan had reiterated that she'd have to give it a hundred per cent; had told her that her reputation had become stained by her poor work ethic and lack of enthusiasm. The *i-D* shoot, he had said, was Eliza's chance to pull herself together and to show the industry that she hadn't lost it – that she was still relevant and professional. But in spite of Jonathan's brutally harsh words, she still found it difficult to focus, and as she stood under the blisteringly hot lights on the set, she couldn't stop herself from shivering, couldn't hide the giveaway goose pimples that always appeared when she was craving a hit. And she especially needed something to take the edge off this morning, as her good intentions of going to bed early the night before had fallen flat with an invitation to a new club night.

Embargo was now the most debauched place to hang out in London – an underground lair where only the very beautiful or the extremely repulsive could play. It was more than just a club; it was a state of mind, and when Eliza had found the secret entrance and walked into the heart of it, she'd found herself in a magical wonderland of grotesqueness, a place where she could be both herself and absolutely nothing at exactly the same time.

She'd danced with underground fashion types with names such as Unicorn and Heaven, she'd laughed with boys smeared in cartoonish body paint, and she'd remembered that she loved drugs not just because they helped her get through her shoots, but because they provided escapism too.

But with the milky morning light – and after the artificial happiness of the drugs had worn off – came the gloominess and the sickness. Eliza knew she was becoming emotionally and physically dependent on chemicals, but normal life – life when she wasn't on heroin – was too insipid, too boring, too lacklustre. The drugs provided her with a warm, hazy fog that shielded her from reality, for hers was an existence that looked glamorous from the outside but was utterly meaningless on the inside.

Eliza often thought back to the conversation she'd had with her mother where Lillie had told her she'd not have a voice as a model. How astute her mother had been, for the once outspoken and political Eliza was now silent: she was a clothes horse who had to keep her thoughts to herself. She was paid to pose and preen in front of the camera, but she wasn't required to speak, and it was during these periods of muteness that she thought of her mother. She couldn't remember the last time she'd phoned Lillie, or the last time they'd had a proper conversation, and the widened gap between them made her feel desperately sad – though not enough to do anything about it. For when Eliza wasn't working, she was smoking heroin, and despite knowing that it was slowly ruining her life, she always needed another hit. She chose the drugs over rebuilding the relationship with her mother – or preparing for a make-or-break fashion shoot that would prove to be the most important of her life.

'Darling, you need to look more alert,' the fashion director said curtly, breaking into Eliza's thoughts. Eliza looked up at him and felt momentarily dizzy. The lights that shone on her face blinded her, and all she could see were stars. 'You need to push the coat off your shoulders and tilt your head slightly to the left. Yes, that's right, do it now.'

Eliza obediently did as she was told, but the fashion director wasn't happy, and the more she tried, the more frustrated the expression on his thin, weaselly face became. Eliza stared at him dumbly.

'Can you tilt your head *more*? And put a bit of energy into it, for God's sake. You're not a new girl straight out of school, so stop acting like one.'

Eliza could hear the annoyance in every word that dripped from his thin-lipped mouth. She pushed the coat further off her shoulders and twisted her neck in an exaggerated pose, but it wasn't enough. She wanted to do well, she really did, but achieving even the basics of what she needed to do felt impossible. She felt as though she carried her ambition in the palm of her hand, and that it was as slippery as water, falling through her fingers and disappearing on to the floor. She wondered what Bertie would have made of her career, of her life . . . and then she tried not to think about it at all.

'The light's changed, so we're going to have to change the lens,' the photographer's voice announced. 'Let's take five, everyone.'

Eliza breathed a surreptitious sigh of relief. She moved her body about to relax her muscles, and then shot a look at the group of girls huddled around a table laden with coffee. She wasn't sure exactly who they were – stylists, fashion editors, make-up artists – but she knew they were in charge and that they were ignoring her. She wanted them to like her – she would have loved some proper girlfriends, as she'd not had even one since she'd lost Alison – but it felt as though they were on a different planet.

Several of the girls glanced over at her, and Eliza tried to smile at them, but none of them smiled back. One of them seemed particularly young and fresh-faced. She had that dewy, healthy look about her that only the very young had, and Eliza wondered when she'd lost her own youth. All she knew was that there was no way she could ever reclaim it.

The girls' voices were hushed, but several words drifted her way. Eliza knew they were talking about how the shoot was a duff one, concluding that she wasn't up to the job. She felt her heroin itch deepen and she desperately needed to scratch it. She'd wanted to wait until she got home until she had a smoke, but her body was giving her little choice – she had to be on form and the only thing that would help was the brown. Her glorious, perfect brown. If she smoked just a bit of it, she'd become the best model in the world – she'd glisten and shine and be mellow and supple.

'I'm just popping to the loo,' she called out, and hurriedly stalked off to the trailer she'd been given to change outfits in. She quickly found her handbag, pulled out her stash, and there it was – the brilliant brown powder that would save the day.

She pushed aside all the foundation and eyeshadow and blusher and lipstick that crowded the vanity table and laid out her foil, her lighter, her powder. Her hands began to shake and adrenalin coursed through her body, and even though she knew it was silly to feel so excited, she couldn't help it. She craved brown all the time. She needed it all the time. And in just a few moments she'd feel better about herself again and this job wouldn't be a disaster.

She flicked the lighter she always carried around with her and placed her plastic tube in her mouth. Others injected, and some used spoons, but Eliza had always preferred this method to get the perfect first hit. She closed her eyes and breathed in, and was just about to relax into knowing that everything would be okay when the trailer door was flung open. There was a stunned, incredulous silence as Eliza looked from her heroin to the fashion director and back again. There was no way to get out of this situation.

'Fancy some?' she quipped. If she was going to get kicked out of the shoot, she was going to do it in style.

She would never be offered another modelling job.

Eliza lay twisted within the dirty sheets of her bed and felt death gently kiss her throat. Her skin was coated in a thin film of sweat, her bloodshot eyes prickled with dryness, and she couldn't stop being sick. She felt as though her body was attempting to purge every cell that had been tainted by the heroin, and all she wanted to do was to sleep it off. Yet she couldn't sleep. She hadn't slept for days.

A shrill, terse ringing began to slice through her headache and she longed for it to stop. The sound of it grew; at first it was bearable, but then it became so loud that it took up all the stuffy air in her bedroom. She gasped for breath and hit at her ears to try to make it come to a halt, but nothing she did could make it go away. At last there was silence, blessed silence, before it started up again, and then Eliza recognised the noise: the ringing was her intercom and someone on the street was relentlessly pressing the buzzer. It could only be Jonathan.

She stifled a groan and pushed her head under her grubby, mascara-stained pillow, but she could still hear the intercom ringing, and the expensive goose-feather pillow she'd treated herself to when her career had been on the up barely took the edge off the noise. Jonathan only visited her flat when he was furious with her, and Eliza knew she didn't have the strength to see him – she could barely hold her head up, could barely focus her gaze. Yet still the intercom rang, and the more it rang, the more it physically affected her. Every blast cut deep into her tender skin, made her head throb, made the barbed-wire knots deep in her intestine twist and turn in agony. She had to stop the ringing. She forced herself out of bed.

'What is it?' she demanded as she put the intercom phone to her ear. Her voice was scratchy and every bone in her body ached; she felt as though she were a hundred years old. 'What do you want?'

As she spoke, she looked at herself in the antique spotted mirror that had come with the flat – the mirror that the owner, Petra, would have looked at in the 1960s. If she felt like death, she looked a hell of a lot worse: her skin was pallid and covered in angry blisters, and her lips were cracked and caked with dried blood from where she'd chewed on them. But her appearance didn't matter. Nothing mattered apart from feeling better.

'It's me.' Jonathan's voice was terse through the crackling intercom system. 'I heard about the *i-D* shoot.'

Eliza paused. She'd lost track of time. She had no idea what day it was and she'd forgotten that she'd been escorted away from the photo shoot. At the time she'd not cared; the heroin had meant she'd just floated away.

'I'm sick,' she said quietly. It wasn't a lie: her withdrawal pains were the worst they'd ever been.

'Let me in,' Jonathan demanded.

Eliza felt her heart sink. She could barely move, could barely think straight. She knew that the only thing that would help her to feel better was more brown, but her dealer had said his supplies were low and he wouldn't have any more for several days. She didn't know if she could last that long. Her bottles of Gee's Linctus had long run out, and she'd swallowed the last of her codeine syrup several nights earlier. She'd never experienced anything like this.

'I don't think you should come up,' she whispered in shame.

Jonathan was silent for the longest time, and Eliza wondered if he'd walked away. But then his voice came loud and clear through the intercom phone.

'That's exactly why I'm going to come up, right now. One of your neighbours has just appeared and she's letting me in.'

'But you mustn't!' Eliza exclaimed. She scratched at her arm agitatedly and was alarmed to see that her scraggly fingernails had drawn blood. Moments later there was a pounding at her front door. She wanted to cry with exhaustion; instead, she turned the lock and wordlessly let Jonathan into her flat, then wearily made her way back to bed, with the assumption that he would follow her.

She knew he would think her bedroom was a mess – a rainbow of clothes was strewn across the floor, and make-up littered every available surface – but apart from smelling sour, the room was relatively clean and respectable. Not that she really cared; how could she care about something so trivial when she'd never felt so bad in her life? Besides, compared to the rest of the apartment, it was a palace.

Eliza had started to get into the habit of bringing strangers she met in clubs – places like Jungle, Westworld and Taboo – back to her flat for come-down parties, and the debris of these could be found in every room. Cigarette papers used to make joints lay on the coffee table, empty Valium blisters were piled up on the arms of the sofas, and wax from candles lit long ago pooled in gleaming white puddles on the dirty wooden floor. The cleaning company had stopped servicing the flat months ago – they'd seen the drugs and had refused to be involved

– and since then Eliza had let her housework slide. She didn't see the point in trying to stay on top of anything.

'Christ, what's happened to you?' Jonathan exclaimed as he took in his client. Eliza huddled under her duvet and stared at a spot on the bedroom wall. She tried to smile but she knew she looked desperately sad.

'I think I've come down with the flu,' she replied in a tiny voice.

Jonathan paced the room. He accidentally stepped on some of her clothes, but Eliza couldn't care less.

'Your career is over,' he began. His voice was expressionless, neutral, but Eliza knew her agent well enough to know he was riled. 'And you need help.'

It was a statement, not a question, and Eliza felt panic rise in her chest. 'It's just a cold. I'll be fine, I'm sure.'

He stared at her. 'Will you?'

His gaze was unwavering and Eliza felt herself falter. Her life seemed to be falling apart, and she so wanted Jonathan to rescue her again, to scoop her up in his arms and tell her that everything would be okay. But nothing would be okay ever again – or that was how it felt. Eliza barely spoke to her mother out of shame at what her life had become, and she desperately wanted and needed a friend.

Heroin filled that void; heroin gave her the hug she needed when she was feeling down. But when its sunshine turned cold, she was left feeling worse than before, and she needed more. She always needed more just to reach that glorious, perfect high.

She felt tears in her eyes. 'I keep thinking of the family whose eighteen-month-old baby died of AIDS, of the thousands of people dying of starvation in Ethiopia. I know my life is brilliant compared to theirs, but it feels so wretched.'

'Why does it feel so bad?' Jonathan asked. He no longer

looked angry; instead his eyes were kind. Eliza wanted to reach out to him, to see if the compassion he felt for her could somehow touch her.

'I don't know,' she whispered. 'All I know is that I don't have anybody, that I'm all alone.' She knew she sounded spoilt and self-pitying, and she hated herself for it.

'There are places you can go, you know,' Jonathan said. 'Places like the Betty Ford clinic in America. They can get you off the drugs, get you back to being you again.'

Fear ran through Eliza's already bruised body. 'I can't do it,' she said. 'Please don't make me go through that.'

It was the first time she had ever seen Jonathan look discomforted, and it alarmed her. He was always so in control; he knew the right thing to say and the correct way to behave in every situation. Jonathan Klein was charming, he was elegant, he was self-assured – but in that moment he looked as scared as she felt.

'If you don't, I'm afraid you'll die,' he said. His voice was quiet, but Eliza knew he was choked up. He looked up from the floor and into her eyes, and she saw something more than professional courtesy in his gaze: she saw that he cared for her.

'I don't need to go anywhere,' she said as firmly as she could. 'I can stop taking drugs any time I want to. I've stopped already, you see. That's why I'm in so much pain.'

Jonathan reached out and took Eliza's hand in his. In the quiet of the Chelsea flat, with only the faintest hint of noise from the double-decker buses that chugged along the King's Road, they sat like that for hours. Despite the terrible sickness, Eliza felt warmth and hope.

Chapter Sixteen

London, recently

Cassie sat on a bar stool at the Dean Street Townhouse and tried hard not to fidget. She felt uncomfortably hot and flustered, but the more she tried to focus, the less she found she was able to, for Eliza Boyle dominated her thoughts and she couldn't push her aside. Even though she knew it was pointless to be concerned about a family member who'd already passed away, she found that she couldn't quite help herself. She had disliked reading about how Eliza had ruined her modelling prospects, and she'd hated discovering how she had so quickly become addicted to heroin. If she could have reached into the pages of the diary to rescue Eliza, she would have done.

Instead, she looked down at the bag that lay at her feet. Inside was her laptop – which held a copy of the business plan she and Ed had been working on – and several of Eliza's diaries, which grew thinner in content with each passing year. Cassie couldn't have explained it to anybody, but she felt better knowing that the diaries were close to her. She felt protective of Eliza's memory and she liked to know that her diaries were safe.

'You look lost in thought,' one of the barmen remarked.

Cassie smiled weakly, then caught sight of her reflection in the mirror behind the bar. Her face was pallid and the shadows under her eyes were heavy, still noticeable under her make-up.

'I am,' she confirmed.

The barman offered her another cup of coffee and she was about to accept when Ed touched her elbow. She smiled at him and asked for two lattes rather than just one.

'And I thought *I* was early,' Ed remarked. He leant towards her and kissed her briefly on each cheek, but Cassie was too taken aback by his appearance to be flustered. She'd known Ed had worked in the City, of course, but she'd never seen him in a suit – when had she had the opportunity? – and she was struck by how professional he looked, how intimidating he would be to her had she not known the man hidden under his London clothes.

'Well, I took the afternoon off work, and I wanted to collect my thoughts away from the noise of my brother and sister,' she explained. 'I like it here. The Dean Street Townhouse always feels like a second home; a refuge, in a way. I suppose that's why I suggested we meet here.'

Ed led her to a small circular table near the window and watched wordlessly as she dropped a brown sugar cube into her latte. She stirred the drink and then pulled out her laptop.

'What time did you say your friend was meeting us?'

Ed looked at his watch, a more expensive-looking one to the one he wore at Beaufont. 'Jake said three p.m., so we've got a while yet. Would you like to go through the business plan again?'

Cassie thought about it, but shook her head. In the week that had passed since she had last seen Ed, she'd been busy: during the days she'd worked at Heritage Books, and in the evenings she'd spent hours putting together some more definite figures for her festival proposal. It had taken several long nights of heavy research and hard graft, but she was confident that what she'd prepared was a good first attempt – especially as Ed had helped her with it.

Cassie wasn't a natural numbers person – she'd always preferred to read and write, had always preferred the arts over the sciences – and when Ed had offered to help her, she'd been relieved. He'd sent her sample business plans, reviewed the work she'd already done, and offered her lots of advice on what a potential investor would be looking for. Superficially he was helping her put together a complex business document, but to Cassie it was so much more than that. She'd never thought she'd be anything but a girl who worked in a bookshop, yet now she was sitting in one of her favourite places in London and waiting to make a presentation to a man who could change not only her life, but the fortunes of Beaufont Hall.

'I think I know the figures off by heart,' she said. 'And I know that you said that not making a profit for a couple of years won't matter, but do you think your friend will see that as an issue?'

Ed shook his head. 'Jake has a fund that specialises in the creative arts. The very fact that you want to do a literary festival will get his interest; being able to forecast a profit several years down the line is the cherry on top of the cake.' He smiled encouragingly, but Cassie noticed that he looked as strained as she felt. 'Jake is fortunate to control a serious amount of money, but he likes to do fun things with it. Something like this is right up his street.'

He pulled at his collar, then grimaced when he noticed Cassie watching him.

'I hate dressing like this,' he confided as he stopped tugging and took a sip of his coffee instead. 'It reminds me of when I used to wear suits like this every day – and how pleased I am to be out of the City.'

Cassie watched Ed's troubled face carefully. 'Was it really that bad?'

His expression softened. 'It wasn't *bad*,' he replied. 'Just fucking awful. I suppose I'd compare it to eating too much chocolate, or smoking too many cigarettes. You end up feeling sick, and just the thought of eating or smoking again makes you feel ill. When I walk the streets of Soho it reminds me of all the drunken nights out, the bad behaviour, me and my mates egging each other on. This is what I wore when I was that guy . . . and I'd like to think I'm not him any more.'

Cassie stared at him until he broke the intensity. 'Well, it's that,' he said slowly, 'but also my suit's now too small for me. Since I've been back in the village, my mother's been feeding me up and I've put on a few pounds.'

Cassie burst out laughing, and the sorrowful mood she'd been in since she'd finished Eliza's diary for 1985 began to disappear. They talked about Ed's life in the City for a while longer, and by the time Jake Walker was shown to their table half an hour later, all her melancholic thoughts of Eliza had been wiped away.

'I think it's safe to say that went extremely well. Jake was very impressed,' Ed remarked several hours later as he pulled off his jacket and rolled up his shirt sleeves.

Their meeting with Jake Walker had lasted longer than they'd planned. After Cassie had discussed her hopes and plans for the Beaufont Festival of Literature, and both she and Ed had answered Jake's questions concerning the finances, her potential investor had left with a firm handshake and a big smile. He'd promised to look into her business plan in more detail, but he'd also said that he was keen to be involved. Cassie was ecstatic.

'It *did* go well, didn't it?' she replied. She felt giddy and light-headed. Despite all the work she'd put into her proposal, she'd not truly believed that Jake would take her seriously, or that he'd be interested in helping her to get the festival off the ground. It would take a lot of money, and plenty more hard work, but should she secure investment, the festival could launch the following year, and eventually there would be a potential revenue stream that would not only help to restore Beaufont Hall to its former glory, but could also maintain the building for years to come. It wouldn't be easy, and it would still take years and years before the house could truly become a family home again, but it was a positive step in the right direction.

'Let's have a drink to celebrate.'

Ed glanced at his watch and then ordered two glasses of champagne. Cassie grinned at him, but he didn't look as pleased as she'd hoped.

'Thank you so much for all your help with this,' she said. She placed her hand gently on his bare arm. 'Being able to save Beaufont means the world to me.'

Ed smiled back, but he looked distracted. 'I know it does; it means a lot to me too.' He handed Cassie a glass of champagne and they toasted their meeting.

Cassie wondered briefly if they were jinxing their good fortune, but she decided quickly that that wasn't the case. Even if Jake Walker chose not to invest in the festival, there would be meetings with other investors; there would be lots of opportunities to find financing.

'Can I buy you an early supper to say thank you?' she asked.

Ed looked conflicted. 'I'd love to stay, but I'm running late as it is. I promised I'd meet Grace – my ex, you know – after work for dinner and drinks . . .'

Ed's words pierced Cassie's good mood and she could feel

her happiness deflate. She tried hard not to let it show on her face but she suspected she'd been unsuccessful. Ed watched her carefully and she wanted to hide away, but instead she took another sip of her champagne and hoped that her hair hid her flushed cheeks.

'Another time,' she said lightly. Suddenly the champagne bubbles didn't seem so lovely and they left a bitter aftertaste in her mouth.

'I wish I could stay here with you, but I promised her that we'd meet,' Ed said quietly, and his words hung in the air.

Cassie concentrated on closing her laptop and placing it back in her bag. She caught sight of Eliza's diaries and decided she'd dine alone and allow the written memories of her distant relative to keep her company instead.

'It's absolutely fine,' she said brightly.

Ed forced out a smile, but he didn't speak. His expression was strained and he suddenly became businesslike: he knocked back his champagne and then stood and awkwardly squeezed Cassie's arm.

'I really should go,' he said apologetically as he pulled out his wallet to leave some money for their drinks.

'You don't have to get that,' Cassie said. 'Please, let me – it's the least I can do.'

'That would be out of the question,' Ed replied. He deposited the money on the tablecloth, then pulled his jacket back on. 'I'll see you at Beaufont at the weekend?'

Cassie nodded. 'Thank you again for today,' she said, and Ed smiled at her fondly.

'It was my pleasure.' He held her gaze for a second, and Cassie thought he was about to speak when the iPhone in his pocket began to vibrate. He pulled it out, tapped a reply to the text message he'd just received, and then disappeared out of the door.

Cassie spent the next hour or so enjoying her own company. She ordered a smoked haddock soufflé – her favourite – and some salad, drank a small glass of white wine, and entertained herself by listening to the conversations of the people around her and rereading some of Eliza's earlier diaries. She started with the first diary, from 1978, and decided to read the entries where Eliza had moved to Soho and had been so happy that she'd felt like she'd been flying. She hoped that Eliza had found such happiness again, and that she'd done so without the aid of drugs. She knew it was unlikely, though. That heroin was likely to have played a starring role in Eliza's death was a painful truth she hoped to avoid, but she knew it was almost inevitable; there probably wouldn't be a happy ending for Eliza Boyle.

After an hour, Cassie had finished her meal and asked for her bill. She'd been about to close the diary when three of Eliza's scrawled words popped out at her: 'Meard Street Gang'. She quickly reread the entry about how Eliza and her friends had named themselves after the road they'd once loitered on, and she wondered how she'd not noticed those words before. For Cassie knew Meard Street well: it was the small shop-lined alley that linked Dean Street to Wardour Street, and was directly to the side of the building she was currently in.

She paid the bill, gathered up her things, and decided to make the most of the crisp evening by sitting on the cold black steps at the side of the Dean Street Townhouse, in front of a closed door that probably led into the kitchens. As she gazed at her surroundings she saw Eliza in every shadow, in the face of every twenty-something who rushed past, and she could easily picture her relative pacing the small pedestrian street in front of her.

Meard Street had been the centre of Eliza's world when she'd first moved to Soho, and as Cassie flicked through the diary entries again she felt a chill run through her. Perhaps it was a coincidence that she was on the same small road on which Eliza had drunkenly laughed with her friends, but perhaps it was something else; for what if she had been drawn to Meard Street because Eliza had once spent time there?

Cassie knew she was being romantic, but she wondered if something had guided her to the place where she now sat. She didn't believe in ghosts, but she did believe in lingering memories, and as she squeezed her eyes shut against the streaming evening sun she could so easily picture Eliza dressed in a grubby lace dress in front of her. She was drinking and smoking with Alison and Raven and Curt before they headed for Gossips.

Gossips. Cassie had spent a bit of time researching it, but apart from knowing it had been on Dean Street, she'd not ever properly discovered the club's location. She pulled out her iPhone, checked her 4G connection, and began to search. Pages and pages of websites appeared, and while they all stated that Gossips had been on Dean Street, none of them offered a more specific address. Cassie ran her hands through her hair in frustration. Then, as a group of laughing teenagers walked past her on their way to Wardour Street, an obvious, and chilling, revelation flung itself in front of her.

She knew exactly where Gossips had been; on a subconscious level she always had.

Her hands shook, but she entered 'Gossips' with '69 Dean Street' – the address of the Dean Street Townhouse – into her phone and pressed 'search'. Before she could prepare herself, the results appeared and she had confirmation that her instincts were correct: Gossips had been right here, in the very building that she felt such an affinity with, the place where she felt so comfortable and at home.

She took a deep breath and kept on digging. The initial website she'd clicked on didn't have any images of the club, so she kept looking through the links on her phone until she found some. The first photo showed a group of teenagers in goth make-up with drinks in their hands; the second was a grainy black-and-white picture of a band on a stage. Cassie knew it was unlikely that she'd stumble across an image of a young Eliza in any of these photos, but as she happened upon a smiling, hard-looking blonde dancing under a canopy made of plastic bats, she wondered if this could have been Alison. She liked to think it was, but she knew she'd never know for sure.

The next set of monochrome photos showed the club from the outside, and Cassie decided it was worth looking at these to see how different the exterior of the Dean Street Townhouse had been in the 1980s. She pinched at the screen of her phone so she could zoom in, and concentrated on the first image in the collection. One of the whitewashed walls of the Georgian building had been decorated with a hand-painted sign that read 'Gossips Discotheque'. Alongside it was a painting of a siren, looking blissful as the wind ran through her long fair hair. As Cassie stared at the painting – which slightly resembled Eliza in her modelling heyday – she wondered which wall of the building it had been.

It was then that realisation dawned.

For to the left of the sign were two black steps that led to the entrance of Gossips. They were the steps on which Cassie was sitting right now.

The first thing Cassie wanted to do was to speak to Ed. She stared at the iPhone in her hands, but she knew that as much as she wanted to, she couldn't ring him. He'd already spent much of the afternoon with her, and he was with Grace – probably rekindling their relationship. Instead she dialled Safia, who'd she'd barely spoken to since she'd started working on her business plan, and begged her to meet her. 'You have to come!' she stressed. Within twenty minutes Safia had jumped out of a black cab, and while she looked flustered and hot underneath her office clothes, her eyes had widened when Cassie shared her discovery.

'The club that Eliza Boyle used to go to was in this building?' she asked incredulously.

Cassie nodded. 'I want to take a proper look around in the basement – that's where the club was. Do you think they'll let me?'

Safia considered this. 'I don't know,' she replied slowly. 'But we can ask.'

The girls walked around the corner and through the main entrance. The hostess who'd seated Cassie earlier was still standing by the reservations computer, and she recognised Cassie and smiled at her.

'Back again so soon?' she asked.

Cassie flushed. 'I've not actually left,' she replied. 'I was wondering if you can help me. A relative of mine used to go to a nightclub that was in the basement of this building in the 1980s. Would it be possible to have a look down there?'

The hostess looked at Cassie and Safia for a long moment and then nodded. 'Let me get the manager to see if he can show you.'

Cassie grasped Safia's hand tightly as they waited. When the manager came over and she explained what she wanted to do, and why, she was surprised at how easily permission was granted.

'I can take you down now if you like,' he said, after he'd introduced himself as Mike. 'But we'll have to be quick – the dinner rush is about to start.'

He led Cassie and Safia past the bar and through the restaurant, then pushed open a set of swinging double doors. They found themselves on the other side of the black door that had been the entrance to Gossips. Cassie was overwhelmed. It didn't take much imagination to pretend that she'd walked into the pages of Eliza's diary, that she'd found a doorway straight into Eliza's life. More than thirty years earlier, Eliza would have stepped through this door, buzzing in anticipation of having the night of her life. And while there was now lots of artificial light rather than the red bulbs that had lit Gossips, and while everything felt clean and sterile rather than debauched and seedy, Cassie knew she could really feel that Eliza had once been here. She didn't know how or why, but she did.

Mike led the girls down the narrow terracotta-tiled stairs to the left of them – and to the right of the old club entrance – and into the basement of the building, which was now being used as the kitchens. The chefs momentarily stopped their prep to stare at them, but Cassie barely noticed. She took in the low ceiling that had once dripped with sweat, and while it was impossible to know for sure where the bar had been, where the stage had been, she could picture the club easily. She could imagine Eliza standing in the middle of the room and dancing in the darkness.

'When this space was Gossips, everything was tiled,' she said, as she recalled an entry from one of Eliza's diaries. 'The ceiling was made up of those white squares you could lift up, and the walls had cheap beige tiles topped with mirrored ones. Those alcoves over there used to hold booths,' she added, gesturing to the side of the room.

'This is amazing,' Safia murmured as a chef squeezed past her. 'To think that we've been coming here for ages, and you never knew that one of your relatives used to work here.'

'The upper part of the building and the roof used to be the Gargoyle Club,' Mike said, cutting into Cassie's thoughts. 'There was a ballroom and a dining room that could only be reached by a rickety old elevator. We don't have the lift any more, and you can only access the old rooftop through one of the hotel bedrooms, but this is where the Bright Young Things of the 1920s used to dance.'

He led the girls back up the stairs and on to the street through the original entrance, and even though Cassie was thankful that she'd finally been in a place where Eliza had once stood, she also felt inexplicably sad. This had been where the beautiful and the damned of the dazzling 1920s – Tallulah Bankhead, Fred Astaire, Dylan Thomas and Francis Bacon – had danced their debauched dances, and where the club kids of the 1980s had lost themselves to the night. But apart from a whisper of a memory of fun and decadence, there was nothing of this history left. She reached into her bag to check that she still had the diaries with her, and wondered what Eliza Boyle had done next.

Chapter Seventeen

London, 1987

Eliza danced as though her life depended on it. She didn't know where she was — she had a vague recollection of walking up some stairs into a squat on Warren Street — but she didn't care. Everyone around her was smiling, laughing, and she wanted to be part of it. She'd been in Embargo when a stranger had pulled her away from the throng and suggested she come to this party. She hadn't agreed, but she'd not protested either, and she'd allowed herself to be swept along by a clammy hand, a crooked smile and a promise of utopia. The man had disappeared almost as soon as they'd arrived — had he vanished in a puff of smoke? Perhaps he had — but as much as Eliza had searched for him, he was nowhere to be found. Instead she was surrounded by people she didn't know, yet they all had something in common: they were all here for a good time — to dance and to surrender all their inhibitions.

The problem Eliza had was that this particular type of good time kept slipping through her fingers. Everyone else seemed to be able to luxuriate in it — to be in the peaceful, calming warmth of heroin or in the clean chemical jolt of cocaine — but being high was elusive to Eliza. She'd been smoking more heroin than ever before, but it no longer had its desired effect. She wanted shooting stars, she wanted that warming heat of relaxation, she wanted to drift away for ever. But it wouldn't come. She now truly understood the meaning of 'chasing the dragon' – she could brush the dragon's scaly indigo skin with her fingertips, but at the last moment it would swish its tail out of reach and she had to pursue it all over again.

It had been over two years since she had promised Jonathan that she'd clean up. She could barely remember what her former agent had looked like, but she could clearly recall the sick feeling in her stomach when she'd lied to him. At the time she knew her assurances were meaningless – her love affair with brown was too far gone. She was enthralled, she was addicted. Nothing else mattered but feeling better, and the only way to feel better was to take more and more and more...

Of course, she'd run out of money. For a while she'd been fine: she'd sold all her belongings and was grateful for her savings account at the Midland Bank. But even though she'd spent as little as possible so she could support her heroin addiction, her money ran out fast. She'd had to move out of the flat in Chelsea, but pride, and fear of being away from her dealers, had prevented her from asking Lillie if she could move in with her. So she had found herself back on the streets of Soho. At the back of her mind she'd always known that her life as a functioning adult in a smart flat in Chelsea was just an act. Soho was where she belonged, only this time she didn't have the strength not to fall down in the seedy shadows.

'You're here,' a voice exclaimed, and Eliza turned to see Raven.

The years hadn't been kind to him – his face was craggy and his eyes were sad – but he still had some of the spirit that Eliza had loved. When she'd spotted him waiting for punters on an alley near Tottenham Court Road, he'd embraced her with open arms and she had instantly forgiven his rejection from years earlier: she needed a friend. Alison and Curt were long gone – to where, nobody knew – but Raven still ruled their tiny bit of Soho. He'd taken her to his squat and helped her find some work, and she had realised that taking all her clothes off and standing in front of a clicking camera wasn't dissimilar to what she'd done for the fashion magazines.

'And you're here too,' Eliza murmured. 'Some man I met at Embargo brought me. He promised he'd sort me out, but he's gone.'

Her eyes darted around the squat desperately as she tried to spot someone doing drugs, someone who would let her ride with them. The underground music scene had changed rapidly in the last couple of years, and Eliza still found it disorientating. People had stopped dressing like works of art and chose instead to wear trainers and baseball caps and brightly coloured T-shirts. The tunes were different too, and they listened to acid house while they grasped at whatever fun they could find in damp abandoned buildings.

'Have you seen anybody doing brown?'

Raven pointed in the direction of a couple of boys in the corner, and Eliza immediately walked over to them. They didn't look at her.

'Can you share?' she yelled over the music. She didn't know what the track was – a girl was singing about 'knowing she wanted to' over various layers of beats – but it didn't matter. The song was about her. She knew it was.

One of the boys shook his head, but Eliza sat down next to them anyway. Her face was pallid and greasy, and her hands shook – she was rattling, and she needed a fix. When the boys produced a syringe, a spoon, a lighter and an old cola bottle filled with water, she watched with interest. She'd never injected before, but she was willing to be taught.

'It will cost you,' the boy with dark hair said.

Eliza stared at him blankly. 'I don't have any money,' she replied. She'd spent the last of it on a fix several days earlier, but she wasn't above begging, stealing or borrowing. Sating her need felt like life or death, and she lived in constant, grating desperation.

The boys looked at each other for a long time. 'If you haven't got cash, I can think of another way you can pay me,' the dark-haired one remarked. His eyes glittered. 'Let's find another room to get to know each other better.'

Eliza didn't care. She knew what the boy wanted from her, and the sex meant nothing; she'd do anything for the promise of getting high.

'I want the brown first.'

The boy roughly pushed the belt on to her arm, mixed the powder with the water and some citric acid, and then heated it up on the spoon. As it cooked, Eliza experienced a moment of doubt – a tiny sense of self-preservation – but she pushed it away. The boy held her gaze as he drew up the syringe, and she nodded.

'Do it,' she said.

As the stranger injected the needle deep into her arm, time slowed down. There were bright colours and a drifting away on a cloud, an incredible feeling of warmth and safety and love, the memory of salty tears of happiness, and pinpricks and bruises. She'd had sex with one of the boys – a sad, fumbled, hopeless fuck – but it barely registered with her. She'd found her utopia again and she was at peace.

Eliza wondered if she was a ghost.

Eliza found that sleeping with men for money or drugs was easier than she could ever have imagined. After her first encounter with the boy at the party, she slipped into an effortless exchange of sex for cash in the clubs that she knew so well. The nights she used to frequent had long gone – the Bat Cave had closed its doors in 1984, White Trash had finished in 1985, and Raw the year before – but Eliza knew the buildings better than anybody; she knew the secret hiding places for trysts and decadence.

For years she had watched the prostitutes in Soho and wondered how they could bring themselves to do what they did. Now she recognised herself in them, in their thin, bruised limbs, their glassy eyes, their matted, dirty hair. Sleeping with men you didn't like wasn't particularly pleasant, but it paid more than nude modelling. For the first time in a long time Eliza had proper money, and she spent it on drugs, on booze, on anything that could numb the pain of a life lost to the underground.

She told herself that this life wasn't for ever. She dressed provocatively, she lingered in corners in nightclubs, and she found that picking up men was easy. Her prices changed depending on what services they required, and within a couple of months she'd slid easily into the side of Soho life that her mother had warned her of when she was a teenager. Lots of her customers were clubbers, but she soon found that it was easier to stand on Meard Street and wait for men to come to her. She joined the ranks of the women she used to stare at when she'd finished her shift at Gossips all those years ago, and she found she actually didn't care about her downfall. Lillie had been right to be scandalised by Soho: it was bitterly horrific.

But it was also Eliza's normality.

One night she watched a group of kids going into Gossips, and she remembered when Soho had been vibrant and fun, a pleasure playground for whoever wanted it. Those who came here now saw what they chose to — and for men it was the over-bright smiles of the girls at the Raymond Revuebar, girls who'd been oiled and buffed and who performed like pros. They didn't see — they didn't want to see — the brittle and broken street girls like Eliza, the girls who'd fallen on hard times and couldn't crack a grin even if they wanted to.

It was one of the mildest winters on record, but Eliza was painfully cold in her thin skirt and top. She felt sick, her whole body ached and she longed to go back to the squat so she could shoot up. A man approached her, but she felt so ill and dizzy that she couldn't concentrate on what he said to her, and after several attempts he walked away. She slumped to the uneven pavement and instinctively placed her hand over her stomach. It took her a while, but the more she thought about it, the more she realised that the symptoms she felt — the awful flu-ishness, the persistent dull headache and the heavy aching in her breasts — weren't heroin-related.

She was pregnant.

She managed to pull herself together and found her way back to the squat, where she sat on the floor and allowed darkness to creep over her. Her head ached from her tears, and when she wasn't whimpering, the howls that left her body made her sound like an injured animal. She knew this was rock bottom, and she knew — for the baby's sake if not her own — that she needed to clean up. Now, and fast.

The first day she stopped smoking or injecting was the hardest: she felt as though the devil had consumed her soul. He whispered sweet nothings about drugs to her constantly, and caressed the longing she had for just one precious hit. And then the withdrawal symptoms came: she shook, she couldn't sleep, she couldn't stop being sick, and she felt restless, uneasy, paranoid, petrified. In her darkest moments she would lie on the floor of the squat and wail. She'd remember how bright life had been when she'd first moved to Soho, and how desperate everything seemed now.

Raven tried to look after her and brought her food, but he was caught up in his addictive life of partying and prostitution. He tried not to take heroin in the squat – he wanted to do that for Eliza – but sometimes he failed, and when Eliza saw him blissed out on a mattress, she felt tortured. She wanted to love the baby inside her but she also despised it for how it had taken over her body. Even in her lighter moments she hated herself – this wasn't the Eliza Boyle she'd wanted to become.

Through her sickness, she tried to think straight. She couldn't face a termination, but she also knew that she had no other options available. How could she bring up a baby? She had little money, she wouldn't be able to work once it had begun to show on her splinter-like frame, and she had no way of raising it.

For the first time in a very long time, Eliza needed the help of her mother.

Eliza pushed several ten-pence pieces into the phone and shakily dialled her mother's number. The phone box smelled of the cigarette butts that frayed in the puddles of stale urine on the floor, and Eliza huddled into the corner and tried to breathe through her mouth. The phone at the other end of the line rang once, twice, and then Lillie Boyle's voice – even crisper on the telephone – rang out: 'Basingstoke five-two-oh-six-four.'

If she'd been feeling better Eliza would have laughed, would have told her mother that nobody answered the phone with their number any more, but she didn't have the heart. Besides, her voice had momentarily left her.

'Hello?' Lillie's voice said down the telephone. 'Hello, who is this?'

Eliza swallowed back a sob. 'Mum, it's me,' she managed to say. Her voice was sticky with tears.

There was a pause, and then Lillie spoke. 'Eliza, for God's sake, I've not heard from you in months. Where have you been? I've been worried sick.'

Eliza shut her eyes and wondered where to begin. Would her mother understand? Probably not. Would she want to be there for her unborn grandchild? Of course she would. She took a deep breath.

'I've got myself into a bit of a mess and I don't know what to do. I need your help.'

Lillie's voice immediately filled with concern. 'What sort of mess?'

Eliza paused again. She'd never been more ashamed of herself than she was at that moment, and to make matters even worse, she desperately wanted something to take the edge off every-thing – heroin, cocaine, speed, weed . . . whatever she could get her hands on. But the ten-pence pieces were being eaten up by her silence, and she knew she had to talk. It was now or never.

'I'm pregnant, and I don't have a job or any money.'

Lillie drew a sharp breath, and Eliza could picture her going into action mode. 'You can come here—' she began, but Eliza interrupted her. Her money was fast running out; she had just eight pence left on the call.

'I can't face getting on the train,' she whimpered. Her with-drawal symptoms were still raging and she didn't think she had the strength. 'Could you come here? To where I live in Soho? It's a bit of a state, but I'll give you the address . . .'

There was a long silence at the other end of the phone.

'Can you come?' she whispered. 'Will you?' She was down to just five pence, and she wanted to make sure her mother would be there for her.

'Of course I can,' Lillie replied. 'Give me a couple of days to get myself together – I need to ask a friend to cover for me at work. I'm assuming you need money, so I'll go to the bank to get some, and then I'll be there as soon as I can. Is Monday okay? I can come sooner if it's an emergency.' It was Friday now, but Eliza could wait a few more days before she fell into her mother's soft, comforting arms.

'Monday would be great,' she replied, and she felt light with relief.

'Darling, I know that things may seem bad right now, but everything really will be okay,' Lillie said quietly. 'A baby is the start of something magical, you'll see.'

Eliza swallowed hard. 'I'm scared,' she admitted, and there was a pause at the other end of the phone. 'I don't know if I can do this.'

'Of course you can,' Lillie said in her no-nonsense manner. It had irritated Eliza when she was a teenager, but now it felt reassuring. 'I was scared when I found out I'd fallen pregnant with you – but having you was the best thing I ever did. You'll see: this baby will change your life for the better and will make you happier than you ever could have imagined.'

Eliza rested her forehead against the grubby window of the phone booth. She so wanted to believe it, but she wasn't sure she had the strength to be a mother, to be the sort of parent that her baby deserved.

'I don't know if I can do this alone,' she mumbled.

There was a long silence before Lillie spoke again. 'But darling, you won't have to do it alone – I'll be right by your side.'

Chapter Eighteen

London, 1988

Eliza sat on her mattress and waited for her mother. When she'd woken that morning, she'd felt lighter than she had in years, and she knew instinctively that today would be a good day. For despite the winter wind that blew through the streets of Soho, the sun still managed to stream through the windows of the squat, and as the weak warmth of it rested on her skin, she realised that she felt calm. The kernel of fear that she'd had over her pregnancy no longer felt like a heavy knot in her stomach; instead it had bloomed into excitement, and it was this excitement that helped to banish the yearning she had for drugs. To add to this, Lillie would be there soon, and Eliza didn't think she'd ever been so excited to see her mother. The baby would be the catalyst for them rebuilding their relationship; the baby would make everything okay again.

As she waited for Lillie to arrive, Eliza cast her gaze over the squat. Despite feeling bone-tired from the pregnancy and ill from her withdrawal, she'd spent the weekend on her hands and knees trying to clean it. She dragged herself out of her makeshift bed and stood by the big fireplace to try to view the two decaying rooms from her mother's perspective. It was a hellish place to live, of course it was, but she hoped that the mattresses on the floor seemed more bohemian than seedy, that the candles they used for light at night-time looked artistic rather than pathetic. Eliza had refused to allow any more parties to take place in the crumbling flat, and without the paraphernalia of drugs and alcohol the rooms scrubbed up well. They were still slightly dirty, still a bit tired and dusty, but no more than most central London homes, where car exhaust fumes stained the windows black.

It was getting on for 9 a.m., and Eliza felt a tiny thrill of hope rush through her. Lillie had said she would catch the 7.18 from Basingstoke, and it wouldn't take her too long to get from Waterloo to Soho. Eliza perched on the windowsill and peered down at the street. Traders had set up their stalls, and the road glistened as though it had been freshly washed. For the first time in a long time, she felt grateful for what she had: she still had her mother, she had a way of making ends meet, and she had a roof over her head. Lots of people had less.

Eliza sat on the windowsill for hours. At first she wondered if there was a problem with the Underground, but as time went on she started to think that Lillie might have missed the 7.18 train. Perhaps she'd not managed to get on it because of all the commuters who would be coming into London. Yet as one hour went past, and then another, she began to worry. Had her mother changed her mind about helping her? She couldn't believe that Lillie would reject her; she would never do that to her – not when she'd suffered that very thing at the hands of her own parents. Lillie might have been a Tempest, but she'd never behave so heartlessly. She just wouldn't.

By the time it got to lunchtime, Eliza could stand it no longer. She stood up, brushed herself down and walked to the closest phone box. She dialled her mother's number again and again, but the telephone in the boxy, nondescript house in Basingstoke rang and rang without being answered. She hung up the phone and tried not to feel dejected. Her good mood had vanished and she felt weary again. She felt tired of life.

She forced herself to eat a cold tin of vegetable soup – for the baby's sake, rather than for her own – and then she curled up in a ball on her mattress. She kept telling herself that Lillie would never abandon her, that she would never repeat history and disown her daughter. But without the drugs to distract her from her insecurities, her paranoia raged, and she longed for the white vapours of burning heroin to take the edge off how she felt; she craved some codeine syrup to help her float away from the hell that she'd created.

She knew she only had to walk a few steps out of the squat to find a dealer; but she also knew that as desperate as she was for artificial happiness, she could never hurt her baby. She curled up tighter under her thin, rough sheets and eventually fell asleep as night consumed the sky.

The next morning Eliza woke and made a decision: if her mother wouldn't come to her, she would go to Basingstoke. She didn't feel well – her pregnancy hormones made her feel sick and exhausted, and her body was still trying to get back to normal after the huge amount of drugs she'd inflicted upon it – but she wouldn't let how she felt deter her; she wouldn't give in to it. She pulled on some clothes, ran her fingers through her knotty, greasy ponytail, and set off for the Tube station.

As she strode along purposefully, she noticed that the streets were quiet – almost too quiet for a Tuesday morning. People spoke to each other in hushed voices, and their expressions were grave. Several of them looked at Eliza sorrowfully, but Eliza just blinked at them in return. Had something happened? Something terrible? The sky was free of clouds and it was a beautiful December day. It was impossible to think that there could have been a tragedy.

She popped into the first newsagent's she came to and paused in the doorway. She told herself that she was being paranoid, being silly – nothing awful could have happened, could it? But when she saw the front pages of the newspapers piled up on the dirty linoleum floor of the shop, she gasped, and when she picked up a *Daily World* and stared at the headline, she felt her legs give way.

The man behind the counter said something to her in alarm, but Eliza couldn't hear him through the pounding buzzing in her head.

Something terrible *had* happened, and it appeared to have happened to Lillie Boyle.

---

35 DEAD AT CLAPHAM JUNCTION
Daily World Special Report

Up to 35 people were killed and 500 injured in a three-train pile-up at Clapham Junction, London, yesterday.

Hours after the crash, between 60 and 100 people were reported to still be trapped in the twisted wreckage.

Three trains were involved in the crash: The 6.14 a.m. from Poole, the 7.18 a.m. from Basingstoke, and an empty train from Waterloo to Haslemere.

The disaster happened at 8.20 a.m. between Spencer Park and Wandsworth Common, when the Poole train ploughed into the back of the one from Basingstoke.

Witnesses described how both rush-hour trains were full, with many passengers forced to stand.

The empty train from Waterloo then smashed into the wreckage.

A chief fire officer described the scene: 'It was sheer bloody hell and the worst crash I have ever seen.'

Hundreds of people were taken from the remains of the trains, with many people still trapped.

For more, see pages 4, 5, 6, 7 & 8.

Dark grey clouds hung dangerously low over Tottenham on the day of Lillie Boyle's funeral. Slashes of rain fell sharply on to the few mourners who hurried into the church, and the wind slapped at the faces of the men who stood in the churchyard. Unlike funerals that found moments of joy by celebrating the life of the person who'd departed into the unknown, there was no happiness here. There was only heartache, regret, and apologies voiced too late.

Eliza sat very still on a wooden pew at the front of St Paul's and thought of her father. The last time she'd been in this church had been on the day of Bertie's funeral, and over the years she'd learnt that time *did* heal: that the twisting stab of bereavement that gripped her heart would ease. But as she sat in the same spot where she'd said goodbye to her father, she wanted to cry out in grief. The memories she had of him were faint, distant shadows, and she couldn't bear to think that her recollections of Lillie would fade away too.

The vicar began the service, but Eliza forced herself to tune out; she didn't have the strength to listen to him rhapsodise about her mother's qualities, not least because he hadn't really known her. All he knew of Lillie Boyle were the bare facts of her life: that she'd been born the youngest of three daughters in Buckinghamshire, married Bertie Boyle and they'd had one daughter. He didn't know how Lillie's nose had scrunched up when she'd smiled with pure, glorious joy, or how her neck had elongated when she was cross and her posture stiffened.

Instead, Eliza thought of the letter she'd sent to Beaufont Hall the day after she'd discovered her mother had died. At the time, she'd been consumed by some sort of madness; a madness that came from her swirling pregnancy hormones, the jittery sickness of not being able to indulge in the comforting hug of drugs, and the black, dark shock that her mother had died on her way to rescue her.

She'd needed release – any sort of release – so she had found a scrap of paper and angrily scrawled a letter to her grandparents. In it she informed them that Lillie Boyle – the daughter they'd so easily discarded – had died, and that they'd never be able to make amends. She didn't know if her grandparents were alive or not; she didn't even know if the Tempests still lived at Beaufont Hall, but writing the letter had been cathartic. She didn't regret sending it, not for a second.

'Lillie Boyle was a good woman, a kind woman . . .' the vicar continued. Eliza tuned him out again to look at the same statue of the Virgin Mary she'd stared at during her father's service. The baby Jesus lay quiet in her arms, and Eliza forced her gaze away. She couldn't think about her baby right now, or what would become of them without Lillie to help; the thin thread that prevented her from falling apart completely was stretched to its limits.

She wanted to close her eyes and to think of absolutely nothing at all, but the vicar had finished his short sermon and there was silence as Lillie's coffin was hoisted on to the shoulders of several faceless, anonymous men. The congregation stood as though they were following some directions that Eliza couldn't see, and then they all walked outside into the harsh wintry weather to watch the coffin be placed next to that of her father.

Eliza was determined not to cry and to be strong, so she focused her gaze on the other mourners as her mother's coffin was lowered into the ground. There was a child in the congregation, a young boy of about seven or eight who wore big bottle-top glasses. His reddish hair blazed against the darkness of his funeral clothes, and Eliza stared at him and wondered who he was. When he pulled a toy soldier from his pocket, he received a stern look from the man who was with him – his father, Eliza presumed. She couldn't think who the man could be, and even though she thought it slightly inappropriate for him to bring a child to a funeral, she was glad they were there. The boy was something cheerful for the adults to focus on; a shot of colour on a dark, miserable day.

The vicar said his final prayer, and then there was silence, utter nothingness. The other mourners began to walk away, but Eliza found she was frozen on the spot. She didn't want to stay in Tottenham, but she couldn't face returning to the squat in Soho. There was to be a wake in a local pub, and she knew she should go, but that would mean making small talk, and what could she talk about apart from her addiction to illegal drugs or the fact that she was pregnant and not in a relationship with the father?

As she tried to work out the best thing to do, there was a cough, a touch on her elbow. She turned around, and her eyes met those of a girl who looked nervous and awkward. Her blonde hair was in a bun and her posture was so upright, so perfect, that she reminded Eliza of her mother.

'We received your letter,' the girl said. She looked to be about Eliza's age, but Eliza couldn't work out who she would be.

'What letter?' she said. She felt weak and faint and she desperately wanted to sit down.

'You sent a letter to my grandparents, Philip and Mary Tempest,' the girl continued.

Eliza said nothing; just stared at the girl in front of her.

'My mother's name is Violet and she was your mother's sister . . . and my name's Rebecca and I'm your cousin.'

Eliza and Rebecca sat opposite each other in a tiny pub close to the church. Eliza could tell it wasn't the sort of place that

Rebecca normally came to. Several out-of-work men sat at the bar, nursing their afternoon pints of ale, and the air was thick with cigarette smoke and the incessant ringing of the fruit machine. A snooker table sat abandoned, and empty crisp packets lay on the table next to them. Eliza gripped her can of Pepsi and stared at the backs of the men.

'I always wanted to meet Lillie when I was growing up, and I often wished she'd return to Beaufont Hall,' Rebecca began softly. Her voice was quiet, but her accent and tone reminded Eliza so much of Lillie that she found that she couldn't help but gaze at her, regardless of the pain. The Boyles had all sounded different to each other – Bertie had had a southern American drawl, and Eliza was proud of her rough, scrambled north London accent, where her vowels sometimes became tangled like knotted weeds growing around concrete. Rebecca was the first person she'd ever met who spoke as Lillie had – in a slow, measured, proper way. She sounded like home.

'My relatives – *our* relatives – hardly ever mentioned her name, but I knew she existed. When I was a teenager, I idolised her and even used to hide away in her old bedroom,' Rebecca continued. 'I loved that she'd managed to escape the restrictiveness of the family and that bloody house. I often wondered how she'd done it and I envied her free spirit and her bravery. I'd never be able to walk away from the family like she did, never be able to cut it in the real world.'

Eliza frowned. 'You make it sound like she chose to leave Beaufont and her family – that she merrily skipped away from all that luxury so she could live on a council estate in Tottenham.'

Rebecca stared at her. 'But she did – that's what my mother told me when your letter arrived. I was the one who found it on the doormat, you see, and because it was addressed to my late grandparents, I didn't think it would be a problem if I opened it. Finding out that you existed – and that Lillie had died – gave me quite a shock. I showed my mother your letter and asked her to tell me more about Lillie, and she said that Lillie had fallen in love with an American and had run away, never to be heard of again.'

Eliza shook her head and gave a sharp, curt laugh. 'My mother's parents – our grandparents – threw Lillie out when she got pregnant. She wasn't married and she'd been having a love affair with a man they believed to be unsuitable, just because he was a working-class American. She didn't *choose* never to see her family again. The Tempests wanted nothing to do with her.'

There was a pause, and Rebecca looked ashen. She'd raised her perfectly manicured hand to her mouth. 'I didn't know that,' she began. 'And my mother couldn't have known it either.'

'My mother missed her older sisters,' Eliza continued. 'We may not have been well off, but we were happy – apart from the cloud that hung over her sometimes. She always said that Violet and Aster were more sensible than her, but she never got over the fact that they never replied to her letters, that they chose to cut her out of their lives as their parents had. It broke her heart.'

Rebecca looked down at her feet. Eliza noticed that they were clad in beautiful suede heels that had been ruined by the mud at the graveside. When she looked back up, Eliza saw that her bright blue eyes were identical to Lillie's – and to her own.

'Maybe my mother didn't receive your mother's letters. I'm sure she would have tried to find her if she could have done.'

Eliza shook her head. 'Then why isn't she here today? Why didn't she respond to my letter and come to the funeral to say goodbye?'

'I don't know,' Rebecca replied in a small voice. She looked uneasy. 'I think she was too upset to come. But I wanted to. I wanted to say goodbye to the aunt I never knew – and I wanted to meet you. I wish I'd known you'd existed, and I'm sure Lloyd and Rose – my other cousins – do too.'

Eliza felt drained. So much had happened, and she wasn't sure she had the energy or strength to get to know Rebecca. Her childhood fairy-tale fantasy of someone from Beaufont Hall appearing to embrace her had finally happened, but now that it had, she wasn't sure she wanted it after all. All she wanted to do was to go to bed, hide herself away under her sheets and wake up in the flat in Tottenham with both her parents alive and pestering her about her homework. She wished so much that she could go back in time. That way she could avoid making all the mistakes she'd made over the years.

'I need to go,' she muttered. She got to her feet, but she felt unsteady and she had to grip at the sticky wooden table to find her balance. The dirty patterned carpet of the pub swirled in front of her eyes.

Rebecca rushed to her side. 'Sit down,' she directed. Eliza fell back on the stool and put her head in her hands. 'Are you unwell?'

If Eliza hadn't felt so deathly ill, she would have laughed. 'I'm pregnant . . . and I'm a recovering addict,' she said instead, and she wondered why she was being so honest with the cousin she'd only just met. She supposed it was because she didn't really have any other choice.

Rebecca's eyes widened. 'Do you have someone at home who can look after you – your boyfriend, or a friend?'

Eliza thought of Raven, then shook her head. As kind as Raven could be, he was also self-centred and selfish. He couldn't be anything else.

'Then you'll come home with me,' Rebecca said. Her voice was bossy and insistent, and Eliza knew she was used to getting her own way. 'You've had a terrible day and you're not in any sort of condition to be by yourself. I'm taking you back to Beaufont Hall.'

Chapter Nineteen

Buckinghamshire, recently

Cassie closed Eliza's diary for 1988 and felt hot tears well up in her eyes. She knew many would consider her grief to be irrational – after all, Lillie Boyle had passed away before she'd been born – but her great-aunt had become as real to her as Eliza had, and she was desperately sad that Lillie had lost her life just as she'd been on her way to rescue her daughter. It was tragically unfair. She shifted on the squishy sofa in the forget-me-not den at Beaufont and wiped away her tears. The important thing was that Lillie and Eliza had come together – in spirit, if not physically – before the former's death.

She swallowed hard and decided to clear her head by taking a walk around the grounds. Back in London, she'd felt as though the city was suffocating her. She'd been on edge waiting to hear back from Jake Walker, and in the end she'd begged Mr Heritage for a few days off so she could escape to the fresh air of the countryside. He had immediately told her to take as much holiday as she needed – she rarely had time off work – and she'd packed up her car and driven to Beaufont. On arrival, she'd installed a microwave in the kitchen, scrubbed one of the smaller bathrooms until it was fit for use, and vacuumed and dusted all the rooms she intended to live in. Beaufont might be falling to pieces, but she could make it her home while she waited to hear if her festival would receive the investment she'd worked so hard for.

She flung open the front door and made her way through the overgrown gardens and desolate-looking orchards. In one garden she found the cracked face of a long-abandoned sundial; in another, she discovered the remains of several broken ceramic pots. She tried to distract herself from the many fraught and demanding thoughts that swirled around in her head, but it was no use: she kept on returning to Eliza's diary, and in particular to the entries in which Eliza had written about Rebecca.

Rebecca had mentioned that she'd known Eliza, of course, but Cassie felt that her mother had somehow misled her; that she had played down her friendship with Eliza so that it had seemed inconsequential. She knew she'd have to read the next diary to discover if that was true or not. Perhaps Eliza had decided she didn't want to get close to the Tempests and the other interactions she'd had with Rebecca had been superficial and polite. But Eliza had desperately needed to be rescued, and Rebecca had tried to fill the void that Lillie had so tragically left. Cassie felt proud of her mother, but she was also slightly cross that Rebecca hadn't mentioned that she'd attended Lillie's funeral. But then she shouldn't be surprised. Rebecca had always disliked talking about the Tempests and hated remembering her family's history.

'Hey there,' Ed's voice called through the bushes. Cassie turned her head in his direction and shielded her eyes from the sun as she tried to spot him through the leaves. 'I recognised your car from the lane, so I thought I'd come and say hello. I didn't think you were coming back until the weekend.'

His glasses glinted in the brightness, and in the sunlight his red hair was ablaze. He looked different to the starchy, professional man Cassie had last seen in London, and she was pleased – she much preferred him like this, when he was relaxed, happy and real.

'I wasn't planning on coming back so soon,' she said with a smile, 'but I needed a break. I was going to ring you in a bit.' She could feel Ed's gaze on her tear-stained face; she knew her eyes would be red, that her nose would be blotchy, and that her weak smile would not fool him for a second.

'Are you okay?' he asked gently.

Cassie nodded. 'I've just been feeling a bit overwhelmed during the past few days. I needed to get away. Putting together the business plan exhausted me more than I thought, and I've been reading more of Eliza's diaries. They're quite harrowing.'

Ed put his hand gently on Cassie's lower back and guided her towards a bench at the bottom of one of the gardens. To her surprise, it looked as though it had recently been fixed. She caught Ed's eye, but he just shrugged and gave her a sheepish grin.

They sat on the bench in companionable silence for several long minutes. For the first time in a long time, Cassie found she felt awkward around Ed; she was unsure of herself and didn't know what to say. So she remained quiet and listened to the sound of birdsong in the trees. The grounds were silent and still, and the longer she sat there, the calmer and more centred she felt.

'Would you like to talk about it?' Ed asked eventually.

He was so kind-hearted that Cassie wanted to tell him everything; she wanted to confide her deepest, darkest secrets and for Ed to sweep her up and tell her that everything would be okay.

But she knew she couldn't. Ed wasn't a literary romantic hero like Mr Darcy or Benedick, who could suddenly make everything better for her because he had secret feelings for her like she did for him. He was her friend and nothing more.

'I'm okay,' she said, and kept her gaze fixed on the back of Beaufont Hall. She'd always known that the house held the Tempest family secrets, but for the first time she was beginning to wonder if she truly wanted to know them. Reading Eliza's diaries was a bit like opening Pandora's box, and she wasn't sure if she had the emotional strength to delve much further into them.

Ed looked at her carefully for a moment and then grinned down at her. 'Well, I have some news that might cheer you up,' he said. Cassie looked at him. 'Jake Walker rang me earlier. He wants to invest in the festival – that is, if you'd still like him to.'

Cassie's mouth dropped open. 'Are you serious?' she whispered.

'Deadly,' he replied, and then he laughed. 'He'd like to have another meeting to discuss the specifics, but it seems that this time next year you'll be hosting the first ever Beaufont Festival of Literature in these very grounds.'

Cassie's eyes filled with tears again, only this time they were ones of joy. She jumped up and hugged him. 'Thank you for helping me,' she whispered into his chest. 'Thank you for helping Beaufont Hall.'

'You're welcome,' Ed replied, but his voice had become stilted. He'd not put his arms around her, and she suddenly became aware that his body was stiff and uncomfortable against hers. She began to slowly untangle herself from him, but before she could free herself completely, he wrapped his arms around her and pulled her closer to him. Cassie could feel her heart racing as he squeezed her tighter, but when she glanced up at him, she realised he wasn't looking back down at her. His gaze was fixed on something in the distance; he appeared sad rather than happy.

'We saved Beaufont,' Cassie mumbled. 'We did it.'

'You did it,' Ed replied, and gently pulled himself away from her.

Cassie crossed her arms against her chest at the loss of warmth from his body, but Ed didn't notice her awkwardness. Instead he looked down at her and grinned – but it was a smile of friendship and shared achievement rather than anything romantic.

'Fancy some food at mine?' he asked brightly, as if their hug – their closeness – hadn't just happened. Cassie was torn: she wanted to spend all her free time with him, but her unrequited feelings of attraction towards him were beginning to make it difficult.

'Sure,' she replied casually, wishing with all her heart that she could get over him, or that he might start to fall for her.

'Is roast chicken okay?' Ed called an hour later from the depths of his refrigerator. 'I have some green beans and carrots too, although some of them may be on their last legs . . . If I'd known you were coming I'd have driven to Thame to get some supplies in. I'm not really much of a cook, to be honest.'

Cassie looked up from her position on the sofa and replied that chicken was fine. She took a sip of the white wine Ed had poured for her – a generous glass because they were celebrating – and tried to focus her thoughts on the festival. But it was hard. Her mind was filled with images of Lillie and Eliza, of Ed and the closeness of his body against hers before he'd pulled away. As far as she could tell, Eliza had never really known love – not the love of romantic novels, anyway – and Cassie knew she didn't want to be in that situation herself. She wanted an all-consuming, desperate passion, and she wanted it to be with Ed. It was heart-achingly upsetting that he didn't appear to want it with her.

When Ed rejoined her, he watched her carefully for a moment. 'You're thinking about Eliza's diaries, aren't you?' he commented.

Cassie nodded, although it wasn't strictly true. 'When I started reading them, I never could have imagined what I'd unearth,' she began. Her voice was soft and quiet, and rather than look directly at Ed, she watched the sun beginning to set. The sky was still a beautiful blue, but the streaky clouds had been tinted a pale pink. 'I'd hoped that they'd been written by a family member, of course, but when I discovered who Eliza and Lillie were, it made the diaries more real. Had they not died, perhaps I would have known them both; I certainly would have known Eliza.'

'It sounds like you've got to know her quite well from reading her diaries,' Ed remarked.

'I have, but it's heartbreaking. I know all her deepest, darkest secrets – all the things she'd have been ashamed of. She was addicted to heroin for years, and the only way she managed to drag herself away from it was because she became pregnant.'

Ed paused. 'She was pregnant?' he echoed.

'She'd been working as a prostitute and then the inevitable happened,' Cassie said sadly. 'She was at rock bottom when she found out, and Lillie was on her way to London to help when she was in the train disaster.'

Cassie noticed a confused expression on Ed's face, so she

elaborated. 'Lillie was caught up in the Clapham Junction rail crash. Do you remember it?'

Ed took a long drink of his wine. 'I remember my parents talking about it, but I was just a kid at the time. I would have been six or seven, something like that. They knew somebody who died in it.'

'Maybe it was Lillie,' Cassie suggested.

Ed shrugged. 'I can ask them.' He paused as he poured them both more wine. They'd already nearly finished one bottle, and the alcohol made it harder for Cassie to ignore her feelings for Ed. She wanted to reach out and touch him. 'But what happened to Eliza's baby?' he asked.

'I don't know,' Cassie replied as she played with the stem of her wine glass. She focused on the conversation at hand. 'In a way, I don't think I can bear to know. I know that Eliza died before I was born, but discovering that her baby died too would be devastating.'

'Maybe the baby didn't pass away?' Ed suggested, but Cassie shook her head.

'I don't think so. I can't help feeling that something happened to the baby, and Eliza was so overcome with grief that she tried to comfort herself with heroin and overdosed.' Her voice was hollow and she was visibly upset. 'I don't think I want to talk about this any more.'

Ed gently placed his hand on her arm, and Cassie found herself distracted by the warmth that came from it.

'Your mother would know what happened to Eliza and her baby,' he said after a moment. 'If you can't face reading the diaries, you could ask her to tell you.'

Cassie shook her head again. 'I can't. My mother thinks I only have a couple of Eliza's earlier diaries – she'd not be happy if she found out I'd lied, if she knew that I have all of them.

Besides, I'm beginning to wonder if this is the reason why she can't bear to talk about her family. When I started to read the diaries I assumed it was Lillie's disappearance that she kept so tight-lipped about, but what if it's Eliza's death that she finds so upsetting?'

'It could be,' Ed said. 'But you'll only know if you speak with her. You really should.'

'I know,' Cassie said in a small voice. 'And I will – but only when I've finished reading the diaries.' She looked at Ed then and saw that he looked sad for her. He was a good friend, and she wished she could settle for that. But she wanted more than just friendship from him.

'Now, let's really change the subject,' she said. 'I know you're not working because you got a humongous pay-off from the City, but would you consider helping me with the festival? I don't think I could pay you the sort of salary you're used to, but I could probably afford something.'

Ed ran his hands through his hair and looked so uncomfortable that Cassie wondered what she'd said wrong. 'What is it?' she whispered.

He shook his head. 'It's nothing . . . It's just that I've been thinking that maybe it's time for me to return to London. When I left, I was in a bit of a state, and I only ever really intended to come back to the village to get my head together, to sort myself out. And you know, I think I've done that now . . .' His voice trailed off.

'So you're moving back!' Cassie exclaimed with forced cheerfulness, although her heart was sinking. 'That'll be great!'

'I'll be in the village for a month or two while I find a new flat, but yes – I'm going back.' He looked up at her, and Cassie was struck by the greenness of his eyes, by the intensity that she saw in them.

'You don't have to, you know,' she said softly. 'You could stay.'

Ed took a big gulp of wine, and silence fell as the scent of roasting chicken filled the air.

Chapter Twenty

Buckinghamshire, 1988

Eliza perched uncomfortably on the overstuffed sofa and distracted herself by meditating on why she felt so out of place. The opulence of the Small Drawing Room of Beaufont Hall swooped upon her senses, and rather than trying to take it all in – from the sea-grey silk wallpaper to the rosy-gold cornicing to the rich Turkish rugs – she focused her gaze on the faded pink and clotted-cream covering of the sofa opposite her. The chintzy fabric had clearly seen better days, yet the vintage furniture added charm and history to the room. Generations of Tempests had reclined on the sofa on which she had chosen to sit, and now Eliza had joined their ranks. She had as much right to be here as Rebecca – who'd deposited her in the room before offering to fetch her a hot drink – yet she felt as if she'd invaded the house by stealth and was an unwelcome guest waiting to be discovered. She told herself to stop feeling so intimidated: Beaufont Hall belonged to her family and had once been home to her mother, even if she couldn't imagine Lillie growing up in this room.

'I managed to find a dusty tin of cocoa powder,' Rebecca announced as she strolled into the room. She placed a mug of lumpy hot chocolate on the gleaming side table next to Eliza, and then cautiously lowered herself on to the sofa opposite with a tentative smile. 'I hope it's okay.'

'I'm sure it will be fine,' Eliza murmured, but she didn't reach for it. Even though she'd allowed herself to be driven here from London, she still wasn't sure if she could, or should, accept any kindness from Rebecca. For wasn't Rebecca part of the family that had broken Lillie's heart?

'How are you feeling now?' Rebecca asked.

Eliza stared at her. Her cousin was flawless, a creamy-skinned vision of perfection whose life had been filled with charm and luck. In comparison Eliza felt dishevelled and dirty; after everything she'd been through, she wasn't sure she'd ever feel clean again.

'I'm okay,' she said eventually, and she realised that it was true – at least of her physical symptoms. She still felt the gnawing craving for heroin, still felt shaky and hungry with longing for it, but her desire had lessened. The blazing fire at Beaufont Hall had warmed her chilled bones, and the ever-present nausea of her pregnancy had eased slightly. 'But I really don't think I should be here.'

'Beaufont is your home too,' Rebecca said softly. 'That is, it can be if you'd like it to be.'

Eliza wanted to pull herself away from her cousin's assessing gaze. She could guess what Rebecca was thinking, and she could see pity in the sharp, familiar eyes that reminded her so much of Lillie.

'I don't need charity,' she said as firmly as she could, but the tone of her voice was fragile. 'I don't need anything at all.'

Rebecca took a sip of her own cocoa and looked fixedly at Eliza. 'But what about your baby?' she asked astutely. 'Does he?'

Her words slashed effortlessly at the performance Eliza was

trying so hard to enact, and she felt herself fall to pieces inside. She needed help, and she needed it desperately, but she didn't think she could take it from Rebecca, or any of the Tempests. Yet this wasn't just about her any more; it was about the tiny baby growing within her, and she couldn't let her family history hurt her child. Not when she had nothing at all, and the Tempests had everything.

'I don't know what to do,' she whispered, her remaining fight deserting her. 'I want my baby to have the start in life he deserves, but I don't know if I can give it to him. I don't know if I have the strength.'

Rebecca came across and sat on the sofa next to her cousin. She took her hand in hers. 'I know I don't know you, but you *are* family. Let me help you; let Beaufont help you.'

'How could you help me?' Eliza mumbled, and Rebecca considered it.

'We can help you financially – although we don't have much – but more importantly, we could *be* here for you. Daddy passed away years ago, so it's just me and my mother rattling around this big old house, at least until I get married and my fiancé James moves in. You could live here, and let us look after you.'

Rebecca's words collided with Eliza's heart. She couldn't remember the last time someone had offered to care for her, or if anyone apart from her parents ever had. An image of Jonathan engulfed her mind, but she banished it out of sight. He'd wanted to be there for her, but she had abused his friendship and lied so she could get her next hit. Would Rebecca become so infuriated by her that she'd give up on her too? Eliza didn't know if she could bear any more rejection, especially if it came from the heart of the Tempest family.

'What would your mother think of me staying here?' she asked.

Rebecca smiled. 'I'm sure she'll want to be there for you too,' she replied, and Eliza shut her eyes and knew she didn't have any other choice.

Eliza had been wary of settling into life at Beaufont Hall – that is, she was sure she'd never truly be able to – but it had only taken a matter of days before she began to feel comfortable. The house was decorated for Christmas, and she fell in love with the roaring fires, the scent of cinnamon in the air, and the two large trees that stood in pride of place in the hall ('We used to keep one in the Great Drawing Room, but I prefer having two here to greet visitors, and Mum lets me be in charge of decorations,' Rebecca had explained).

Rather than being made to feel like a visitor, Eliza had been left to her own devices, and she'd spent hours exploring every inch of Beaufont. When her heart ached with the loss of her mother, she would go and sit on the rug in what Rebecca had said was Lillie's old bedroom. She'd try to imagine her mother looking down at the rose garden through the window, or reading on her bed. When she wanted company – which didn't happen often, as she was still coming to terms with everything that had happened – she sought out Rebecca or her fiancé James, who'd perfected the art of being able to chatter away about absolutely nothing at all.

The one person Eliza stayed away from was Violet.

Violet Tempest was an older, more severe-looking version of Lillie, who carried herself as the matriarch of the family despite not yet being sixty. At mealtimes, Eliza felt Violet's cool gaze upon her, and she knew she was watching her, assessing her. But when she dared to look up to meet Violet's gaze, she found that her aunt would be looking elsewhere, and she wondered if she'd imagined being the focus of her attention. Eliza would toy with the healthy food on her plate and wonder if Rebecca had been entirely truthful with her. For while Violet didn't appear to mind Eliza's seemingly permanent move into Beaufont Hall, she wasn't warm or friendly towards her either. She kept her distance from her niece, and Eliza was happy for her to do so. When they did meet – on the stairs, in the Great Drawing Room – Eliza was polite, but she couldn't quite forgive her aunt for not keeping in contact with Lillie after she had been banished from the family home.

'Do you have everything you need?' Rebecca asked one afternoon as Eliza curled up on the sofa in her favourite room.

She loved everything about the tiny den, which she'd adopted as her own: she adored the forget-me-not wallpaper, the poppies on the tiles by the fireplace, the squashy sofa placed opposite the window. It was the one room in the majestic house – apart from the small guest bedroom in which she slept – in which she felt entirely at peace.

'I think so,' Eliza responded, holding up a small biscuit-coloured book. 'I found this in the library and thought I'd give it a try.'

Rebecca sat down next to her and took the book with a wistful smile. 'My mother used to read this to me when I was little,' she remarked as she turned the pages. 'Every night before I went to sleep I'd beg for my favourite story about how Milly Molly Mandy goes blackberrying. It was her favourite story when she was young too, so she never really minded.'

'I like the one about how Milly Molly Mandy makes a penny go a long way,' Eliza admitted, and Rebecca smiled at her again.

'I think your mother enjoyed that story too,' she replied, and handed the old book back. 'I once heard my mother and Aunt Aster recalling how Lillie used to make lemonade for the gardeners, but she always wanted flower seeds in return.'

Eliza was fascinated. 'Do you know many stories about when my mother was young?' she asked, but Rebecca shook her head.

'Not really,' she replied. 'When I was growing up, Lillie wasn't really mentioned. I was born five years after she left Beaufont, and by that time she was a memory, a ghost. Discussing her was something that upset everyone, so I learned not to. My mother could tell you lots of stories about their childhood if you asked her...'

As Rebecca's voice trailed away, Eliza thought of how Lillie had grown up with all this splendour, and wondered if it had been difficult for her to live in the mean little flat in Tottenham or the tiny house in Basingstoke. She supposed that the love that Bertie had showered her with would have more than made up for it.

'I will, in time.'

Rebecca toyed with a cushion and looked as if she were turning words over in her head. In the end she decided not to say whatever was on her mind, and instead shot a gentle smile at Eliza's small bump.

'How's the baby settling in?' she asked, and Eliza was relieved that she had changed the subject.

'Oh, he's fine,' she replied. 'It's quite a strange sensation, you know, being pregnant. Would you like children?'

Rebecca nodded. 'As soon as James and I are married we intend to start straight away. Even when I was a little girl it was my ambition to live here with my own family. It's all I've ever really wanted. I know that forging a life for myself outside of Beaufont isn't for me. Creating happiness here is what I want to do.'

'Well, you're doing a terrific job looking after me,' Eliza said warmly, and when Rebecca smiled back, she realised that this was what family was meant to be about: unconditional love.

*

Eliza had been asleep for only a few hours when she woke abruptly in the middle of the night. She'd dreamt that she was in Soho, behind the bar at Gossips, and when she woke, she half believed she was back in 1982. The actuality – that she'd been asleep in a bedroom at Beaufont Hall – was far more surreal to her than the dream had been, and it took her several minutes to adjust to her new reality.

She had just closed her eyes again when she heard a sound, the sound that had woken her. Rather than allowing herself to fall back to sleep, she strained to see if she could recognise it. It could have been a baby crying, or perhaps a cat mewing, and she instinctively and quietly climbed out of bed to open her bedroom door. She was met with silence. But after a moment she heard it again, and she crept along the dark corridors of the first floor towards the noise. There was little light, but she felt her way along the hall until she found herself outside Lillie's old bedroom. She could make out the gentle flickering of candlelight from under the closed door, and she was about to leave when she heard the cry again: a human sob ineffectually muffled. She stood there uncertainly, but before she could make a decision as to what to do next, she found that her hand had turned the doorknob.

She discovered Violet curled into a ball on Lillie's old bed, her face crimson and dripping with tears.

'I'm sorry, I didn't mean to disturb you,' Eliza began, but Violet had already sat up and was staring at her with unnerving intensity. Eliza started to back out of the room, but Violet held her hand up.

'Lillie?' she croaked, and Eliza froze. Nobody had ever mistaken her for her mother before.

'It's Eliza,' she said firmly but as gently as she could. 'Lillie's daughter Eliza.'

She didn't want to be in her mother's old bedroom late at night, and she certainly didn't want to be trapped within it with one of the Tempests. She would always feel a strong sense of loyalty towards her mother, and comforting her aunt was something she didn't feel able to do.

'Eliza,' Violet repeated slowly, and Eliza watched her aunt's mouth form the word as if she'd never said it before. 'Eliza.'

'I need to sleep,' Eliza muttered, but before she could escape, Violet spoke again.

'Don't go,' she instructed, and it was then that Eliza noticed that her aunt was fully dressed; she clearly hadn't yet gone to bed. Sodden handkerchiefs littered the bedroom floor, and old sepia photos of Lillie – photographs Eliza had never seen – were spread out all around her. Despite feeling desperately uncomfortable, Eliza found herself rooted to the spot, her eyes trained on the photograph closest to her.

'I want to tell you the truth,' Violet mumbled. 'I owe you that much at least.'

Eliza faltered. She longed to be back in her own bed, but she found herself instinctively drawn towards her aunt.

'Please sit down and let me tell you what really happened between your mother and the rest of the family,' Violet said, and Eliza knew that however unpalatable it might be, she needed to know.

She needed this to heal her.

Chapter Twenty-One

Buckinghamshire, 1960

Violet Tempest was not having a particularly good year. She was bored by her husband – a man she'd only really married because he'd been the first to ask, and her father had approved – and she felt continually wretched that she hadn't yet fallen pregnant. Her sister Aster had recently and rather effortlessly given birth to a beautiful daughter named Rose, but despite being older *and* married for longer, Violet had yet to conceive. It certainly wasn't for lack of trying, however much she dreaded those moments with her tiresome wet blanket of a husband.

After numerous visits to the village doctor, and several to a specialist in Oxford, she and her husband had been decreed perfectly healthy and had been gently informed that they'd be blessed with a baby in time: that they needed to be patient. When the doctor had delivered his diagnosis – in what Violet had considered to be a patronising and rather over-rehearsed manner – she'd wanted to scream. She was twenty-four years old and she wanted a baby *now*. Of course, she hadn't let her expression betray her emotions – that wouldn't do at all – but as soon as her husband had delivered her back to the comforting surroundings of Beaufont Hall, she'd cried her heart out.

If only tears could help make a baby; she had plenty of those within her.

As well as feeling as though her body had betrayed her, Violet was also listless, and spent much of her time wandering around Beaufont Hall looking for things to do. Her husband spent long periods away because of work – he'd taken a small flat in London because of his increasingly late nights in the office, which didn't exactly help with her campaign to start a family – and her sisters were distracted. Aster, of course, was now a full-time mother and barely left her cottage, but her youngest sister Lillie didn't seem to be around much either. Ever since she'd been on her first unaccompanied visit to London, she'd had her head in the clouds, and Violet knew she had been sneaking into the city when she'd claimed to be visiting local friends. When she returned, she almost always smelled of alcohol and cigarettes, and Violet was tempted to tell their parents what she was up to. But she hadn't said anything, not yet. She wanted to see what Lillie had to say for herself first.

She strode from the morning parlour towards Lillie's bedroom with that very purpose in mind. She was the eldest daughter, and therefore it was only proper and correct that she should ask Lillie what was going on. Violet had always known she was to spend the rest of her life at Beaufont – she would inherit it after her father died – and therefore it was her responsibility to uphold all the Tempest family traditions and values, and to make sure her sisters did the same. If she had children – *when* she had children, she told herself – they would be expected to behave properly too. She secretly hoped for a boy, an heir, who would pick up the mantle. Beaufont Hall had been dominated by women for far too long, and Violet had nothing but sympathy for her father, who'd been completely outnumbered. No wonder he spent all his time in his study, no doubt reminiscing about his time in India. She envied him being able to daydream about exotic locations and a more civilised way of life; she wished she had memories to escape into when the anguish of wondering if she was infertile overwhelmed her.

When she reached Lillie's bedroom, she knocked on the door and pushed it open, but her sister was nowhere to be seen. Violet sighed and was about to turn on her heel when she noticed that the bedroom felt different. It was a small room – one befitting the youngest, least important daughter – but Lillie had always made it homely, and liked to leave the window open so the scent of the rose garden below could drift up to where she slept. But today the window was tightly closed, and the room felt cold and without spirit. Violet pursed her lips and took a closer look around. As her eyes drifted across the room, she noticed with a start that Lillie's dressing table – normally covered with trinkets and fashion magazines – was bare. A quick look at the wardrobe showed that it was empty, and as Violet cast her eyes towards the bed, she realised that Lillie's beloved teddy bear, Ann, was not there.

She paused for a moment and wondered what she should do. Her instinct, of course, was to alert her father to the situation, but she wasn't entirely sure if there actually was a problem, and she wasn't one to plummet into ridiculous female hysterics – at least not until she knew all the facts. Perhaps there'd been a misunderstanding and Lillie had decided to change bedrooms. There were plenty of empty rooms on this floor of Beaufont alone, and she might have decreed that this bedroom, with its wallpaper of girls in fashionable outfits, was too childish for her. Violet swept out into the corridor and began looking in all the empty rooms to see if her sister was in one of them.

But she wasn't. There was no sign of her anywhere.

Violet decided to go to her own bedroom to try to collect

her thoughts, and it was when she entered her room that she saw the letter lying on her bed. Her name was written on the envelope in Lillie's distinctive hand, and at that moment Violet knew that something bad had happened. Lillie hadn't changed bedrooms. She'd decided to change her life.

31 May 1960
Tottenham, London

Dearest Violet,

By the time you read this, I shall have left Beaufont. I hope you aren't too upset with me. You probably are, but I simply couldn't help myself. I've left a letter for Mummy and Daddy and Aster in the Great Drawing Room, but I've written to you separately because, darling Vi, I wanted you to know the absolute truth — I've left for your sake, and for no other reason. I fear that if you're not already livid with me, you may be about to be, but I need you to know that everything I've done has been out of love. Please believe me when I say this is the absolute truth.

Oh darling Vi, I can hardly believe it myself, but I've fallen deeply for a man. His name is Bertie, by the way, Bertie Boyle, and he is everything I've ever dreamed of. I've not known him long, but he's already everything to me. And this is the part that will shock you the most — I'm pregnant. I know you'll disapprove because we're not married yet and I've only been seeing him for two months, but this is all I've ever wanted. I've gone to London to marry him and then we'll have to be vague about my due date. It's not ideal, but we're so happy together that we can hardly wait to meet our child. How we're going to be able to wait seven months I have no idea!

The thing is, the moment I discovered I was pregnant, the first thing I thought of was of you, and the troubles you've had falling pregnant yourself. When Aster delivered Rose, your face was a picture of joy, but Vi, I know you as well as I know myself, and I could see how haunted you were that she had produced a child when you've not yet been able to. I simply couldn't bring myself to be the reason for you to experience that hurt again, and I knew that if I stayed at Beaufont you'd have seven months of watching me bloom. So Bertie and I have decided that we will see out the pregnancy in London — we've found a small flat in north London, as you can see from this address — and we'll not come back to Beaufont until you're happy for us to. I long to be at home, but I couldn't ask for you to watch another pregnancy that isn't your own, not unless you were perfectly happy with it.

Of course, I've not told Mummy and Daddy I'm pregnant — could you imagine their faces! — but I'll send a letter home as soon as Bertie and I are married and we feel it's an appropriate time to share our news. I hope you'll keep our revelation under your hat for now. I know you will; I'd trust you with my life.

I have one more thing I need to share, and I know you will be as open-minded about this as I am. Bertie is a wonderful man — he's musical, hard-working, handsome, and has integrity, which I am in awe of. But he is also American. I'm not sure how Mummy and Daddy will react to the news that I'm to marry a poor foreigner rather than Jack or Kit or Charles.

So I beg of you, lovely Violet, when they read the letter I've left for them, could you please try to be on my side? I know they look to you as the person who understands more modern times, and I know — just know — *that if you can soften the inevitable blow, things will be agreeable in time.*

*I love you, always, and I look forward to your letter in
return.*

Your Lil x

Violet stared at the letter incredulously and felt a dull pain
in her heart. Lillie was *pregnant?* Tears filled her eyes, and she
fell on to her bed and smothered her face with a pillow so her
desolate cries wouldn't ring out throughout the house. At this
particular moment, she couldn't care less that Lillie had run
away to marry an American; all she could think was that her
youngest sister had managed to conceive without even trying.
Violet would be the last of the Tempest girls to start a family
– that was if she ever managed it at all.

A chill ran through her body as she thought of her parents'
reaction to Lillie's news. They didn't know she was pregnant,
but they would be intrigued about this Bertie Boyle fellow
who'd stolen her heart. Would they be put off by the fact that
he wasn't English and from a good family? Her father probably
would be. But Violet knew – just as Lillie did – that they would
come around to the idea in time. Lillie had always been slightly
different from both Violet and Aster, and behaving in such a
modern way was almost expected of her.

Violet clenched her fists tightly and wondered what to do
about this sorry mess. She was grateful that Lillie had considered her feelings concerning her pregnancy – however stoical
she liked to think she was, she wasn't sure she had the strength
to watch another sister's body blossom with new life, or to see
her face flushed with love – but she couldn't help but be jealous,
as well as furious.

She stood rather suddenly and, without truly thinking about
what she was about to do, strode to the Great Drawing Room,

located the letter Lillie had left for her parents, and threw it in the fire.

'Where on earth is your sister?' Mary Tempest asked as the family sat down for dinner. The table had been laid perfectly: the silver gleamed, the crystal glasses glittered, and the food looked delicious. Violet wasn't particularly fond of grouse, but she knew she wouldn't have to eat any of it, not once she'd delivered her news.

She looked at her mother and father and swallowed hard. 'She's not here,' she said somewhat lamely, and her father looked at her sharply.

'We can see that for ourselves, Violet. But where exactly is she? Run along and fetch her,' he commanded, as if Violet was ten years old rather than a married woman.

Violet suddenly wished that her husband had been able to come home that night. Although he was rather cowardly, he would be an unwitting ally; someone to provide comfort after the terrible thing she was about to do. She took a deep breath and then opened her mouth to let the lies drift out of their own accord.

'She's in London, Daddy,' she began. 'She left a letter for us. I have it here . . . though perhaps it would be better if I shared it after we've eaten . . .' She knew her parents wouldn't be able to eat dinner while there was an air of mystery over where their youngest daughter was. However Victorian they could be sometimes, they always put their children first.

'A letter?' Mary asked in bewilderment. 'She went to London and left a letter? Why on earth would she do that?'

Violet lowered her eyes. She knew that what she was about to do was wrong, but she didn't feel she had any other option. She could either tell her parents the truth about her sister, or she could amend Lillie's version of events slightly so that the next seven months of her own life were happier.

'Because I don't think she's planning on coming back to Beaufont.'

Philip Tempest rose to his feet and Violet watched his ivory napkin flutter to the ground. 'Hand me the letter,' he instructed, and she slipped the note out of her pocket. She'd spent an hour writing it that afternoon, perfecting both Lillie's handwriting and a new truth, amended ever so slightly from the real one.

As Philip read the letter, Violet watched him carefully. Her father was a great man – everybody said so – and she had grown up wanting to be just like him. She knew he had been disappointed to sire three girls, and she'd gallantly accepted the unspoken challenge that as the eldest, she'd have to be as much of a man as she could be. She was the heir to Beaufont Hall, and she took her lead in how she behaved from her father rather than her mother. But she'd never seen his composure shaken before, had never seen his face grow pale or his hands tremble. He sat down again and looked at his wife.

'Lillie has run away to London to be the wife of an American,' he said as calmly as he could, but both Mary and Violet knew that his steady voice hid a less than anchored demeanour. 'She's written that she's fallen in love with him, and that she no longer wishes to live at Beaufont – that she knows we'll never accept her fiancé and she wants nothing more to do with any of us.'

Mary Tempest clutched her napkin tightly and Violet watched her begin to cry. As she stood and comforted her mother, she felt conflicted. She disliked herself for being the bearer of such horrid, untruthful news, but she couldn't help but be secretly relieved that her parents had believed the letter she'd penned.

'But Daddy,' she said, her diamond-cut vowels hiding her

deception, 'that doesn't sound like Lillie at all. She's always been wilful, but she would never be so hurtful. This must be that man's influence over her.'

Philip stared at the letter in front of him. 'We must find her,' he said. 'No matter how hard it may be — and it will be hard if she has already married and taken this man's name — we must track her down and talk some sense into her. It's our duty as parents. I can accept whoever she wishes to take as a husband, but I cannot accept that she's walked out of our lives for ever. I won't.'

'May I please see the letter again?' Violet asked, and Philip handed it to her wordlessly. She cast her gaze on it, despite knowing the contents off by heart.

'She hasn't included an address, and she's written that she doesn't want to be found, not yet. She says she'll write again in time, but for now she wants to be left to enjoy her new life.'

'She doesn't know what she's saying,' Mary said sorrowfully, and Violet felt a pang of guilt. She loved her parents and would never want them to suffer, but the alternative was worse. 'I agree with Violet: this man of hers has led her astray.'

'She doesn't mention her fiancé's name,' Violet continued. Her eyes remained fixed on the heavy cream parchment in her hand. 'It would be impossible to find her, however hard we tried. So what should we do?' She shifted her gaze to her father, who stared blankly into the distance. He didn't speak for several moments, and Violet knew he was turning over every option in his mind, desperately attempting to think of a way to find his youngest daughter and bring her home.

'We have to let her find her own way,' he said eventually, and Violet felt a tiny stab of triumph sweep through her. She ensured it didn't show on her face. 'She says she'll write in time, and we need to trust that she will. We've raised her well, and we need to have faith in that.'

Violet nodded and looked down at her plate of food. Suddenly her appetite had returned.

2 June 1960
Beaufont Hall, Buckinghamshire

Dearest Lillie,

I've tried several times to write this letter to you, tried to make it eloquent and as pleasing as possible, but I fear there is no easy way to say what I need to tell you. Please do sit down, and please prepare yourself for the worst.

When Daddy found your letter he was livid – furious, in fact. I tried my best to talk him around, but he won't stand for you marrying an American of no social standing, and he said that the thought of you having children with your fiancé would be the absolute worst thing you could do to the Tempest name. Mummy was very quiet about the whole thing, but I'm afraid she feels the same as Daddy. You know that even if she didn't, she'd never go against him.

Lillie, darling, this is so very hard for me to write, but you need to know that our parents have said they want nothing more to do with you – that they no longer think of you as their daughter. Please leave this with me; give me time to talk them around. I'm sure that I may be able to soften their opinion, and when I have, I'll let you know. In the meantime, I don't think it a good idea for you to write to the house. Leave it for a while; let the air cool and the waters calm. Do not do anything to anger them further.

I'll write you to again in time to let you know how things are. Until then, I'll think of you often and with fondness.

Love to Bertie, who I look forward to meeting one day, and keep well — you'll be a mother soon, and I look forward to being an aunt to your child.

Violet x

It wasn't until five years later, after Violet had eventually given birth to Rebecca — who would be her only daughter despite several more half-hearted years of trying — that the enormity of what she'd done back in 1960 began to haunt her. As she watched her small blonde daughter sleep, she couldn't help but think of Lillie, the sister she'd betrayed so badly because of her own jealousy. Rebecca reminded Violet so strongly of Lillie in both looks and disposition that she wondered if this was what the hippie movement called 'karma'; if having a daughter who was the spit of the woman she'd been so disloyal to was what she deserved.

Lillie had written to Beaufont only twice more. The first letter was a sad reply to Violet's news that she'd been disowned by their parents; the second contained a message that she'd given birth to a beautiful baby girl whom she'd named Eliza. Lillie explained that life in Tottenham was hard, but that she was happy, and she asked Violet to share the news of her baby with their parents to see if it would soften their feelings towards her. Both times Violet screwed up the letters and burned them without replying; she couldn't think of how she could undo the lies she'd told, and life was easier if she didn't think of Lillie or her new niece.

Her parents stopped planning how they could track their youngest daughter down, stopped talking about her because it hurt too much, and eventually life at Beaufont Hall shifted. Nobody ever forgot about Lillie, but they'd found a way to move on without her.

Violet lived in fear that Lillie would one day turn up; that both she and her parents would discover what she'd done. But despite sensing the ghost of her sister in the garden – a flash of long hair beyond the lilac hydrangeas, the sound of humming as she trailed through the orchards looking for fallen apples – Lillie never returned to Beaufont. She had been led to believe that the Tempests wanted nothing more to do with her, and Violet never heard from her again.

Chapter Twenty-Two

Buckinghamshire, 1988

Eliza stared at Violet in dismay. She'd spent her whole life wondering why the Tempests had disowned Lillie, and she couldn't quite believe that the elderly lady in front of her had been the source of so much pain. The flickering shadows from the candlelight whipped across Violet's face, and as Eliza stared at the self-pitying tear stains on her cheeks, she felt herself grow angry. The woman in front of her was a monster who'd carelessly thrown her youngest sister away out of jealousy and spite.

'My mother spent her whole life wondering why her parents had rejected her so ruthlessly,' Eliza said angrily. She kept her voice low and quiet so she'd not disturb Rebecca, but she couldn't keep the tone from being both tight and distressed. 'She had no idea that you were behind it, that you'd cut her off from the rest of the family because she was pregnant with me.'

Violet couldn't raise her eyes to meet Eliza's, but her hands grasped her handkerchief so tightly that her knuckles turned white. 'I've regretted it every day of my life,' she said quietly. Her blue eyes — Tempest eyes — began to water again. 'I want to make amends, and since I can't apologise to Lillie, I'd like to do so to you.'

Eliza was astonished. She ignored the tears falling down

Violet's face and crossed her arms over her chest. 'There's nothing you can ever do or say that can make up for this,' she said bluntly. 'My mother had a happy life regardless of the decisions you made, but we always lived with a sense of rejection; a sense that the Tempests never thought we were good enough.'

Violet picked up an old photograph from the bedspread and gazed at it remorsefully. 'I'm glad she was happy,' she said faintly, and looked at Eliza. Her once-sharp eyes were cloudy, and her hands were shaking. 'I spent years searching for her, you know,' she continued, as if she was oblivious to the dark stare Eliza had cast in her direction. 'But I never found her. I'd forgotten her married name, you see. I so desperately regretted throwing all her letters on the fire... so regretted not writing down her address, the name of her husband, the area in London in which she'd chosen to live.'

Eliza thought of the estate where she'd grown up and compared it to the faded splendour of Beaufont Hall. She couldn't imagine Violet Tempest picking her way through the litter and discarded cigarette butts of Tottenham; couldn't imagine her walking up the concrete steps to the tiny flat that her parents had made their home.

'I'm glad you never found us,' she said sourly, and this time she didn't bother to lower her voice. 'I'm glad my mother never saw you, or discovered how you'd betrayed her. It would have broken her heart all over again.'

She watched her aunt swallow hard. 'I'd do anything to turn back time,' Violet said weakly. 'Anything at all to make amends. I always thought I'd have many more years to find her, and that in time we'd eventually meet again and I could explain everything. I never expected her to forgive me, but I hoped we'd be able to find a way to have some sort of relationship;

that she'd be able to come back to Beaufont with her family to show them who she was.'

'We knew who my mother was,' Eliza said in a voice she didn't recognise. It chilled her, and she was stunned to realise she was capable of such anger. 'Lillie wasn't the carefree person who lived at Beaufont, perhaps, but she was a better person because of what you did – she was strong, she was resourceful, and she was in love. Maybe she had those qualities before she left Beaufont, but I think she found courage within herself after you sent her that deceitful letter. I think she managed to break free from the Tempests when she read it – and thank God she did if you're an example of the family she came from.'

Violet looked despondent, and Eliza was glad. Her mother had fought hard for everything she'd loved, and Eliza was proud to be able to stand up for her.

'Please let me try to make it up to you,' Violet said weakly. 'Please let me – and Beaufont – look after you. Let us do this for you now your mother is gone.'

Eliza's legs wobbled but her resolve was strong. 'There's nothing I'd like less, and I know that my mother – if she was alive – would feel the same. Lillie made her way in the world without the support of her family and I can do the same. I've never needed the Tempests, and I never will.'

Her aunt reached out for her. 'Please,' she begged again, but Eliza shook her head. It was too late. Violet clutched at her chest and fell backwards on the bed, and the stricken expression on her face turned to one of deep, agonising pain.

Eliza peered at her and wondered what on earth she should do. She wanted to walk away – to pretend she'd never encountered her aunt this evening, to pretend she hadn't been told the dark family secret that Violet had kept to herself for nearly thirty years – but she couldn't bring herself to do so.

'Are you okay?' she asked reluctantly, but there wasn't so much as a flicker of movement or acknowledgement from her aunt. 'Violet? Can you hear me?' Still Violet didn't shift, and Eliza stared at her. Something was badly wrong.

She raced towards Rebecca's bedroom and hammered on her door until her cousin appeared. Rebecca's sleepiness quickly gave way to alertness, and she looked at Eliza in alarm.

'Is it the baby?' she asked breathlessly, and Eliza shook her head. She wasn't sure she could speak, or if she could, what she would say. She pulled on the sleeve of Rebecca's dressing gown and tried to drag her towards Lillie's old bedroom, but Rebecca stood firm. 'What on earth is the matter?' she asked sensibly.

Eliza found her voice. 'It's Violet... your mother.' She swallowed. 'I think she's dying.'

Rebecca stared at her in disbelief, as if Eliza was playing a particularly cruel practical joke. When she realised she was serious, she ran to the telephone at the other end of the corridor and phoned for an ambulance as calmly as she could. Eliza watched her comfort Violet as they waited for the emergency services to arrive, and while she felt sorry for Rebecca, she realised that for her aunt she felt absolutely nothing at all.

'Mummy's had a heart attack,' Rebecca said wearily as she flopped on to the armchair in the small den. It was the following evening, and Eliza had been huddled up reading *Charlie and the Chocolate Factory*, but as soon as Rebecca had walked into the room, she'd put the book down. Her cousin's face was pale and her hair was tangled, and Eliza felt nothing but compassion for her. 'The doctors told me to come home to sleep; they said they'd phone if she takes a turn for the worse.' She frowned. 'As if I could sleep at a time like this.'

Eliza pulled the blanket she'd draped around her shoulders

closer to her body and offered her cousin a small, sympathetic smile. In the dark, cold night, Rebecca seemed fragile and exhausted. Eliza suddenly realised that it was Christmas Eve, but it was unlikely there would be much cheer in Beaufont Hall over the next few days.

'Can I make you a drink, or some soup?' she offered, but Rebecca shook her head. Her gaze fixed upon Eliza, who shifted slightly. Rebecca looked as though she had something on her mind other than her mother's condition.

'What were you and Mummy doing in Lillie's old bedroom so late last night anyway?' she asked quietly. 'I noticed there were photographs of Lillie on the bed, and handkerchiefs all over the floor, but I can't quite work out what was going on. Was Mummy telling you stories about their childhood?'

Eliza considered how she should answer the question, whether she should edit events for the benefit of her cousin, but she quickly dismissed the idea. Violet's story had taught her that however unpalatable the truth, and however much it might hurt other people, honesty was the only option in situations like these.

'I found her in there,' she said simply, and Rebecca looked confused. 'I'd been asleep but I heard someone crying. When I followed the sound, I discovered Violet on Lillie's old bed, surrounded by photographs of my mum.'

'Had she already collapsed?' Rebecca asked, and Eliza shook her head.

'She wanted to tell me about my mother . . . about how Lillie came to be ostracised by the rest of the family. She confessed that Philip and Mary hadn't dismissed her for falling in love with Bertie; that it was she who'd manipulated Lillie into believing that she'd been rejected.'

Rebecca became extremely still. 'I know I should probably

ask you to explain, but I don't think I have the strength to process a revelation so big tonight.' She leant back and rested her head against the high back of the chair. 'Do you think you can forgive Mummy for what she did?'

Eliza shook her head. 'I don't think I ever will,' she said softly, and she could see fresh hurt in Rebecca's eyes. Her cousin had experienced an appalling day, with more pain possibly yet to come, but Eliza couldn't soften her words. She felt remorse at further upsetting her, but she had to be true to herself; she had to be honest. 'My mother lived believing that her family wanted nothing to do with her, and when my father died she had nobody at all – not even me. Not really.'

Rebecca's usually perfect posture relaxed into a slouch. 'I understand,' she said eventually, and both girls fell silent, with Rebecca unable to meet Eliza's eyes. A light patter of rain fell outside, and Eliza wondered if it was cold enough to turn to snow. She couldn't imagine Beaufont Hall in the summer, and she wondered if she'd be here long enough to experience it; if Rebecca would allow to her to stay given that she'd probably triggered her mother's heart attack.

'I don't think I'll be able to leave in the morning,' she said eventually, 'but I can leave after Boxing Day if the trains are running again. I can go back to where I was living in London.'

Rebecca stared at her incredulously. 'Why would you leave?'

Eliza looked down at her lap. 'Because it was during her confession that your mother had her heart attack. I wouldn't blame you if you hated me because of it.'

Rebecca continued to gaze at Eliza; then, quite without warning, she burst out laughing. 'Are you always so melodramatic?' she asked, and Eliza bit her lip in confusion. 'Of course I don't blame you. To be honest, I'm relying on you to be here. If Mummy does . . . well, if things take a turn for the worse, I'd appreciate you being around. James could come and stay, but I like your company. Since you've been here, Beaufont doesn't seem so empty, and it feels happier. The house was built for a family, and you're part of ours.'

Eliza considered her cousin's words. Violet's confession was proof that the Tempests hadn't disowned the Boyles, yet she wasn't sure she'd ever be able to change the way she thought, if she could ever outgrow her insecurities. She'd once again presumed she was being rejected, and had once more assumed the worst.

'I'll stay,' she said faintly, and then realised what she was agreeing to. She took a deep breath and committed herself to doing the right thing. 'And when Violet comes home, I'll help you nurse her until she's better.'

Rebecca looked surprised but quickly composed herself. 'I'd understand if you didn't want to be around my mother,' she said sympathetically, but Eliza shook her head.

'I don't think I'll ever be able to forgive her for what she did, but I'm not going to run away from her or from Beaufont Hall. I'll learn to accept what happened, and I promise I'll be around to help you through whatever happens next.'

Rebecca was just about to thank her when the telephone began to ring.

The two girls froze and looked at each other. They knew without question that Violet had passed away.

Chapter Twenty-Three

London, recently

'There's so much I want to talk to you about,' Cassie said to her mother in a tight, quiet voice, 'that I don't quite know where to begin.'

Cassie had been in her bedroom, reading Eliza's diaries, and she'd become so stunned by what she'd learnt that her eyes had grown wider and wider. She'd been slightly surprised when she'd first seen her mother's name written in Eliza's shaky hand, but then – despite Eliza's spidery handwriting becoming neater with her sobriety – the contents of the diaries became more and more shocking. Cassie couldn't get her head around everything she'd found out, and she knew she could no longer put off speaking to her mother. She'd stalked through the house until she'd found her, and then stared at her accusingly.

Rebecca looked back at her daughter in surprise. She'd been sitting on the sofa in the living room – a chintzy pink and cream sofa from one of the drawing rooms at Beaufont Hall – folding up the dresses that Henry and Alice hadn't used for their production of *A Midsummer Night's Dream*. Swathes of velvet and antique lace lay in puddles at her feet, and Cassie looked at the musty dresses that had once belonged to her grandmother and found she no longer cared what happened to them. She was furious with Violet and what she'd done to Lillie Tempest.

'Darling, what on earth is the matter?' Rebecca asked, but her voice wavered, and for a moment Cassie could picture her self-assured mother as a younger woman; a nervous, uncertain woman who'd timidly approached Eliza Boyle at Lillie's funeral because it had been the right thing to do.

'Eliza wrote about everything in her diaries,' Cassie replied simply, holding up several water-stained notebooks in shades of red and blue. 'She wrote about how you persuaded her to live with you and Granny at Beaufont... and then she described Granny's confession about what she did to Lillie. I can't believe I didn't know any of this.'

Rebecca looked as though she wanted to snatch the diaries out of her daughter's hands. Instead she darted her eyes away from them and stared straight into Cassie's blue eyes. 'I thought you said you'd not discovered any more diaries,' she said quietly.

Cassie shrugged. 'I just didn't tell you,' she replied. 'How could Granny have done that to her own sister? And why didn't you tell me how close you and Eliza became?'

Rebecca's normally cool composure was shaken. 'I told you that I knew Eliza,' she said eventually. 'I showed you a photograph of me and her together, and I told you that we were becoming friends when she passed away.'

Cassie frowned. This was true, of course, but she still felt as though her mother had misled her.

'But what about what Granny did to Lillie – why didn't you tell me about that?'

'Because I was ashamed of what she'd done,' Rebecca replied crossly, and then she sighed and bit her lip. 'Now, how many more of Eliza's diaries do you have in your possession?' she asked. Cassie knew there was no point in being evasive.

'There's just one more,' she replied. 'The one she must have written before she died.'

Rebecca was lost in thought. 'I knew that she kept diaries, of course,' she said eventually, 'but I never asked her what she wrote about – and nor did I ever read them, not really. After she died, I bundled them up and put them in the library for safe-keeping, and I suppose I must have forgotten about them. Your father and I had just married, you see, and we were so busy finding a home in London that they slipped my mind . . .'

'She wrote about her life,' Cassie said simply. 'She wrote about how bored she was when she lived at home with her parents, how exciting it was when she moved to Soho, but she also wrote about the more difficult parts of her life – about when her parents died, her addiction to heroin . . . Mum, we really need to talk about this, it's important to me.'

Rebecca nodded. 'I never wanted you to find out about all this, and I certainly never wanted you to discover what your grandmother did,' she said.

'But why?' Cassie asked.

Rebecca gave her a faint smile. 'Because ever since you were little, you've idolised anything to do with the Tempests. You put your grandmother on such a pedestal that I couldn't bear for you to know the despicable things she was capable of.'

'I don't suppose you ever talked to her about it?'

Rebecca shook her head. 'I'd grown up hearing whispers about my missing aunt Lillie, and I'd hero-worshipped the idea of her. I knew she'd left Beaufont Hall and no longer spoke to anyone in the family, but I assumed she'd chosen to do that herself. I thought she had rebelled against family and tradition, and when I was a teenager I found this idea attractive. I used to spend hours in her bedroom wondering what she was like, what she was doing. I pictured her having a gay old time in London; I imagined her attending glamorous parties and having midnight dinners with debonair gentlemen.'

'The truth was quite different, wasn't it?' Cassie said, and Rebecca nodded. 'She lived on a council estate in London with little money and little hope.'

'That's true, of course,' Rebecca said, 'but she was in charge of her destiny, and she made her own choices. She met Bertie at a party in Chelsea in 1960, and within a couple of months of that first meeting she'd packed up her belongings and run away to be with him. She may have had little in terms of material possessions, but she had love – real love – and I've always thought that more important.'

'Lillie thought so too,' Cassie said softly. 'Do you think her parents – your grandparents – would have accepted Bertie and Eliza if they'd known about them?'

Rebecca looked directly at her daughter, and Cassie could see sadness in her eyes. 'I like to think they would have,' she eventually replied, 'but who knows? My mother stole that opportunity for her.'

'I can't believe Granny did that,' Cassie said. 'I know I never met her, but I just can't believe anyone would be so cruel to their own sister. I'd never do that to Alice or Henry.'

Rebecca smiled sadly. 'My mother was always uptight and controlling. I used to think it was because of her upbringing, but I think the guilt she felt was probably eating her up inside. It would have been a hell of a thing for her to live with, and I think that was punishment enough for her – and in the end Eliza thought so too.'

They sat in silence for a moment, each lost in their own thoughts. Eventually Cassie cut into them.

'Mum, would you like to read Eliza's diaries?'

Rebecca's eyes became misty. 'I don't think I could bear to.

And I have to say that I really don't like the idea of you reading any further. Her last months were happy ones, and she was full of hope for the future, but I really would rather you didn't read any more.'

'I'd like to know what happened to her,' Cassie said in a small voice, and as she watched a solitary tear trickle down her mother's face, she knew that Rebecca would keep no more family secrets from her. 'I don't think I want to know tonight, but once I've read Eliza's final diary, will you tell me how she passed away?'

Rebecca nodded sadly, and Cassie stood and embraced her tightly.

Buckinghamshire, recently

Cassie walked through Beaufont Hall carrying two mugs of tea and realised that since she'd read the majority of Eliza's diaries – and now knew of the darkest Tempest family secrets – the house felt different. The undercurrents of the mansion, which had previously been dominated by the righteousness and Victorian values of Violet Tempest, had shifted slightly, at least for her. For Cassie could now sense the subtle ghost of Eliza within the austere walls; she could see a tiny imprint of the pluck and spirit that Eliza had carried with her throughout her life. Cassie stood in the doorway to the forget-me-not den and breathed in the scent of the room. Was it serendipity that she loved the room at Beaufont that Eliza had thought of as her own, much like the coincidence that she felt comfortable in the building that had once been Gossips? Or could it just be that this room had been singled out by both of them because of the lack of boastfulness in its decor, the lack of ostentatiousness in the way it felt?

She leant her head against the door frame and wondered how often her mother had stood in that exact same position. She'd have seen Eliza pregnant on the sofa in front of her; there would have been a blanket draped around Eliza's shoulders and a book taken from the library in her hands. She thought then of Rebecca and how kind she'd been to Eliza, and how strong she'd been for her. Cassie had never felt particularly close to her mother – not in the way she'd have liked to – but after reading Eliza's diaries, she felt as though she'd seen a different side to Rebecca, and she loved her even more for it.

'What's up?' Ed asked, looking up from his iPhone. He'd been fiddling with it when Cassie had gone to the kitchen to make them cups of tea. He looked strained and tired, but Cassie was too caught up with the imagery in her head to properly notice.

'I was just thinking about my mother and Eliza, and the time they spent in this room,' she admitted. She handed him his mug, and as his fingers brushed hers, she tried not to respond to it. No matter how comfortable she felt with Ed, she'd never stopped reacting to his touch. She'd probably never stop being attracted to him – her feelings were too strong to ever disappear.

'I think I'll probably read Eliza's last diary in here,' she continued quickly. 'I know I'll never know for certain, but I like to think she'd have written some of the entries on this sofa.'

'It will probably be quite hard for you to say goodbye to her,' Ed said softly, and Cassie was once again struck by how perceptive he was.

'I know,' she admitted in a small voice. 'I just wish I could make amends for what my grandmother did . . . I wish I could somehow go back in time to save both Eliza and Lillie.'

Ed placed his mug on the floor and patted Cassie's arm somewhat awkwardly. 'I know we can't magically make a time machine appear, but you *are* saving Beaufont Hall – and that's quite a feat in itself.'

Cassie nodded and thought about the festival. She'd not done much work on it since Jake Walker had said he'd invest, and she knew that she needed to leave her job at Heritage Books and start concentrating on it. The first thing she wanted to do was to set up an office at Beaufont, install high-speed Internet and move into the house more permanently. That hadn't been a big or difficult decision to make when she'd thought that Ed would be in the village, but now that he was moving back to London, she wasn't sure if she was looking forward to being here quite so much. Beaufont would be a much lonelier place without him.

'How are you, anyway?' she asked. 'When do you think you'll be moving to London?'

Ed shifted his gaze to the window. 'I've decided I'm not going to go,' he said eventually.

Cassie felt her heart soar but she told herself to try and ignore it.

'Is Grace going to move here instead?'

'Grace?' Ed asked.

'I thought you were moving back to London to be with Grace,' Cassie admitted, and Ed laughed.

'That was never on the cards,' he said.

'But I thought . . . I thought that when you went to meet her that time, you were getting back together with her. I thought she was the reason you were leaving Beaufont.'

Ed shook his head. 'I saw her to apologise for how awful I was when we were together. It was cathartic, in a way – we're now in a much better place. I think we might even be able to become friends in time.'

'So why *were* you going to move back to London?' Cassie asked. She tried to keep her voice steady, but her heart was racing. She was delighted that Ed wasn't going to move away, but at the same time she was dismayed – seeing him more often would make it harder for her to keep her feelings for him in check.

Ed swallowed, and Cassie watched his Adam's apple shift in his throat. 'I just thought it was the right thing to do – it had always been my plan, and it made sense to stick with it. But I'm not the same man I was in London, and I don't think I'd be happy there. Not really. It was my mother who made me realise it – she gave me quite a talking-to.'

Cassie found she could picture the scene between Ed and Valerie Winter perfectly.

'The thing is,' Ed said slowly, 'my mother also thought that I was moving back to London to get away from you – which wasn't the case at all.'

'Why would she think that?' Cassie's voice was only just louder than a whisper.

'She assumed I had feelings for you and that I was scared of them,' Ed said with a short laugh. 'I told her she was being ridiculous, that I've been helping you with the house and the festival and that's all, but Mum thought there was more to it. I told her it wasn't true, of course,' he said hurriedly.

'Of course,' Cassie echoed, but she felt crushed. Hearing Ed confirm that he didn't like her in that way was a bitter blow.

'I mean, we're friends, aren't we?' Ed said, and Cassie nodded. 'I'm not the sort of man who'd ever want to ruin a friendship by letting sex get in the way of it. I've seen so many mates lose their female friends that way, and I like you too much to risk that – as attractive as you are.'

'You're absolutely right,' Cassie murmured, although inside she felt as though her heart was splintering into a thousand sharp little pieces. 'Why ruin a good friendship?'

'And if the offer is still open, I'd love to help you with the festival,' he continued. 'I can't think of anything I would like to do more.'

Cassie swallowed hard. 'Even though I'll only be able to pay you pennies?' she asked.

'Even if you can only afford to pay me with cups of tea and biscuits,' Ed said with a smile, and it took everything Cassie had to be able to smile back at him.

Chapter Twenty-Four

Buckinghamshire, 1989

James Cooke had been fidgeting nervously at the front of the chilly village church for the past ten minutes, and Eliza was about to go and offer him a few reassuring words when the organist played the first notes of Bach's Air on the G String. James stopped pulling at his collar, stood extremely still for a split second, and then turned on his heel to watch his fiancée enter the church. The tense, anxious expression on his face relaxed into an excited smile when he caught Rebecca's eye.

Rebecca, of course, looked beautiful. The current fashion was for embellished shoulders and puffed sleeves, but she had remained true to her traditional values and was dressed in her mother's wedding gown – an ivory satin dress from the late 1950s. The square neckline displayed her delicate collarbones, the chiffon bow accentuated her narrow waist, and the full skirt of the dress floated gracefully over the floor as she walked slowly down the aisle towards her husband-to-be. Her vanilla-blonde hair was swept up into a haughty chignon, and diamonds glittered at her ears, but they couldn't distract from the antique Tempest family tiara. It wasn't extravagant, and nor was it particularly in vogue, but Eliza had never seen anything so exquisite. Glittering diamonds and natural rosy pearls sat on delicate yellow gold, and as Rebecca glided past the pew in which she sat, Eliza wondered if one day she too would marry; if one day she'd be able to wear the Tempest tiara. She hoped so.

Behind Rebecca trailed two bridesmaids in peach ballerina gowns – both of whom Eliza knew to be the daughters of one of her cousin's school friends – and a familiar-looking boy of about nine years of age. Eliza observed him carefully as he scowled in his sailor outfit and straw boater. He pushed his smudged glasses up his nose, and it was then that she saw a flash of reddish-brown hair under his hat. Of course, she thought, it was the son of Alan Winter, the man who looked after the house. Eliza smiled at the boy encouragingly, and when he glared at her in return, she had to stifle her laughter. He clearly hated what he'd been asked to wear.

After a wedding ceremony full of classic, time-honoured prayers and quiet contemplation about the life on which Rebecca and James were about to embark, the couple were pronounced husband and wife. Polite applause rang through the church, and as Eliza clapped, she felt her baby kick. He'd been remarkably active recently, keeping her awake at night as she desperately tried to find a comfortable position to sleep in, and he felt low in her body. He wasn't due for another month, and even though Eliza was counting the days until she could meet him, she hoped he'd hang on until Rebecca was back from her Italian honeymoon; her cousin had said she'd hold her hand during the delivery.

Eliza considered how generous Rebecca had been to her, and she felt grateful and blessed. If it hadn't been for Rebecca, she wasn't sure what would have happened to her. Would she still be on Meard Street, turning tricks despite a flowering, pregnant belly? Or would she have begun to shoplift instead, looking for a fast way to make money that didn't involve spreading her legs? The life that she had inhabited a year ago seemed so repulsive to her now, and thankfully so far away. For the first time in her life, she felt just like everyone else . . . and that was good enough for her.

Eliza found her place setting in the large marquee that had been erected in the grounds of Beaufont, and was pleased to see that she'd been put next to Alan and Valerie Winter and their son Edward, who was currently causing quite a scene, throwing a tantrum over his boater hat and jumping up and down on it instead of sitting in his chair. Valerie remained cool and poised. Eliza envied her calm and hoped her own mothering skills would be as impressive.

'He has to get it out of his system,' Valerie proclaimed as she helped pull out Eliza's chair and watched her settle into it. 'If he doesn't destroy that wretched hat now, he'll be in a terrible mood all afternoon. I don't quite know what Rebecca was thinking, putting him in that outfit.'

'I do,' Alan said. 'I imagine she saw Prince William dressed in something similar for Prince Andrew's wedding and thought it would be the thing to do. Rebecca is a stickler for doing things properly – just as Violet was.'

Eliza smiled. The Winters seemed to know her cousin well.

'When is yours due?' Valerie asked.

'Next month,' Eliza replied, and Valerie gazed at her thoughtfully.

'It's a boy,' she said knowingly. 'You've got a rather neat bump, and everyone says that when it's a boy, the bump is more to the front.'

Eliza smiled. 'I've always felt like he's a boy,' she confided, placing her hands on her stomach lovingly. 'Was your bump to the front when you were carrying Edward?'

'I think so, but I felt huge all over – I *was* huge all over, unlike you.' Valerie glanced at Edward for a moment and noticed that he was cramming bread into his mouth. She smiled apologetically at Eliza and then shook her head at her son. 'Edward, stop that this instant – you'll spoil your appetite.'

'Don't care,' the boy replied sullenly.

Valerie turned back to Eliza with a fixed, determined beam. 'I was told that the Terrible Twos were the worst part of childhood, but nobody thought to mention the Naughty Nines. I don't know what has got into him today.'

'Don't like weddings,' Ed piped up. 'Don't like love. It's boring.'

Eliza laughed. She enjoyed Ed's spirit. 'One day you'll meet a girl and feel differently,' she offered, but Ed rolled his eyes.

'I won't,' he said stubbornly. He looked at Eliza's stomach. 'You have a baby in you. Can I see it? Is it a boy baby?'

Valerie coughed. 'Edward,' she warned, 'you're being rude.'

But Eliza touched her arm. 'I don't mind,' she said, and turned to Ed. 'I do have a baby in me, but you can't see him just yet. You'll be able to in a month's time, though, when he comes.'

Ed eyed the bump suspiciously.

'If you put your hand on my stomach and keep it there for long enough, you may be able to feel the baby kick. He might grow up to be a footballer, like Gary Lineker,' Eliza continued gently.

Ed left his chair and stood in front of her. He reached out cautiously and placed his small palm on her stomach. As if on cue, the baby kicked him.

'I felt him move!' Ed exclaimed, turning to his mother in surprise. His large green eyes were wide in wonder. 'I didn't know babies kicked mummies. Did I kick you a lot? Did I do it very hard?'

But before his mother could reply, he turned back to Eliza. His pleased expression had turned into one of horror.

'But how is the baby going to get out of you?' he asked in alarm.

Eliza was momentarily thrown, and was grateful when Alan handed Ed the entire bread basket and told him to run along and play. At least he'd not asked how the baby had got into her, she thought. The 'when a mummy loves a daddy' explanation definitely wouldn't work with her.

After a starter of salmon mousse and a main course of lamb and mint sauce, the wedding guests were happy and sated. Ed was running around the marquee with the two bridesmaids – whose peach dresses were already looking remarkably grubby – but Eliza was exhausted and looking forward to retiring to her bedroom. Alan Winter had been telling her what it had been like to grow up at Beaufont, and even though she wanted to listen to him carefully, she found she couldn't concentrate: her stomach hurt and she wondered if she had indigestion.

'When I was a child, there was a maze in one of the gardens – one of those large jobs made from carefully tended hedges,' Alan said. 'I used to get lost in it several times a month, but eventually I remembered the paths in and out and became quite the pro. One hot summer evening one of the Labradors – I can't recall his name: it may have been Goldie, or something like that – got stuck in the maze. Aster was sent down to the village to fetch me, as I was the only one who could rescue him.'

'Did you find him?' Eliza asked.

Alan nodded. 'I managed to lead him out, but as soon as he'd been freed from the maze, he jumped in the pond and proceeded to cover the whole house with water and mud. The family weren't best pleased.'

'When I was little, I used to lie in my box room in Tottenham and imagine children playing at Beaufont Hall. I felt so envious,' Eliza said. 'In my head it was like a palace – and it sounds like it was a bit.'

'It would have been once upon a time. But when I was a child it seemed more spooky than regal. I'm not ashamed to admit it scared me,' Alan confided. Eliza could easily picture him as a young boy: his dull red hair would have been brighter, and he would have been skinny, with a face full of freckles just like his son. 'I was convinced there were ghosts and goblins lurking behind closed doors and that they were going to eat me alive, but as I got older I began to appreciate it more. It's not the prettiest of buildings, admittedly, but once you're inside and you give yourself up to it, it begins to feel like home. Well, that's how I feel, even though I've never technically lived here.'

'It does,' Eliza agreed, and then she felt a sharp tugging in her abdomen and her back. She took a quick breath and gripped the edge of the table.

Valerie looked at her with concern. 'Are you okay?' she asked.

Eliza nodded. 'It's probably nothing,' she said, but then it came again, stronger, and she doubled up in pain. The chatter of the wedding breakfast came to a halt and all eyes were on her.

Valerie gave her an excited smile. 'I think you're in labour,' she said.

'But it's too soon,' Eliza whispered, pale with shock as Alan helped her to her feet and scrabbled about in his pockets for his car key. He handed it to his wife.

'I'll fetch Rebecca and meet you by the car,' he said.

As he walked away, Eliza felt another tug of pain – and it was then that her waters broke, and fluid mixed with blood trickled down her thigh.

Chapter Twenty-Five

Buckinghamshire, 1989

Rebecca knew that her wedding dress was becoming creased and bloodied, but she didn't care. She willed the Winters' white Ford Escort to drive faster, and as soon as they pulled up outside A&E, she started screaming for a doctor, a nurse, a student – anyone who could help Eliza. She knew that she and Valerie were causing quite a scene as they helped Eliza through the double doors to the hospital, but she couldn't have cared less. All that was important was Eliza and her child; nothing else mattered.

'The baby isn't due for another month,' Eliza repeated over and over again as she doubled up in pain. 'This has to be a false alarm – it's too soon.'

Rebecca brushed Eliza's hair away from her face and tried to force a natural-looking smile over her worried expression. 'It may be too soon, but your son has chosen to upstage me on my big day.' She struggled to keep her voice light; she knew for Eliza's sake that it was important to.

She quickly found a seat for Eliza to perch on and then rushed to the reception desk and demanded that she be seen by a doctor at once. She watched the receptionist's mouth hang slack in shock and she wanted to shake her – it couldn't have been the first time she'd encountered a soiled bride barking orders at her.

'Just get a doctor, will you?' she hissed before returning to her cousin.

'Is it meant to hurt so much?' Eliza asked Valerie as she gripped the sides of the orange plastic chair. Her knuckles had turned as white as her face. 'Is it going to get worse?'

Valerie took Eliza's hand in hers. 'It will,' she admitted. 'But it will be worth it, I promise.'

Eliza nodded, but her eyes began to lose focus and she'd started to mumble. 'This is all my fault,' she said softly. 'This is because of the drugs, because I didn't look after myself...'

Rebecca didn't know what long-term damage the drugs had done, but she knew it wouldn't do Eliza any good to think that way. 'That's a ridiculous thing to think,' she said sharply. She rarely felt scared, but there was something about Eliza's expression, about the amount of blood that had stained her sailor-style maternity dress, that chilled her to the bone. 'The baby has decided to come early, that's all. Look, here's a doctor. Can you manage to walk through to the ward? We can find a wheelchair...'

Eliza used all the energy she had to push herself up from the chair and troop through to the chaos of A&E. Nurses and doctors rushed around as they dealt with a car accident that had come in an hour previously, and the smell of disinfectant and unwashed bodies assailed their nostrils. Rebecca kept talking softly to her cousin, trying to distract her from the sound of sobs and moans coming from various curtained cubicles, but she knew Eliza could barely hear her meaningless, empty words.

Eliza suddenly stopped and reached her hand out towards a mint-green curtain as if to steady herself. As she touched the material, she looked surprised that it wouldn't take her weight.

She fell to the floor in the cloying agony of another contraction, and even as Rebecca was trying to make her come round, trying to stop her from slipping into unconsciousness, she knew it was no good.

She heard the soft footsteps of nurses running towards them, but she couldn't take her eyes from Eliza, who looked as though she were sinking into the cold tiles under her body. Her cousin muttered something, but Rebecca couldn't make out the words she was trying to form before she passed out.

Several hours later, Rebecca found herself glaring at the unsympathetic doctor who stood at the end of Eliza's bed.

'You've lost a lot of blood and are continuing to do so,' he said in a matter-of-fact tone, and Rebecca wanted to stand up and slap him for being so cold, so cruel. 'You mustn't fall asleep. You must stay awake for a while longer.' He muttered something unintelligible, then demanded that Eliza sign a sheaf of consent forms, all of which she barely glanced at.

She had been left attached to various machines and monitors, which bleeped away distractingly, and Rebecca told herself she absolutely mustn't cry. She swallowed down her tears.

'Have I been drugged?' Eliza managed to ask.

Rebecca took a deep breath. 'You've had lots of medicine,' she managed to say, although it was hard to get the words out. 'You're bleeding quite heavily and you've been in the operating theatre so the doctors can try to work out what's wrong.'

Eliza stared at her as if Rebecca had spoken in a foreign language. 'Why am I bleeding? Should I be?'

Rebecca shot a pleading look at Valerie, who answered on her behalf. 'I don't know why you're bleeding, darling,' she said gently.

Eliza shut her eyes for several moments and then opened

them in alarm. 'But when will it be time to have the baby?' she asked in a shrill tone.

Rebecca felt sick to her stomach. 'Eliza,' she began in an unsteady voice, 'you've *had* the baby. Don't you remember delivering her?'

She watched Eliza's eyes widen in shock as she tried to look down at her stomach. She could tell that her cousin was trying desperately hard to remember what had happened.

'I've had a baby?' she asked, and she leant back against the pillows and smiled, a dreamy, contented smile. Rebecca knew that she was in considerable pain, but at that moment it was clear that all Eliza felt was love. 'Where is he?'

'She's in the NICU because she was so early,' Valerie explained in a slow voice. 'But you mustn't worry – the doctors think she'll be okay. She's small, but perfect. She's beautiful.'

Eliza frowned at her. 'I'm having a *son*,' she said calmly. 'I think you must be confusing me with someone else. I'm having a son who I'm naming Bertie after my father.'

Rebecca felt herself wobble slightly, and it was then that the tears that had threatened to spill for so long finally slid down her face. She wiped them away furiously. She would not cry; she would not upset her cousin.

'Eliza, you've had a difficult birth and the doctors are concerned about the amount of blood you've lost,' she said as matter-of-factly as she could. She could hear the emotion in her own voice and she hoped Eliza would not. 'But I assure you, you have a daughter.'

Eliza watched her but didn't say a word.

'The doctors tried to stop the bleeding, but they couldn't,' Rebecca continued. 'So now you need to have a transfusion. You might also need an operation . . . A hysterectomy. Do you understand?'

'I've had a baby?' Eliza asked again. 'A girl?'

Valerie nodded. 'I'm going to go and see her in a minute. She's gorgeous, really very beautiful. She looks just like you.'

Eliza squeezed her eyes shut tight, as if she were trying to picture her daughter. When she opened them again, they were filled with disappointment, and Rebecca knew that she couldn't remember.

'Have I held her?' she asked eventually.

'You saw her for a moment,' Rebecca replied, 'but you weren't able to hold her. She's too small. She had to go straight to the NICU and you weren't very well after she was delivered.'

'Will you go and see that she's okay, please?' Eliza asked Valerie with as much authority as she could manage. Valerie looked at Rebecca, who nodded at her. 'Please? Please can you check on my baby?'

Valerie squeezed Eliza's hand one final time and left the room. When she'd gone, Rebecca began to stroke her cousin's hair gently. Eliza closed her eyes, and even though Rebecca wanted her to find peace, to find calm, she knew she mustn't let her fall asleep. She called out her name, and Eliza opened her eyes and looked directly at her.

'I wanted to say thank you,' she said softly. 'I wanted to say thank you for helping me.'

Rebecca's eyes filled with tears again, only this time she didn't wipe them away, for Eliza's eyes were brimming too. 'You don't need to thank me for anything,' she managed to say. The upset in her voice was desperately apparent. 'You need to rest for your transfusion. You haven't got long until you go back into theatre.'

'That's why I need to say it now.' Eliza's voice was low, like a whisper. 'I really don't feel well. I'm feel like I'm already a ghost.'

'What can I do?' Rebecca asked softly. Tears ran down her face like hot rivers and fell on to Eliza's frail arm.

'Just make sure my daughter has the life I wished for her,' Eliza managed to say. 'I wrote something in my diary: I wrote what I want for her. Please make sure she has it, that she reads it . . .' Her voice trailed off, and she closed her eyes again.

Rebecca knew that they were running out of time, that her cousin's fight was disappearing with her final sigh. She screamed for a doctor, but as they bustled in and began to work on Eliza, she knew that it was too late. The beeps of the heart monitor faded into white noise, the doctors all suddenly froze and then melted away, and Rebecca realised that Eliza was not moving – and that she'd never move again.

Chapter Twenty-Six

London, recently

Cassie held her mother's hand and cried. She cried for Eliza, the determined, messed-up girl who had died before she'd fully been able to change her life around for the better, and she cried for the baby who'd never known her mother. She looked up at Rebecca's face and her mother offered her a sad little smile. It was a smile that spoke of pain and of secrets, but Cassie found she couldn't quite smile back. Poor Eliza.

She wiped away her tears and looked towards the fireplace. On the mantelpiece was an innocuous, happy wedding photograph of her mother and father, but Cassie now realised that every time Rebecca looked at it, she'd be reminded of Eliza, and how her cousin had passed away on what had begun as such a happy day. Suddenly Rebecca's hesitation about talking about her past – and her family – became clear. No wonder she'd wanted to move away from Beaufont Hall and her sad memories; no wonder she and Cassie's father had moved to London for a fresh start.

'I knew there wasn't going to be a happy ending,' Cassie said slowly, 'but I assumed that Eliza would have passed away because of her drug addiction. I feel terrible for thinking that.'

Rebecca looked down at the carpet. 'It would have been hard

for you to draw any other conclusion,' she replied. 'I so wish that you hadn't read the final diaries, or that you'd told me you had all of them. I'd always planned to tell you about Lillie and Bertie and Eliza, but I wanted to do it in my own way, and in my own time.'

'I understand now why you were so reluctant: losing Eliza must have been awful for you,' Cassie commented.

'It was,' Rebecca confirmed. She too glanced at the wedding photograph. 'Sometimes that day only feels like yesterday, and the pain is still remarkably raw. But other days I'm able to pretend it didn't happen. Watching a cousin die – a cousin you quickly grew to love as a sister – never leaves you, you know. That's why I don't like to speak of Eliza, and that's why there aren't any photographs of her on display in the house. It's easier to pretend it didn't happen sometimes, although she is always there with me. She never really left me.'

'Do you have more photographs of her?' Cassie asked.

Rebecca nodded. 'A few: some from when we lived at Beaufont together, and several of her at our wedding. I'd wanted her to be a bridesmaid, but she refused to do it in her condition. To be fair, she was rather large.'

Rebecca stood and rummaged through some cupboards until she found an intricate wooden box with stars carved into it. Cassie recognised it instantly. She'd always loved it as a child and had believed that the locked box contained magic. When she'd been small, Rebecca had always refused to allow her to play with it, and her voice had grown sharp when she'd tried to. Cassie now understood why.

'Eliza wasn't like everyone else, of course,' Rebecca continued. She pulled a tiny silver key from her soft cardigan pocket, and Cassie realised that she had been waiting to reopen this box for a long time. 'She was wild and troubled and was always looking for something to save her from boredom, but apart from James, she was the person closest to me, and I loved her deeply.'

She opened the box and began to pass the photographs to her daughter.

'This is Eliza and Valerie before the ceremony,' she said.

Cassie's eyes hungrily scanned the photo, and she was gratified to see that despite the harrowing years of drugs and prostitution, Eliza looked well. She no longer looked like a model – her face was too full, and her body was obviously large with the pregnancy – but she was happy and healthy, and there was no hint of the ill health that would consume her later that day.

'And here's one of Eliza with Edward Winter. He really didn't like that sailor suit, as you can see.'

Cassie took the photograph from her mother and her eyes immediately went to the nine-year-old Ed rather than to Eliza. His expression was one of frustration, but Cassie recognised his green eyes hidden behind the oversized 1980s-style glasses. She felt a tug in her heart and forced herself to look at the image of Eliza instead.

'And this is the hardest photograph for me to look at. It's of me and Eliza just after your father and I married,' Rebecca said simply.

Cassie gazed at the photograph and felt her eyes begin to fill with tears again. The shot wasn't a professional one, and it had been taken when the girls weren't looking at the camera, but it was beautiful. Rebecca and Eliza were arm-in-arm, their heads turned towards each other, and they were grinning such happy, joyful grins of love and friendship that Cassie found it a difficult photo to examine. They had had everything in the world to look forward to – a new marriage, a baby on its way – and it seemed unbelievable that only hours later Eliza would be dead.

She handed the photograph back to her mother, who stared at it wordlessly. She looked drawn.

'That was the last photo to be taken of us together,' Rebecca said quietly. 'Alan Winter took it at the wedding reception, and he gave it to me on the day that James and I moved out of Beaufont. It broke my heart to leave, but I couldn't stay there: the ghost of Eliza was everywhere, and I couldn't cope with it. I know Eliza would have thought me silly, that she would have said I was being ridiculous, but I had to leave – *we* had to leave. So James found this house – which we thought was perfect for a family – and we moved in. London was meant to be a fresh start . . . although that would have been impossible, of course.'

Rebecca's gaze held Cassie's intently, and Cassie shifted uncomfortably in her seat. She felt as though her mother was waiting for her to ask something, but she couldn't think what it would be.

'Is Eliza buried in the village with the rest of the Tempests?' she asked eventually.

Rebecca shook her head. 'We buried her in Tottenham with her parents. Your father and I discussed whether she should be buried in the family crypt, but in the end we felt it best that she return to be with Lillie and Bertie.'

'And what about the baby?' Cassie asked. 'Was she buried in Tottenham too?'

Rebecca turned to her daughter in astonishment, and for a long moment she couldn't speak. Her face was pale and her hands shook.

'Eliza's daughter didn't die,' she managed to say.

Cassie stared up at her mother and felt the familiar feather-light chill run up and down her body. It was the same feeling that she'd last felt on the steps of Gossips. She was aware of something in the very back of her mind – a memory, perhaps

– shifting slightly. But the more she tried to grasp at it, the further away it drifted.

'What happened to her?' she asked in a whisper, but she already knew what the answer would be.

Rebecca rummaged around in her keepsake box until she found an envelope. She opened it slowly and pulled out several faded pages of notepaper. Cassie recognised the paper instantly as that of Eliza's later diaries, and when she saw Eliza's distinctive handwriting on it, she suddenly felt afraid.

'Mum,' she said slowly, 'why do you have pages from Eliza's diary?'

Rebecca looked more upset than Cassie had ever seen her, but she handed the thin pieces of paper to her carefully.

'Because Eliza asked me to give them to her daughter when the time was right . . . and my darling, that time is now.'

Chapter Twenty-Seven

Buckinghamshire, 1989

Eliza sat on the peony-patterned rug in her mother's childhood bedroom and chewed thoughtfully on her pen. She'd pushed the window open slightly so that a crisp autumnal breeze could air the room, and as she leant back against the wall, she tried to picture Lillie playing here as a child, or experimenting with make-up as a teenager. But try as she might, she couldn't imagine her mother in her younger incarnation, couldn't picture her asleep in the old-fashioned single bed, or brushing her long golden hair at the mirror on the creamy-white dressing table.

The few photographs she had of her mother showed a happy, carefree teenager – a girl who looked as though her impending adult life wouldn't faze her, regardless of what it held. It wasn't until Eliza had seen these photographs, and Violet had confessed to what she'd done, that she had really considered who Lillie Tempest had been before she'd left Beaufont. She regretted not taking the time to get to know Lillie properly – instead she'd lazily accepted a version of her mother that she'd taken for granted – and she wished there was more of her here at Beaufont to make up for that: more photographs, more letters, even some diaries like Eliza's own.

It was this that had prompted her to try to write a diary entry for her unborn child. She had no intention of allowing her child to read her diaries until she was long gone, but she'd grown up in the shadow of her mother's past, and she didn't want that for her own son or daughter; she wanted her life and her history to be open and secret-free. But Eliza *did* have a secret, and she wanted to record it in her diary just in case she never got a chance to sit down and share it with her child. She just hadn't expected it to be so hard for the words, the truth, to come.

She frowned and kicked off her shoes, pulled off her favourite multicoloured glass earrings, and swept her hair up into a messy ponytail. Then she shifted her position so she was more comfortable, stared at the blank page of her diary for several minutes and then began to write.

My darling child,

There's so much I want to tell you, and I'm struggling to find the words to express my thoughts, but I'll start with the three that are the most important and come so easily to me: I love you.

There's not a day that goes by when I don't think of my own mother, and I wish so much that I'd known her better. Lillie was brave, she was gentle and she was kind, but I became so swept up in my own life – my hedonistic, hellish life – that I never got to know her imperfections or the things that truly made her who she was. I loved my mother but I didn't know her as a person, not really, and this isn't what I want for you. It's always been important for me to know who I am and where I come from, and I imagine it will be the same for you. That's why these diaries, these scrawled, confusing notebooks in which I've written since I was a teenager, will one day be yours. Because I want you to know the real me; I want you to know about who I was before you were born.

There's one diary entry that's missing from the collection, and it's one I need to write down because it's important that it's documented somewhere safe. I never lied to myself in my diaries, but I was so ashamed of some of my actions that I couldn't face writing them down. This is the heartbreaking denial all addicts have: we are so remorseful that sometimes we pretend that things we do haven't happened.

I wrote that the last time I saw Jonathan Klein was in my flat in Chelsea when I promised I'd try to clean up ... but I also saw him several years later, when he came across me on Meard Street in Soho. I was sitting on the steps to Gossips and at first he didn't recognise me. When he eventually did, I saw that he had tears in his eyes. He told me that he'd assumed I'd died, and I felt so awful that I nearly ran away. I wanted to crawl under a rock because I was so ashamed of myself and how I'd treated him.

Instead, Jonathan persuaded me to come back to his house and he made me dinner. I wasn't hungry — I was high, of course — but his small act of kindness reached me and warmed me in a way that drugs never could. I was so grateful for his care and attention that I wanted to show him what he meant to me, so we fell into bed. It was the loveliest night of my life.

Yet when I woke in the morning, all I could think of was getting another ugly hit of drugs. The light was a dull, milky grey, and I dressed and walked out of Jonathan's house and life without a second glance. It's something I'll always regret. That night he admitted that he'd always loved me — yet I carelessly threw his feelings away.

But despite my being so casual about him, Jonathan got to me. I saw his face every time I shot up; I saw the sadness in his eyes every time I found a dark alley to take a customer into. Before too long I discovered I was pregnant, and I knew *without question that the baby inside me was his. You see, I'd always taken those early 1980s posters about HIV and AIDS seriously, and whenever I worked I used protection. The only time I didn't was when I was with Jonathan. His love for me swept me away.*

So, my darling child, your father is Jonathan Klein, and you were created from our love. You may not be born yet, but I imagine you to be a miniature version of him, a child who is quiet but fearless, a child who loves to read like his father and loves music like his mother. You'll be soft and gentle like your grandmother Lillie, but you'll also have a stubborn streak like both Bertie and me. You'll be beautiful, of course – how could you not be – and you'll have the glorious blue eyes of the Tempests.

Darling child, I want you to learn from the mistakes of my life, and to flourish despite everything I did wrong. I want you to be the happy ending for Lillie and Bertie and their tragic lives, and I want you to be the happy ending for me too. I can't give you anything much, not at the moment, but I can give you the gift of my love and of my truth.

I love you.

Eliza xxx

Eliza closed her diary, put down her pen, and cried for everything she'd lost and for the happy future she hoped she'd have.

Chapter Twenty-Eight

London, recently

Cassie refused to allow Rebecca to catch her eye. The living room of the London town house had filled with a tense silence – the silence of nervous, worried anticipation – and not a sound could be heard. Rebecca shifted uncomfortably and reached out to touch her daughter's arm, but Cassie pulled away. Her movement wasn't an unkind one, but it was one that suggested that she needed a few more moments to fully understand what she'd read, to comprehend what she'd just been told. For long minutes Cassie and Rebecca sat together in the still quiet, and when Cassie finally found her voice, it was raspy, as if she'd never spoken before.

'Eliza is my mother,' she stated, as if saying the words out loud would make it feel more real. Then she said it again, this time louder, stronger: 'Eliza Boyle is my *mother*.'

She finally glanced up at Rebecca, and saw fear and upset in her eyes – the Tempest eyes that she'd inherited, although they'd been passed down from Eliza and Lillie rather than from Rebecca.

'She is your biological mother, yes,' Rebecca said softly, and she let a finger trail against the gleam of the photograph of her and Eliza on her wedding day. 'Eliza asked me to adopt you if she passed away, and it never crossed my mind not to. From the moment I saw you, I loved you with all my heart.'

Cassie thought of how grave and sad that final conversation would have been for both Eliza and Rebecca, and she wondered how her mother – how Rebecca, she meant – could have stood to have a living, breathing memory of Eliza in her house. All her life Cassie had thought she looked like James Cooke or Violet Tempest, but the reality was different – her mother was Eliza Boyle, and her grandparents were Lillie and Bertie. She was still a Tempest, but not in the way she'd always assumed she was. She felt dizzy at the thought of it.

'Sometimes I see such remarkable flashes of Eliza in you that it takes my breath away,' Rebecca confided quietly. 'You're not as extrovert as her – you must be more like your grandmother Lillie, who I think had a more gentle disposition – but your expressions and your demeanour are so like Eliza's, especially when you're determined to have your own way. And you're as beautiful as her, you really are.'

'But why didn't you tell me she was my mother sooner?' Cassie whispered.

Rebecca looked at her adopted daughter sorrowfully. 'Because I couldn't bear to,' she admitted. 'Your father and I love you as though you're our own flesh and blood, and we didn't know how best to tell you that you weren't, or how to tell you about Eliza. We would have told you one day, of course we would have, but we weren't yet ready to. It seems as though Beaufont Hall had other ideas, though.'

'If I'd not found Eliza's diaries, I'd still be in the dark, wouldn't I?' Cassie asked sadly.

Rebecca held her daughter close to her. 'I'm sorry that you had to find out this way.'

Cassie remained quiet for a long time as she considered her

mother's words. Would she have behaved differently had she been put in Rebecca's situation? The more she thought about it, the more she wasn't sure. What else could Rebecca have done?

'Does anybody else apart from Dad know that I'm adopted?' she asked. She was sure that Alice and Henry wouldn't know, but there must have been family friends who had been aware of Eliza's death and her baby's adoption.

Rebecca smiled sadly. 'We lost touch with a lot of people who'd attended our wedding after we adopted you,' she admitted. 'We couldn't run the risk of them accidentally mentioning it in front of you.'

'But Valerie and Alan Winter know the truth,' Cassie stated, and Rebecca nodded.

'They do – they were a great comfort to me after Eliza passed away – but Edward doesn't know. After you'd visited them, Valerie phoned me to talk about you. She'd not seen you since you were a tiny baby, and meeting you as an adult – as a woman who so resembles Eliza – gave her great pleasure. Alan, too . . . He's worked as hard as he could for you on very little money to try to keep Beaufont from completely falling to bits.'

'What do you mean, for me?' Cassie asked. Rebecca took another deep breath.

'Beaufont Hall belongs to you, darling,' she said quietly. 'It always has done.'

Cassie looked at her mother in confusion. 'But that's not possible – the house belonged to Violet and then it was passed on to you. Wasn't it?'

Rebecca paused, and her silence forced Cassie to look up at her. 'Before Mummy died, she left Beaufont Hall to Eliza,' she said simply. 'She was so consumed by guilt at what she'd done to Lillie that she wanted to make amends in the only way she knew. She loved Beaufont – perhaps more than any other

Tempest had done – so she transferred the deeds to Eliza before she confessed to her. It was her way of saying sorry.'

Cassie felt her head begin to spin. She knew she ought to be pleased that Beaufont Hall was hers, but all she could think about was how her real mother and grandmother had been wronged, and how the house could never make up for the alienation and sadness that Lillie must have felt.

'Darling child, I'm here for you as much as you need me to be,' Rebecca said softly, and her words reminded Cassie of what Eliza had called her in her diary. Eliza had been so sure that she was to be born a boy, and that she was going to be called Bertie.

'Mum,' she began slowly, 'is my middle name Alberta because Eliza planned to call me Bertie if I'd been a boy?'

Rebecca nodded. 'James and I thought it would be a good way to honour your biological grandfather,' she said, and despite the crushing sadness of the day's revelations, Cassie found that she managed to smile through her tears.

As Cassie drove up the long driveway to Beaufont and peered through the gaps in the trees, she thought the house had never looked lovelier. It was winter now; the cold had kissed every blade of grass and every tree so that it all glittered with a silvery frost. The air was crisp, the sky was a bright blue, and as the house itself came fully into view, Cassie stared at it as though seeing it for the first time. All of this was hers. It was the home that her grandmother Lillie had left to begin a new life, the home in which her mother Eliza had spent the remaining days of hers, and soon it would be a home and workspace for her.

She parked in her usual spot and wasn't surprised to see that Ed's car was already there. He had agreed to meet her at the house so they could start to measure up some office space, and Cassie was looking forward to seeing him.

After Rebecca's revelations, Cassie had not returned to Beaufont for several weeks. Instead she'd said her goodbyes to Mr Heritage and Heritage Books and spent most of her time in her bedroom, where she'd read Eliza's diaries again and again with fresh eyes. Sometimes she'd ventured into central London to see Safia, and they'd almost always gone to the Dean Street Townhouse. She'd drawn strength from knowing she was Lillie Tempest's granddaughter and Eliza Boyle's daughter. Every time she looked in the mirror she could see more and more of Eliza staring back at her, and even though she didn't know what Jonathan Klein looked like, he'd seemed kind and friendly from the emails they'd exchanged. She hadn't yet told him that he'd fathered a baby with Eliza, but she suspected he might have guessed. She looked forward to meeting him and getting to know him, should he be open to it.

She watched a kite fly over the house and then got out of her car, her boots crunching on the gravel. The front door was open and Ed had appeared in the doorway. He was in his socks and had a scarf around his neck to keep him warm, and Cassie couldn't keep the smile from her face. She'd missed him.

'You're a sight for sore eyes,' he called out as she approached.

She stuck her tongue out at him, and then laughed as she recalled the photograph of him at her mother's wedding.

'So are you,' she replied.

They walked along the flagstone floor and automatically found themselves in the forget-me-not den. Cassie reached into her bag and found the picture.

'Look at this,' she said. She passed it to Ed, who glanced at it and grinned, recognising himself.

'What a horrible little boy I was,' he said. 'I remember that wedding – but whose was it, and who's that woman I'm standing next to?'

Cassie stared at him for a moment, and then explained how the photograph had been taken at Rebecca and James's wedding, and that it had also been the day she'd been born. As she went on to tell him that she was Eliza's biological daughter, and that Eliza had died shortly after she'd been delivered, Ed stared at her in astonishment.

'That's an awful lot to absorb,' he commented, and he reached for her hand and enveloped it within his. Cassie felt a blush begin to bloom on her cheeks, but she also found she didn't seem to mind Ed seeing her flushed. 'How are you feeling about it all?'

She considered this for a moment. 'I feel lucky,' she admitted. 'I've got the two best parents in the world, but I'm also the biological daughter and granddaughter of two women I greatly admire. Eliza definitely wasn't perfect – and I hated reading about how she became addicted to drugs and fell into prostitution – but I'd rather know the real version of her than a sanitised, untruthful one. She had the same strength that Lillie had, and I feel blessed to know that I've hopefully inherited that too.'

'Of course you have,' Ed said as he squeezed her hand in his. 'Not many people would decide they want to save a decrepit family home and then go out and find a way to actually do it. It's amazing. You're amazing.'

Cassie felt winded as his words hung in the air between them. She forced herself to look up at him, and when she saw how he was gazing down at her – as though he thought she was the most wonderful person in the world – she glanced away. Something had changed between them since she'd last seen him, and she wondered what it could be.

'I think you're amazing too,' she murmured. 'I never would have been able to raise the money for the festival without your help, and the house probably would have fallen apart without you.'

'I think you need to give Beaufont more credit than you do. Underneath the cobwebs and the superficial rot, it's stronger than it looks,' he said mysteriously.

Cassie looked at him in confusion. 'What do you mean?' she asked, but Ed just smiled at her.

'Come with me.'

Ed led Cassie down the corridor. He kept her hand tight in his, and every so often he looked at her and smiled. As they approached what had been one of the drawing rooms, she was surprised to find that he had slowed his pace, and when they stood in front of the closed wooden door to the room, he dropped her hand. It felt cold without his wrapped around it.

'I wanted to show you this,' he began, and he pushed open the door to the drawing room.

Cassie stared in astonishment. The wooden floors had been varnished; they shone under the light that filtered through the new glass windows. The walls had been washed a soft dove grey, and on them were several beautiful oil paintings of the valleys outside. A huge iron chandelier hung from a stunning ornate ceiling rose, and the Victorian-style cornicing had been completely restored. Cassie walked wordlessly into the room and gaped at Ed.

'Did you do this?' she asked. 'Did you do this for me?'

He nodded proudly. 'I had some help, of course, but I wanted you to have another room to live in while we start to restore the house. I wanted to make you happy.'

Cassie twirled around and took in the room. 'It's gorgeous,' she whispered – and it was. The colour scheme slightly resembled the tones of the forget-me-not den and of Lillie's old bedroom, and she found she could picture exactly the sort of furniture she'd like, and how she'd be able to sit in the room in the evening and read. 'I love it.'

'There's something else, too,' Ed said, and he led Cassie over to the fireplace. On top of the marble mantelpiece was a small black-and-white photograph. It had faded with age and one corner was missing, but it showed three girls in a line. 'It's Violet, Aster and Lillie Tempest when they were children,' he said. 'My father found it in one of his photo albums and asked me if I thought you'd want it. I felt sure that you would.'

Cassie examined the photograph. Two of the three girls stared solemnly at the photographer, but the third – the youngest – gave a sweet, soft smile. Cassie smiled back at her and then grinned up at Ed.

'I know her life was short and there was lots of unhappiness,' she said, 'but I think the love that Lillie and Bertie had for each other saw her through the dark days. I think that in many respects she was lucky – luckier than Violet ever was.'

Ed nodded and swallowed hard. 'I hope to be able to give you that same love,' he said quietly, and Cassie stared up at him in shock.

'What do you mean?' she whispered for the second time that day.

Ed looked uncharacteristically bashful. 'I mean that, if you'll have me, I'd like to be able to show you just how special you've become to me.'

Cassie's mouth dropped open. 'But ... I thought you didn't like me like that. You never gave me any indication that you had any feelings for me.'

Ed looked shamefaced. 'I was attracted to you the moment I saw you,' he admitted. 'But I couldn't let you know how I felt until I was ready. When I was in London, I wasn't a very nice person: I was obsessed with work, with making money, and

I treated girlfriends badly. I liked you so much that I wasn't prepared to take a chance in telling you how I felt. I wanted to be sure that I'd treat you the way you deserve. Because you deserve only the very best.'

'You *are* the best,' Cassie replied in a small voice.

Ed smiled. 'I'm not, but if you'll give me the chance, I'd like to make you gloriously, blissfully happy. I've fallen in love with you, and it's not something I'm taking lightly. I've been scared of my feelings, and it's taken me a while, but I realise that I want to nurture and cherish you. I want to make you as happy as Bertie made your grandmother.'

Cassie felt Ed's hands squeeze hers tightly, and then she felt a sudden peace and calm that she'd never experienced before. She was in Beaufont Hall – the place she'd always felt she belonged – with the man she'd always dreamed that she'd one day meet.

'You already do,' she replied, and then Ed leant down to kiss her.

Epilogue

Buckinghamshire, last autumn

The grounds of Beaufont Hall were packed to capacity. Tents of every colour littered the fields surrounding the house, and the sound of laughter floated on the light breeze. The sun warmed the people who stood in excited, happy groups under the vintage bunting that hung from every tree, and the scent of hog roast filled the air. Soft music from an acoustic rock band playing 1960s Cliff Richard classics could be heard from one tent, and the booming voice of an author on the literary bestseller list came from another. Children with purple butterflies painted on their faces chased after one another with hands sticky from candy floss, and couples relaxed against hay bales. The first Beaufont Festival of Literature was undoubtedly a success.

'This is amazing,' Safia exclaimed as she watched the crowds. In her hand she held a book that had been signed by her favourite author, and her face was flushed pink from the sunshine.

'It came together, didn't it?' Cassie remarked with a grin.

Safia beamed at her. 'It more than came together – this is the highlight of everyone's September. It's astonishing.'

'It was bloody hard work to put it all together in time,' Cassie said. 'And I wasn't sure I'd be able to do it. I might not have done if it hadn't been for Ed and his support.'

The girls turned to see Ed laughing with Jake Walker in the VIP area. Both men held flutes of champagne, and as they caught Cassie's eye they raised their glasses to her. Cassie blushed under their gaze, but she was no longer shy; she was just deliriously happy. A few metres away from them stood Rebecca and James, and Cassie was pleased to see that her parents were laughing with Jonathan Klein. It had taken several months of dinners for Cassie to open up to him and to admit that she was his biological daughter, but when she'd finally told him the truth, Jonathan couldn't have been more delighted. He was a quiet man – in many ways she was extremely similar to him – and she was enjoying getting to know him. When he spoke of Eliza, she could see the love in his eyes.

'My mother once told me that some of the Tempests would have had reservations about the idea of a festival,' Cassie said as she turned back to her friend. 'But I can't help thinking that even the most constrained of them would have loved this. In fact I know they would have done – it's brought Beaufont Hall back to life.'

All weekend she had been unable to shake the feeling that the ghosts of her family surrounded her. She could picture her great-grandparents watching the festival from a drawing room window, and she could sense Violet smiling at the crowds from under a tree – even though she'd never have let her hair down and joined in. It had taken time, but Cassie had eventually been able to accept and forgive what Violet Tempest had done to Lillie, and she now thought of her great-aunt fondly. She hoped that Violet had found peace.

'And what do you think Eliza would have thought of it?' Safia asked.

'She'd have loved it,' Cassie replied instantly. And as she looked up at the vanilla clouds floating in the deep blue sky, she knew that Eliza was looking down at her, that she was enjoying what her daughter had managed to create. All her life Cassie had felt loved and looked after, but it wasn't until she'd finished reading Eliza's diaries that she realised those feelings hadn't just come from Rebecca and James; they had come from Eliza too. It had been Eliza's spirit that had led her to find a sense of sanctuary in the Dean Street Townhouse; it was Eliza's honesty and bravery in her diaries that had provided her with the courage she'd needed to save Beaufont Hall. Eliza might have only met her daughter for a few brief minutes before she'd passed away, but her legacy – and the impact she'd had on Cassie – lived on.

'Fancy a dance?' Ed asked, interrupting Cassie's thoughts.

She looked up at her boyfriend and smiled. 'I'd love to,' she replied.

Ed led Cassie deep into the crowds of people dancing under the blazing sun, and as they looked for a space to call their own, Cassie felt certain that each and every one of the Tempests was looking down at her. They could see Beaufont Hall coming back to life, and they were celebrating alongside her.

'I've been looking forward to this dance all afternoon,' Ed murmured into her ear, and as he swirled her around to the music, something caught her eye. She stopped dancing and stared through the crowds, but she couldn't find the people she was convinced she'd just seen. For underneath the bunting, and a little further into the shadows, she could have sworn that she'd spotted Lillie Tempest and Bertie Boyle dancing close together, just as they had done on the very first night they'd met.

She hoped they were having fun.

Author's Note

This novel is not a true story, but the London in which it's set – the London from the 1960s to the present day – is very much real. Anyone who's ever lived in London sees ghosts of themselves in the areas in which they once lived, in the pubs they once drank in, and in the alleyways in which they got up to no good. This is a novel about that London; the London that's created from our collective memories.

Soho has always had a grip on me; as a toddler in the early 1980s my grandparents took me to Hostaria Romana, an Italian restaurant at 70 Dean St. This building is now – of course – the Dean St Townhouse, two proud Georgian buildings that have hosted everyone from King Charles II's mistress in the 1600s to the bohemians who ate, danced and played at the Gargoyle Club from the mid-1920s. It is this continual adding of history upon history that makes Soho so special.

However, Soho is being demolished at an alarming rate. Change in cities is unquestionably inevitable, but rather than building around what has come before, developers are scrubbing and scouring at layers of history to make way for new-build, luxury apartment blocks and a high-speed train line. In doing so, Soho not only loses its memories and its glitzy, grubby beauty, but it also loses its people: the local traders, the musicians, the lovable reprobates and the raconteurs.

Save Soho is a lobbying group dedicated to preserving the spirit of the area. If this novel has made you fall in love with Soho as much as I am and you're interested in finding out more, please visit www.savesoho.com. Thank you – IPF, London, October 2015.

Acknowledgements

This novel took blood, sweat and tears to write, rewrite and then rewrite again; the effort I put in was matched by my editor, Kate Mills, with patience, insight and invaluable editorial suggestions. Without Kate, this book would be comparable to something scrawled on a toilet door by the bastard child of Irvine Welsh and Judy Blume. So thank you, Kate, for saving me from myself – and for everything.

Grateful thanks to everyone at Peters, Fraser & Dunlop (especially Michael, Fiona and Jemma), all those past and present at Orion Books who helped Kate when she was fed up with me (Jo, Jemima, Bethan, Gaby and Elaine), kind strangers who became friends as they guided me through their memories of Soho in the 1980s, the patient staff at the Dean St Townhouse / Soho House & Co, my family (Peter and Harry especially), friends (Hannah, Holly, Tom, Lindsey, Little Adam, Ronnie, Roz), the men who didn't quite understand what I was trying to achieve with this novel . . . and, finally, the men who did.